ABOUT THE AUTHOR

Melissa Hemmings was born in Nottingham. Having put a pin in a map it landed her up in the Bristol Channel. Not enamoured with the prospect of living on a sandbank, she decided to cheat and moved the pin down a bit. As a result, she upped sticks to live by the sea in Somerset, whereupon she awoke one day and decided to open an organic delicatessen. This sort of behaviour has blighted Melissa's life and, whilst it has, undoubtedly, afforded her a very rich and eventful time of things, she now finds herself in need of a sit down.

Hence the advent of her love of writing. She has always written. All manner of things; from stern letters of complaint to poetry, as well as having the pleasure of ghost-writing others' literary works.

She is also an artist and when she's not writing, she's creating pictures. All artwork promoting her books are hers and more can be found hung on people's walls, in books and magazines.

This is Melissa's third novel.

OTHER BOOKS BY MELISSA HEMMINGS:

Observations From The Precipice

Meanderings Of A Cuckoo

FORTITUDE AMONGST THE FLIP-FLOPS

By

Melissa Hemmings

FORTITUDE AMONGST THE FLIP-FLOPS

Published by Happy Mayhem Media Ltd

20 – 22 Wenlock Road, London N1 7GU

This is a work of fiction. Names, characters, businesses, places, events and incidents are either the products of the author's imagination or used in a fictitious manner. Any resemblance to actual persons, living or dead, or actual events is purely coincidental.

The rights of the author of this work has been asserted to her in accordance with the Copyright, Designs and Patents Act 1988. No part of this book may be reproduced in any form, by photocopying or by any electronic or mechanical means, including information storage or retrieval systems, without permission in writing from both the copyright owner and the publisher of this book.

ISBN: 978-0-9927277-7-2 (Paperback)

First published 2022

Text Copyright © Melissa Hemmings 2022

All Rights Reserved

Cover Illustration Copyright © Melissa Hemmings 2022

A CIP catalogue record for this book is available from the British Library

For my second chance

When life gives you lemons, make ~~lemonade~~ lemon drizzle cake.

Eliza Wakeley

Acknowledgements and thanks for all who have supported me on my writing journey.

If you're reading this, I would presume you have read the other two books in the trilogy which preceded this one. If you picked this up on the off chance because the title appealed to you, then you'll not have a clue what's going on which, I think we can both agree, is rather unfortunate.

For the other readers who have been waiting patiently for the conclusion of Eliza's exploits then you're in luck. I have conjured up another book-load for you. There might be more, I don't know yet. My mind is a peculiar tangle of waffle just clambering to spill forth to others, whether they like it or not.

With a bit of luck you will like it. If not - ah well, it's all part of life's rich tapestry and all that... One man's meat is another man's poison... What doesn't break you makes you stronger... You get my gist. I'll crack on.

Chapter One

Eliza's Social Media Post: *We must be willing to get rid of the life we've planned, so as to have the life that is waiting for us. The old skin has to be shed before the new one can come. Joseph Campbell*

Jude drove into the car park of the Billington Gazette and turned off the engine. Eliza looked across at him from the passenger seat.

Eliza: "I don't see why I have to go in. You said I could work from home."

Jude: "What I said was, you can do most of it from home. It has, however, caused a great deal of consternation amongst the other personnel and words like 'favouritism' have been bandied about within my earshot. I can do without a revolt in the office; they're quite a nice bunch. It's still part time, you can be around people and some of it can still be done from home. It will be good for you to spend some time with them; you might make some new friends."

I don't want any new friends. I've got Lydia.

Eliza: "I've met old long hair and Gaz."

I said that out loud, didn't I? Tut.

Jude: "Old long hair?"

Brave it out, like it's the most normal thing in the world to refer to people in such a manner.

Eliza: "Her, who was with you at Vertigo."

Jude: "Charlotte. She's very nice."

Eliza: "Is she indeed."

Jude gave her a sideways glance.

Jude: "Are you ready now? Can we leave the car?"

I'd rather not if it's all same.

Eliza, huffing: "If we have to."

Jude: "Your enthusiasm for your first day at work is truly heart-warming."

Jude got out of the car, went round to open Eliza's door and she shuffled out. He motioned to her to follow him and led the way across the car park into the office side entrance of the Billington Gazette. She trailed along behind him and was led into an open plan office with several people sat at their desks. They all sat to attention as he strode in.

Jude: "Good morning, everyone! Please let me introduce our new recruit, Eliza. Eliza will be joining us on a part time basis. She'll be responsible for the new agony aunt, or is it person feature, these days? I don't know, quite frankly, but for the purposes of this introduction, she's an aunt. She'll be typing up the classified adverts and, of course, other ad-hoc work as required by the team. In response to general feelings aired, she'll be working alongside you here for the most-part."

The gaggle of staff murmured hello and nodded their heads with mutual satisfaction that their opinions had been taken on board.

From running my own business to ad-hocer in the blink of a bad balance sheet.

That's Kenneth's fault that is. That and poor management by Lydia and me, perhaps?

No, it's because Kenneth opened up FunkyFurn and made us look rubbish.

That and we sold his stock at twice the price and customers only had to get in the car to Billington to buy them direct. Whatever.

Anyway, it's done. I am officially a part time ad-hoc person and newspaper agony aunt. I'm completely under qualified for both but if Jude doesn't care, then who am I to be concerned. It'll keep Tom in chocolate buttons and cookery classes.

I wonder if that's a phase, the fixation Tom has with knowing how to make Baked Alaska. I shall have to see if it's a known developmental stage.

Oh, people are staring. Stop thinking and say hello.

Jude: "I thought you could help her settle in, Charlotte."

Eliza shot Jude a look.

Oh, you didn't tell me Charlotte-long-hair was going to be looking after me. She thinks I left a poo down a toilet in Vertigo.

Charlotte curtly nodded and slapped a smile on her face.

Charlotte-long-hair: "It would be a pleasure."

I sense you didn't really mean that.

Jude: "Wonderful. Make her feel at home, she's not been in an office environment for a few years."

Yes, alright. Too much information.

Make the social misfit feel at ease.

Charlotte: "Of course, I'll take her under my wing."

To be honest, I don't fancy going anywhere near your wing.

Jude smiled broadly at Charlotte.

Charlotte flushed under the warmth of his grin and let out a little sigh.

Jude glanced at his watch then turned to Eliza.

Jude: "Right, I must get on, I'm running late so I'll leave you in Charlotte's capable hands. She will do the introductions and show you where everything is."

With that, he whisked off back out of the door they had just entered, leaving a shoulder slumped Eliza stood alone with the rest of the office staring at her.

Could this be any more awkward?

Charlotte-long-hair: "Right then, I'll show you where you can sit."

Eliza: "Ok, thanks."

Charlotte cleared a pile of old newspapers from a spare desk and waved her hand towards it.

Charlotte: "There."

Eliza smiled, put her handbag under the desk and, under the unstinting gaze of Charlotte, gingerly sat down.

Charlotte-long-hair: "Let me introduce you to everyone."

Eliza quickly stood back up again.

Charlotte wafted her hand around in various directions.

Charlotte-long-hair: "That's Valerie, that's Mandy and Gaz is over there somewhere."

Valerie and Mandy's arms popped up in a wave above their monitors and then they went back to typing.

Charlotte-long-hair, continuing: "There's others, but you can only probably remember a couple of names in one go. I'm part Finnish so have amazing memory retention."

Unlike me, who you assume to have the mental capacity of a carp.

She thinks I'm stupid. I need to redress this and get on an even footing.

Eliza: "I've met Gaz before and you, of course."

Finnish brained Charlotte-long-hair, disdainfully: "Indeed. I remember you from the nightclub."

Eliza: "For the record, let me just say, that poo wasn't mine. I felt obliged to deal with it."

Fingers stopped tapping keyboards and silence momentarily descended on the office.

That's it, redress the stupidity.

Perfect, just perfect.

Gaz came into view and wandered over to them.

Gaz: "Hey, bomb laydee! You's shaggin' the boss now? Got yourself a little job out of it! That's cool, innit?!"

He extended his arm for a hand shake and Eliza involuntarily shook it, somewhat stupefied by the turn of events.

I need to go home.

I'm not cut out for human interaction.

I need tables. I can strip them.

The tables have gone. There are no more tables.

The furniture has left the building.

Gaz: "I owes you a favour, laydee. You and your crazy mouth got us the best exclusive with Barney from BLOB. We was contacted by the nationals over that. I nearly defected to The Star but I's got loyalty. I's not affected by the lure of tabloidture."

Charlotte-long-hair: "I thought they offered less than you were getting here?"

Gaz: "Whatevers. My heart lies in Billington."

Gaz thumped his chest in solidarity and Charlotte rolled her eyes.

Valerie and Mandy stood from their desks and wandered over. Eliza sized them up and ascertained that Valerie had quite a lot to size up on the bosom department. She had chosen to wear a cerise nylon blouse which was straining to contain her buxom form; her bosoms resting on the waistband of a cinch-waisted black, pleated skirt. The whole ensemble looked as if it was constricting every muscle movement whilst it did its utmost to contain the contents of a once, undoubtedly, fabulous hour-glass figure.

Ooh, I used to wear a skirt like that in secondary school. How very retro.

If she takes in a deep breath and exhales in an unabashed fashion, her blouse buttons are in danger of pad-oinging off and taking my eye out.

I imagine she walks in the front door at the end of the day, releases everything and takes a good gulp of air.

Mandy, on the other hand, was as thin as a racing greyhound with poker straight hair which she'd tied back in a severe pony tail. She was wearing top to toe Lycra which clung to every sinew of her wiry body.

Goodness, everything about her is built for speed.

I wouldn't be surprised if she gets her neighbour to open her front gate every morning and she runs, full pelt all the way to work.

I bet she hasn't got a rabbit. She wouldn't be able to trust herself.

Voluptuous Valerie: "Oh, you're the one! We've heard all about you, haven't we, Mandy?"

Mandy the Greyhound: "Yes! You've given us our most talked about articles; not a lot goes on around here other than listed building consents and Billington in Bloom."

Voluptuous Valerie, continuing: "There was the bomb, of course. Then Barney in rehab and the rare Dickens' book which sold at auction. You're quite the sensation."

Eliza: "Oh."

Gaz: "Me boss is probably with you to ensure we keeps the exclusives. You's a walking catalogue of errors. Something's bound to 'appen with you in tow!"

I feel a bit wobbly. I think I might cry.

Eliza shot a look at Charlotte who was smirking.

Mandy came to Eliza's rescue.

Mandy the Greyhound: "Shut up Gaz. Ignore him, he's a twat."

Gaz looked suitably admonished.

Gaz: "Oh, sorry laydee. No offence intended."

No, but lots taken.

Can you call people twats in an office situation these days and not be reprimanded? I thought I read an article about acceptable parlance in the workplace. I don't think that was in there.

Charlotte had clearly had enough of the introductions.

Charlotte-long-hair: "Well, that's the hellos over with. Let's all get on with this week's edition, shall we?"

There was a collective nod and everyone drifted off to their respective desks.

Charlotte-long-hair: "Eliza, I have some filing that needs doing. I'm so busy I just don't have the time. Jude has seen my potential and given me more responsibility so I have to sort next week's edition in his absence."

Jude? Isn't he Mr Hardy to you?

Get in the right century Eli, you're not in the 1960's now.

It's all dress down and first name terms these days in the workplace.

Gaz is wearing jeans with rips in them. When did that become the norm?

Hang on....

Eliza: "In his absence?"

Charlotte arched a perfectly sculptured eyebrow.

Charlotte: "Yes, he's up at Head Office for the next few days so I'm standing in for him. Did he not mention it to you?"

Eliza looked surprised.

Eliza: "No."

Charlotte looked delighted.

Charlotte-long-hair: "Oh, I would have thought what with you being 'together' he'd have said."

Oh, stop it.

Eliza: "I'm sure he'll tell me at dinner tonight."

Charlotte-long-hair: "I doubt it. He's halfway to Scotland."

What a truly marvellous first day this is turning out to be.

Eliza: "Where's the filing?"

Charlotte waved her hand in the direction of a mass of precariously stacked paperwork and Eliza's eyes widened.

Eliza: "Have I got to do all that today?!"

If you say yes, I'm going to have to hit you.

Charlotte-long-hair: "No, we need to sort out that agony aunt column of yours this afternoon. As the readers don't know anything about it yet, we had a thought shower and made up some problems for you to answer to get the stone rolling."

Ball. Ball rolling.

You had a what? A thought shower?

Can you imagine your disappointment if you'd shampooed your hair and instead of water a load of thunks came out of the shower head? You can't rinse off suds with ideas.

How would you capture a thought shower? Does someone sit under it and catch all the words and make sentences with them? What if they get them in the wrong order?

Uh oh, she's looking at me. She's expecting me to move.

Charlotte was looking at Eliza, impatiently.

Eliza: "Ok, I'll make a start then."

Charlotte nodded with satisfaction.

Charlotte-long-hair: "It needs alpha, numeric, edition and genre. All in those cabinets over there. Ok?"

I haven't got the faintest idea what you just said.

Eliza: "No problem."

Charlotte's phone rang and she picked it up.

Charlotte-long-hair, with a definite telephone voice: "Good morning, thank you for calling the Billington Gazette, home of local news for over one hundred years. You're speaking to Charlotte Anderton, marketing and interim editor, how may I be of assistance to you today?"

You could pay their phone bill due to your unnecessarily long introduction.

Charlotte felt Eliza watching her whilst on the phone and she sharply motioned for her to get on with her filing.

Tut. To say I feel completely out of my comfort zone would be an understatement.

But it is my first day; it's bound to be a bit of a learning curve. Let's face it, I'm not used to mixing with normal people.

For the past few years I've have had Tom, Lydia and Mr Hicks as primary company. That's not equipping one for society.

Just keep your head down and do your best.

Number of misfiled items at the Billington Gazette that morning: *Thirty-eight.*

Chapter Two

Surreptitious Social Media Meme: *Where there's tea, there's hope. Arthur Wing Pinero*

Ten thirty came and Eliza was parched.

I've been randomly plonking bits of paper in slots for over an hour.

I would have normally had four cups of tea by now.

I know, I'll curry favour and shall ask if anyone would like a beverage.

Eliza wandered over to Charlotte.

Eliza: "Would you like a cup of tea?"

Charlotte looked up from her keyboard and peered at a purse-lipped Valerie who had stopped typing.

Charlotte-long-hair: "Er, no thank you, Eliza. We don't have hot drinks until eleven and Valerie makes those, don't you, Valerie?"

Valerie nodded.

Voluptuous Valerie, tightly: "I do usually, yes."

Tea rules. Who'd have thought?

Eliza: "Oh sorry, I was just a bit thirsty."

Charlotte-long-hair: "There are plastic cups by the water cooler, you may have water."

What is this? Boot camp?

Voluptuous Valerie: "You can make them this time if you like, Eliza. My warts are playing up and the middle toe on my flip-flop is proper biting."

Eliza: "Can I make it now?"

I am not a number; I am a free woman.

If I want tea, I shall have tea and I shall have it when I want it.

Charlotte-long-hair, tersely: "Eleven o'clock please, Eliza."

Or maybe not.

Eleven o'clock came and Eliza sprung into kettle duties, armed with a ream of instructions to follow for each person's particular preference.

Ten minutes later, Eliza came back from the office kitchen with a tray laden with mismatched mugs and caught Charlotte stealing a glance at her watch.

Were you timing me?

She handed a "you don't have to be mad to work here but it helps" mug to Mandy.

Mandy, flatly: "That's not my mug. I have Wallace and Gromit on mine."

Eliza: "Oh sorry, I've washed them all so it doesn't matter."

Mandy tutted and made it clear it did matter very much, actually, and begrudgingly took her tea.

Eliza passed Wallace and Gromit to Valerie.

Valerie seized the cup and took a glug.

You see Charlotte, she was thirsty at ten thirty as well.

Valerie then proceeded to gag and pull a face.

Voluptuous Valerie: "Did you put my sweetener in?"

Eliza: "Oh no, sorry! But look there's a pack on your desk."

Voluptuous Valerie: "They're my emergency pack."

Eliza: "Doesn't this constitute an emergency?"

Voluptuous Valerie: "No."

What constitutes a sweetener emergency other than not having any sweetener in your drink?

My brain cannot cope.

Ignore and walk away.

Eliza shrugged and moved on to Gaz, leaving an annoyed Valerie opening her emergency sweeteners.

Gaz: "Thanks, bomb blighted, bangin' the boss, Barney from BLOB bothering biatch! That's illiteracy, innit? Just like Gaz of the Gazette. I were born for the job. I'm in charge of doing the headlines because of my unique handle on the English language."

Charlotte-long-hair, huffing: "You're illiterate. You mean alliteration."

Gaz: "Same thing."

Gaz leant in conspiratorially and whispered loudly to Eliza.

Gaz: "She likes split hairs."

I don't doubt.

Charlotte was just about to say something else but instead gave him a withering look and beckoned to Eliza to bring her coffee.

Charlotte-long-hair: "Right guys, gather round. We need to bang our heads together and chew the nettle about this new column."

Sounds painful.

I'm sure even cows avoid chewing nettles.

I think she might mean chewing the fat or grasping the nettle.

Shall I correct her?

Perhaps not. She's doesn't seem the type to take critique of merged idioms well.

Charlotte-long-hair: "We need to think of a strapline. It needs to be succinct, brief, snappy and to the point."

Unlike you.

Gaz: "So give me the gist. Eliza's gonna be a guiding light in times of confusion, yeah? Helping others in their hour of need? Easing the burden and the everlasting pain of everyday life and making it more bearable?"

Christ, I'm Florence Nightingale.

Charlotte-long-hair: "Erm, along those lines. Maybe not quite so extreme."

Gaz: "I gotcha. Leave it with me."

Charlotte-long-hair to Eliza: "I'll email over the problems we've thought up for you to answer and we'll put them in this week's paper. We must illustrate to the readers as to the nature of the problems we want to receive. We don't want the general public barking up the wrong bush."

Eliza: "Or tree."

One too many in a short space of time. It was my duty to correct her.

Charlotte-long-hair: "Huh?"

Eliza: "Barking up the wrong tree."

Charlotte-long-hair: "Yes, exactly. As I said. Now let's buckle down. There's much to do. We can't be dawdling and sitting idle."

I strongly feel her vocabulary could be edited.

The rest of Eliza's day was spent with much muttering and pen chewing as she tried to solve the dilemmas created by the various staff from the Billington Gazette.

Tester Letter: *Dear Eliza, The staff at the Billington Gazette are wicked, especially the photographer, Mr Gavin Wild. I think he should be given a promotion and pay rise. Do you agree magnificence should be acknowledged? Regards, wondrousness-should-be-rewarded-with-whopping-wages-and-wealth.*

Tester Letter Reply: *Dear wondrousness-should-be-rewarded-with-whopping-wages-and-wealth. They are indeed a marvellous bunch of people. The editor is particularly heavenly. I also like the new agony aunt; she's said to be very good. She deserves tea whenever she wants to aid her ability to answer really hard life problems.*

Chapter Three

Inspirational Social Media Post: *Beautiful Sunsets need Cloudy Skies. Paulo Coehlo*

Later that evening, an exhausted Eliza pulled up outside Lydia's new house. She dragged her bones out of the car and banged on the door.

It was flung open and Lydia's face popped out.

Lydia: "Get in and creep; Tony's asleep."

Eliza: "Oh, sorry. Is he ill?"

Lydia: "No. It appears I've got him for the 'afternoon nap' years of his life. He drops off mid-dinner sometimes, which is a blessing, quite frankly, as he eats so loudly, I could stab him in the windpipe with his own fork."

Eliza: "Maybe you've got Misophonia and need therapy."

Lydia: "I don't know what that is but it sounds painful. I don't need therapy; I need separate mealtimes."

Eliza: "Has Tom been good?"

Lydia: "Of course, he's never any trouble. Well, that's not strictly true but I blame Lewis for any of his minor flaws."

Eliza: "I do too; it saves introspection. Him and my mother; she has a lot to answer for."

Lydia ushered Eliza in towards the lounge where they found Tom slumped in front of a silent television with subtitles on.

Tom: "'Allo mum. How was Captain Kirk?"

Did I inadvertently tell him I was visiting the Starship Enterprise?

Captain Kirk. Quirk, lurk, shirk, work... Work, that's it!

Eliza: "Tiring. I'm not sure I'm a team player."

Tom: "You inherited that from me. I get in trouble in PE cos I won't pass the ball."

Eliza: "Can we go, please?"

Tom: "Yeah, I haven't the foggiest what's happenin'. I can't read in me head."

Lydia: "Sorry, Tom."

Tom: "It's Ok, pen shunners need their sleep. Their bones are worn out with years of carrying shopping bags."

Lydia gasped and she started to rub her chest.

Oh dear, no.

Out of the mouths of babes.

Eliza, quickly: "Tony's mature, not retired Tom. There's a big difference."

Tom shrugged and got up from the settee, brushing crumbs from his lap on to the carpet.

Tom: "He looks old to me."

Just then the lounge door opened and naked, save for a loosely belted burgundy, velour dressing gown, Tony shuffled in.

Oh dear. No one attending primary school needs to witness that.

Eliza went over and blocked Tom's view.

Tom's right, he does look old.

He's crumpled like an old porn star's black satin sheet which has seen plenty of action but definitely better days.

Tony, smiling: "Ahh, the delightful Eliza. I thought I heard your delicate tones."

A worn-out porn star with the voice of melted butter.

Eliza's insides squirmed slightly and let out an involuntary growl.

Lydia, snapping: "For god's sake put some clothes on, Tony. Tom's here and Freya will be home soon."

And me. I'm here and I don't want to see so much of you, quite honestly.

Tony, laughing: "My apologies, I shall bid you farewell until next time."

Yes, off you go. You and your voice; put some pants on.

Tony left the room and there was a slightly awkward silence which Tom, thankfully, broke.

Tom: "Right, let's get you home, me old china. You need to put your plates up."

Eliza: "I do."

They moved towards the front door and Tom pulled his coat on.

Lydia: "When are you next off work, darling?"

Eliza: "Thursday."

Lydia: "Shall we meet at the Merrythought Café at ten?"

Eliza: "Ah Lydia, that'd be wonderful!"

I've not seen as much of Lydia since she moved in with Tony.

It's lovely that we've met people but I do quite miss the "just us" days.

Tom: "Fanks Auntie Wydia for the biscuits. Mum normally limits me; I've never had half a packet before."

Eliza widened her eyes at Lydia.

Lydia, shrugging: "Soz. Can't harm, can it?"

No, copious amounts of unrefined sugar and fat never harmed anyone.

Eliza ushered Tom out of the door.

Eliza: "Thanks again."

Lydia: "Any time. I'll see you on Thursday."

Second Tester Letter: *Dear Eliza, A new person has joined my place of work who I hope doesn't expect preferential treatment just because they're fraternising with the management. What are your suggestions to ensure a cordial working relationship as I expect all rules to be adhered to and beverage times respected? Regards, I-will-not-be-your-escaped-goat.*

Second Tester Letter Reply: *Dear I-think-you-mean-scapegoat, I shouldn't worry, I want a quiet life. I'm absolutely shattered after hours of fraternising with the management every night; I can barely walk I'm that fraternised out. With reference to the beverage concern; I shall purchase a flask. I wish to offer you a poignant quote which you might want to reflect upon: Some minds are like concrete: thoroughly mixed and permanently set... No one wants a concrete mind, do they?*

Chapter Four

9.55pm Bashed out Social Media Meme: *A good relationship starts with good communication.*

Later that evening, Eliza had put a biscuit filled Tom to bed and was flumped down on the settee. Norris seized the opportunity to have one-on-one cuddles and jumped on her lap, wiping his purring, dribbling face on her chin.

Eliza: "Do you have to do that?"

Norris continued to rub his face against hers.

Eliza: "Apparently so."

Eliza tickled him and tried to guide him down to her lap.

Eliza to Norris: "You'd not go to Scotland and not tell me, would you? I wonder why he didn't mention it. He's not messaged me to see how my first day was or tell me if he's got there safely. Shall I text him and appear nonchalant? I don't want to come across as needy. What do you think?"

Norris slid down her front and laid spread-eagled on his back on her lap, purring loudly.

Eliza: "I take that as a yes. I'll use you as a phone rest."

Eliza rested her mobile on Norris's tummy and composed her text to Jude.

Eliza's text: "Hi, how's your day been? Hope you've had a good one. xx"

Eliza to Norris: "That's a nice, non-needy text. Let's watch TV whilst we wait for his reply."

Eliza placed mobile beside her and flicked through the channels whilst periodically looking at her mobile in case he'd replied but she'd not heard the very audible "ping".

Ten minutes went by without a reply and a twitchy Eliza prodded a snoozing Norris.

Eliza: "Shall I send him another one? Maybe it didn't go. Scotland might have poor signals and they get lost in the mountains."

Norris squirmed, let out a silent mew at being prodded and went back to sleep.

Eliza: "That's a yes. Ok."

Eliza's text: "Hi, I hope you're ok. In case you're wondering my first day went well. xx"

You're obviously not remotely wondering.

Ten minutes more went by and Eliza nudged Norris to ask if she should send another message. Norris awoke and gave her a look of disdain. Having had enough interruptions, he jumped off her lap and went and nuzzled up to a slumbering Ellington.

Thanks for your support, cat.

Eliza texted again.

Eliza's text: "Hi, I understand you've gone to Scotland. That's a long way. It must have been sprung on you suddenly as I'm sure you would have told me. Maybe you did and I've forgotten. xx"

Puts the onus on me a bit there, even though it's completely your fault.

After watching the news to see if there had been a pile up on all the roads from England to Scotland, Eliza composed another message.

Eliza's text: "I'm worried. Have you been injured or been involved in a head on collision in which you've died? I read an article where roads up there can be perilous. Please reply even if you're deceased. xx"

I've watched the news; Scotland has not been hit by an asteroid.

Be reasonable.

He's lived for nearly forty years without a head on crash. Why would he suddenly have one now, this evening?

Because that's life that is.

It does that. It giveth and it taketh away.

I'm proper cross and concerned.

How can he put me through this worry?

Eliza glared at her mobile and started stabbing out another text.

Eliza's text: "If I ever went away, I'd be sure to text you when I set off and during the journey as I know you'd be concerned. I'd also cock tag you when I arrived sagely. xx"

That shows that I'm thoughtful.

I'd never give him cause for concern.

Eliza reread her latest text.

Cock tag you when I arrived sagely?

Tut.

Eliza's text: "Contact you when I arrived safely. It was predictive text."

He'll think I've got hooves for fingers.

That's because I was hammering the message out with rage and worry. I ended up sending gibberish.

He'll think I'm crackers.

Move away from the phone.

Eliza harrumphed and looked at the clock.

I have to go to bed.

She dragged her weary bones upstairs to her room and started taking off her work clothes when something on her bed caught her eye.

She shuffled over with her trousers round her ankles and saw there was a box of chocolates and a card perched on her pillow.

She ripped open the envelope to the card and read it.

Eli,

Thank you for a wonderful weekend.

Just to let you know, I'll be up at Head Office this week.

I hope your first week goes well and I'm so sorry I won't be there with you.

Enjoy the chocolates and imagine me there with you.

See you on Friday.

J xx

p.s. Save me the nutty ones!

Oh. My. God.

She went to get her phone and promptly fell over her half-mast trousers.

After yanking off her trousers and glowering at them, she grabbed her mobile and hesitantly re-read the texts she'd sent.

When did I become like this?

I'm unhinged.

Years of chakra bettering, ruined in a stream of bunny boiler texts.

Just then her mobile started ringing.

Aargh! It's Jude.

What do I say?

Nothing.

Hang up.

Eliza pressed ignore on her phone and dropped it like a hot potato onto the bed.

Certifiably mental.

You've been waiting all evening to hear from him and when you do, what do you do? You hang up.

He's alive. That's the main thing. Either that or it's the police who now have his phone and are ringing around his nearest and dearest to tell them the devastating news.

Do they do that?

The Bill was cancelled years ago; I have no idea.

I'm sure they turn up at your door. That way, they can put the kettle on whilst they tell you the news and they soften the blow with a cup of tea and a custard cream.

The mobile started ringing again.

Eliza peered over at it on the bed and Jude's name was flashing.

Pick it up, you stupid cow.

Pretend you're so not bothered about his welfare, you fell asleep.

Eliza, sleepily: "Hello?"

She let out a loud fake yawn into the mouthpiece.

Jude: "Eliza? Have I awoken you? I'm so sorry, go back to sleep."

Too dramatic.

Eliza, perkier: "No, no, it's ok."

Jude, cautiously: "I've, er, just received a number of texts from you. My phone ran out of battery life on the way up and I've only just got to the hotel to charge it. It's always a bit full on when I get up here."

He sounds unsure.

Come up with something to try and mitigate the madness.

Eliza: "I had a headache so I've taken a large number of tablets. I think I'm having a reaction against them and it's making me act in a way I wouldn't normally."

Diminished responsibility. Excellent!

Jude, shocked: "You've taken tablets?! What sort of tablets? How many have you taken?!"

He sounds worried.

Maybe a drugs overdose wasn't the best justification, after all.

Haul it back in.

Eliza: "It's fine, they were herbal. One big wee and they'll all be out. Anyway, less about me. How was your trip? Thank you for the chocolates. You should have left them downstairs; I've only just found them."

Then you wouldn't have been deluged with mobile madness.

Jude: "I was worried Ellington might eat them."

Ah, he's so thoughtful.

Eliza: "It was a lovely gesture."

Verbal communication prior to leaving would also have been a lovely gesture but chocolates ease the annoyance.

Jude: "How was your first day?"

I had an existential crisis.

Eliza: "I had a wonderful time."

Jude: "Ah that's good, I did say they were a nice bunch. I was wondering, to make up for me missing your first week at work, if you'd like to go away for the weekend with me?"

A romantic weekend away!

Like in films!

Eliza: "That would be lovely!"

Jude: "Ok, I'll sort out where, if you can let me know when is suitable for you with Tom and the pets."

They're not strictly pets. They're family but you're not to know that yet.

Jude: "I'm shattered, Eli. I have a big day tomorrow so I'll say goodnight. You probably need to get some sleep too. Don't forget to go to the toilet before you drop back off."

Erm. Bit weird.

Eliza: "I don't need to go."

Jude: "Your tablets. Make sure they're out of your system before you go back to sleep."

Oh, my herbal overdose.

Eliza: "Absolutely. Will do. I'm weeing as I speak. I'll be as clean as a whistle in a jiffy."

Just no, Eli.

Jude: "That's nice. Night Eli."

Eliza: "Night Jude."

Eliza caught her reflection in the cheval mirror as she put down her phone; stood in her pants and socks with a fully clothed top half.

That's a sight to behold.

Put that with the verbal incontinence and imaginary herbal drugs overdose, you really are quite the catch.

Final Social Media Meme before lights out: *It's Better to be Absolutely Ridiculous than to be Absolutely Boring – Marilyn Monroe*

Chapter Five

Billington Gazette's front page:

We are proud to introduce 'Dear Eliza', our new mentor in life feature:

Billington Gazette's MILF

Guaranteed to lighten your load

Thursday came and Eliza was sat in the Merrythought Café with a fidgety Lydia.

Eliza: "You've got gossip. Spill the beans."

Lydia: "I've bought a defibrillator."

Eliza: "What?! In case Tony keels over on the job? I know he's knocking on a bit but isn't that a bit extreme?"

Lydia: "It's for me; for my face. He said it's gone a bit saggy."

Eliza: "And you think jump-starting it is the cure? Did you read that on some dodgy blogging website?"

Lydia: "It does make my cheeks shudder a bit, I do grant you, but I do think I look more alive."

I'm sure administering that much power to your face with your heart still beating is a bit dangerous.

Possibly life-threatening.

Eliza peered across the table at Lydia's face.

Eliza: "It looks a bit red."

Lydia: "I used the harshest one, it's akin to pumice stone. I think I'll only use that on my feet in future."

A look of dawning crept across Eliza's face.

Eliza: "Defoliator. A face defoliator. As in exfoliating all your dead skin away. You've bought one of them."

Lydia: "Yes, that's what I said. However, I do think it's a bit rich Tony moaning about me getting wrinkles. It's not me who makes a bending over noise."

Eliza: "Eh?"

Lydia: "He groans 'ooooh-there-she-blows' when he straightens up; it's very disconcerting. He isn't even aware that he does it. I walk out of the room now when I spot him going down to tie his laces."

Eliza: "Oh my, that and the snoozing before dark."

Lydia: "Exactly. I might be starting to wilt under the weight of gravity but I'm vibrant and full of vigour. He's full of lifelessness and lethargy."

Can you be full of lifelessness?

Eliza: "Age comes to us all, Lydia."

I am a giver of wise words.

Lydia: "He said I needed to get fit."

Eliza, indignantly: "No, you don't! You're fine. Don't let a man dictate your hip size, Lydia. You are not a dress number, you are a powerful, independent woman."

Lydia: "Yes, yes. Calm down, Germaine Greer. I was thinking, if I showed willing by buying some Lycra and doing some lunges, it might encourage him to join me. He could become all long distance runnery and weather beaten. I find that craggy look quite seductive. I need something to fire up the loins; it's gone a bit dwindly in that department."

Lydia pulled a face full of derision.

Dave approached their table and started to lift the tea pot off the tray in order to place it on the table.

Eliza: "Dwindly? As in he hasn't got a very big willy? Or he doesn't last very lo... DAVE!"

Eliza shot back on her seat as Dave promptly dropped the full tea pot onto the floor, smashing it and splashing Eliza with hot tea, as it did so.

Dave, hollering over his shoulder: "BELINDA! Get the mop!"

He turned his attention back to Eliza and leant over her, haphazardly trying to wipe down her leg with the corner of his apron.

Dave, flustered: "Sorry Eliza, are you scalded? Please say you're not. Apart from the fact I'd hate the thought of damaging your porcelain skin, I'd have to find the accident book. I could do without a claim; my insurance is extortionate enough as it is. It's the hobs; the cuff on your cardigan can go up like a flare."

Eliza: "It's alright, it only went up my leg a bit. Are you ok? You're not normally so clumsy."

Dave: "You said the word willy. I wasn't prepared for that utterance from your lips at this time of day."

Lydia: "The word willy can be used any time of day, Dave. That and ball sack. We have no boundaries."

Dave started to visibly shake as he fervently tried to dry Eliza's lap. Eliza shot a look at Lydia and shook her head. Lydia grinned, cheekily.

Eliza batted a perturbed Dave away.

Eliza: "Please stop, Dave. You might injure yourself. Just another pot of tea, perhaps?"

Dave: "Yes, yes, sorry. Of course."

Dave turned his head slightly and hollered over his shoulder again.

Dave: "BELINDA! Another teapot required!"

Belinda, from less than a metre away: "Alright, Gobby, keep your wig on; I'm right here."

She thrust the mop at him and slouched off back towards the kitchen. Dave half-heartedly swished it around the tiles, bent down and picked up the smashed pieces of china and put them in the pocket of his apron. He straightened up slowly and muttered "straighten-up-the-mast" under his breath as he unfurled to his full, stooped height and shuffled off after Belinda.

A look of horror spread over Lydia's face.

Uh- oh.

Lydia, leant forward: "Did you hear that?! Dave's got a bending over noise, as well. Oh my god, I've got a Dave!"

Dave approached their table with the new pot of tea.

Eliza: "Nah, you don't. He doesn't have a voice that makes you willing to instantaneously drop your knickers."

Dave juddered as he sought to rescue the second pot of tea.

Dave: "Shit, bollocks!"

Dave fumbled with the pot with both hands and hastily flung it on the table. He started blowing his burnt hands and stared long and hard at Eliza.

Eliza, shrugging: "Sorry."

Dave nodded by way of acceptance of her apology and went off to serve another customer whilst shaking off the pain from his hands.

Lydia: "Can we meet up again next week? I miss you."

Eliza: "Of course, I miss you too. I'm working from home on a Thursday so don't do anything."

Let's hope no one from the Gazette is in here and overhead that.

Make amends, just in case.

Eliza: "What I mean, of course, is that I will work really hard and extra late so I am able to meet you to receive newsworthy news that may be able to go into the paper, thus being a proactive researcher with my ear to the ground on the Billington streets; never off the job."

Lydia looked at her, somewhat bemused.

Lydia: "Yes, well whatever. That's set then, darling. Every Thursday we shall meet up for a natter."

Mentor in Life Feature letter: *Dear Eliza, I've got it all going on. I'm beautiful and I have a dog called Prince Harry who I keep in a bag under the counter at work. I do the best make-up and can talk dirty with my eyes shut. I'm miserable, though, there has to be more to life than being drop dead gorgeous with men falling at your feet. Luv, Sasha-when-talking-dirty.*

Dear Sasha-when-talking-dirty, Life's a trial when you're beautiful; my friend has this trouble. It clouds people's judgement. Just be safe in the knowledge one day you'll be old and the world will look upon you less favourably. So, enjoy being one of life's stunners. Revel in the vacuity of society - set up an Instagram account and share with the world your fabulous drawn on peacock eyes.

Chapter Six

Social Media Meme: *If you can't get rid of the skeleton in your closet, you'd best teach it to dance - George Bernard Hicks*

It was Monday morning and a full complement of Billington Gazette staff were sat at their desks when an apoplectic Jude strode out of his office holding the previous week's paper.

Jude, sternly: "Who is responsible for the Dear Eliza acronym and strapline?!"

Ooh he's cross. He looks ever so manly when he's cross. Passionate. All moody and ornament flingy.

Hang on, why's he cross?

Gaz stood gingerly and raised his hand.

Gaz: "It was me with the abbreviation. It's the way we speak now. We are in a busy continuum; there ain't no time for full words. To sell paper copies we need to appeal to the urban masses or they'll just MSN it."

Jude, spluttering: "Urban masses? The most exciting thing that happens round here is a goat running amok on the dual carriageway."

Gaz: "I dunno, your missus has added quite a few column inches over the past couple of years."

Jude's stance stiffened.

Jude: "Leave our relationship out of this, please. It is not pertinent. What is pertinent is you printing that she's the paper's MILF and she'll lighten anyone's load."

Oh dear god.

Jude turned to a sheepish looking Charlotte.

Jude, angrily: "Why didn't you proof this? You said you wanted more responsibility. This was your opportunity whilst I was away. We're a laughing stock with Head Office."

Charlotte-long-hair, flustered: "I did proof read it. I have no knowledge of such parlance. I didn't know MILF meant Mother I'd like to Fuck."

Valerie gasped and there was a plop as a shocked Mandy dropped a half-eaten protein bar into her smoothie.

Eliza shot her hand up in the air and Jude looked at her, enquiringly.

Jude, sighing: "Yes, Eli?"

Eliza: "No one said the meaning of MILF. She just said it then without any prompting."

Charlotte gulped loudly.

Jude glared at Charlotte and she flushed under his stare and looked away, awkwardly.

Ooh, there's an uncomfortable silence. Shall I fill it?

It's the law, I must.

Eliza: "Perhaps, it was a mistak..."

She was cut off by Jude raising his hand to silence her.

Fair enough, silence is not illegal in a newspaper office.

Jude, quietly: "Charlotte. My office, please."

She's been rumbled.

Charlotte scraped her chair back and glowered at Eliza as she followed behind Jude towards his office.

Jude guided Charlotte in and shut the door, leaving a silent office all staring at Eliza.

Eliza: "What? Why is it my fault?! Why didn't you know what it meant, Gaz? You're at one with the urban masses."

Gaz, shrugging: "Yeah, well we kinda knew that dubbly entendre but thought it'd escape the recognition of the geriatrics in Billington. Them the ones what buy the paper, innit. None of them would've heard the phrase; I've been down the bingo hall - there ain't one of them I'd show my rod of steel to."

The whole office simultaneously blanched at the notion.

Gaz looked towards the closed door to Jude's office and continued.

Gaz: "Old Lotty and I's, we have a competition going on. Who can get the best caption printed and get away with it; we've had some pearlers. This one would have topped the current leader."

Eliza: "What's the current leader?"

Gaz: "One-armed Man Applauds Generosity of Billington's Residents."

Voluptuous Valerie: "Oh, I remember that one."

Gaz: "That one was a nine. We run a points system – ten is maximum awesome and a two is a must try harder. It's a complete malarky."

Mandy abandoned fishing her protein bar out of her smoothie, went over to Gaz and put her hands on her hips.

Mandy the Greyhound: "You twat, Gaz. Your titting about reflects on the paper as a whole, especially Jude being editor."

Jude's door opened and a red-faced Charlotte almost fell out. She stopped, straightened up and squared her shoulders as she stalked back to her chair; avoiding eye contact with a gawping workforce.

Voluptuous Valerie, cautiously: "Are you alright, Charlotte?"

Charlotte plonked a fake smile on her face.

Charlotte-long-hair: "Marvellous. Never better, right as rain. There will be an announcement in due course."

Voluptuous Valerie, nervously: "Oh! What's that then?"

Are you leaving?

That'd be handy, I wouldn't have to do your filing.

Charlotte-long-hair: "I can't tell you; it's top secret."

Gaz: "Top secret?! We ain't no chicken recipe, Lotty. We ain't KFC."

Valerie, twiddled nervously with her blouse and looked anxiously at Mandy.

Voluptuous Valerie: "What if we all get the sack?"

She then broke wind, loudly.

Voluptuous Valerie: "Oops, 'scuse me, that felt like a wet one."

Oh, that's pleasant.

Mandy's jaw dropped whilst Valerie fanned the air.

Voluptuous Valerie: "It's my IBS, any upset in my composure and I guff uncontrollably."

Nice.

Jude stepped out of his office, ran his hands through his hair and motioned for the assembled personnel to listen.

Oh, his beautiful face is ashen. I need to kiss it all over. Little butterfly kisses.

I need to then kiss his wonderful neck and work my way down to his tanned, broad shoulders.

I need to melt away the stress by nuzzling his chest.

I'll slowly kiss down to his tummy button and…

Oh my giddy aunt, I'm getting all unnecessary in the workplace. Now, I'm sure that definitely is illegal.

He's talking.

How long has that been going on?

Jude: "…so anyway, they said they're going to arrange for you all to go on a training course. It'll team build as well as address the allowable content in their family of local newspapers."

Eliza stuck her arm up in the air and Jude raised his eyebrows, enquiringly.

Jude: "Yes, Eli?"

Eliza: "They?"

Jude: "As I said, Head Office."

Eliza: "Oh, sorry. I missed that bit."

I was kissing your naked body.

Valerie popped her hand up.

Jude: "Yes, Valerie."

Voluptuous Valerie: "Is this the announcement in due course?"

Jude: "I'm sorry, what do you mean?"

Voluptuous Valerie: "Charlotte said but she wouldn't say because we were a secret recipe."

Jude looked at Charlotte who was shaking her head, rapidly at him.

Charlotte-long-hair, mouthing to Jude: "I never said that."

Voluptuous Valerie, continuing: "We're not all getting the sack then?"

Jude turned his attention back to Valerie.

Jude: "No, there's procedures to follow before any personnel can be removed from their position, Valerie, so please don't worry. I have told Head Office this was an innocent error and we will happily take on board their suggestions to make the Billington Gazette an informative, local paper. A training course is the perfect way to show our commitment."

Valerie let out another loud fart as she visibly dropped her shoulders.

Voluptuous Valerie: "Sorry. That was a relief one."

Jude shot Eliza a look as she stifled a giggle and smiled at her.

Charlotte watching the exchange, huffed and coughed. Jude quickly stopped smiling and clapped his hands together.

Jude: "Right then troops. Let's get this week's edition cracked on with; no more dubious acronyms and lots of interesting articles, please. I'll let you know when

Head Office send me the training dates for your diaries."

Eliza watched as he went to go back into his office. Feeling her gaze, he turned slightly and winked at her as he departed.

Ooh, me innards have gone.

I could just run after him and throw myself on his lap top.

Mentor in Life Feature letter: *Dear Eliza, My husband has just walked out on me to be with a woman half my age. I am devastated. Where do I go from here? Yours, lost-and-alone.*

Reply: Dear lost-and-alone, When my ex-husband left me for a woman with black bra straps, I fell apart. However, over time I realised it was the best thing to happen to me. I look at what life he is living now and I celebrate the fact it is not the path I am on. My husband leaving me gave me the opportunity to date a man who made me think I was having stroke when I met him. Take this quote with you: "Always look to the sun and the shadows will be behind you." Stay strong, the best is yet to come.

Chapter Seven

Billington Gazette Headline: ***Not Such a Merrythought. Billington Café Owner Foots the Fee for Customers' Free Footwear Due To Foolish Floor*** (Pun Points – seven)

Eliza tugged at Tom's sock.

He had fallen asleep in front of his latest fixation, a cookery programme.

Culinary catatonia.

Ellington, from across the room, opened an eye and watched Eliza failing to stir a slumbering Tom. He stood and stretched; his floppy jowls reverberating as he yawned. He loped over and stood by Tom's foot.

He looked up at Eliza, silently seeking Eliza's permission.

Eliza: "Be my guest."

Ellington then grabbed the hem of Tom's trousers with his teeth and proceeded to drag him off the settee.

Tom was unceremoniously deposited onto the floor.

Tom opened his eyes and started batting away Ellington.

Tom: "Oi! Gerroff, you hairy mutt!"

Eliza: "Stand easy, Ellington. Your work here is done."

Ellington gave two wags of his tail and went back to where he was sleeping, previously.

Eliza: "Tom, we need to get you in the bath and then bed. I'm off early tomorrow for my weekend away with Jude and I need to drop you off at Lydia's, first thing."

Tom: "Ooh, that's exciting."

Eliza: "It is. I will miss you, though."

Tom: "Yeah, I know you will. It's because I've got it all going on."

Eliza: "Modesty being the main thing you've got going on."

Tom: "Don't worry about me; I'll be eating as many cakes and biscuits I can pick up. Auntie Wydia has no portion control. It's brilliant."

Eliza: "Indeed. I can rest easy."

Eliza and Tom wandered up to the bathroom and Eliza started running Tom's bath whilst he disrobed.

Tom: "Mum, Charlie says I'm his brother from another mother."

Eliza, swishing in the bubble bath: "That's nice, dear."

Tom: "I told him; I've already got one of them with Orson."

As if I need reminding.

Eliza, still swishing: "Indeed."

Tom: "Charlie says he's from the hood. It sounds proper scary."

Eliza stopped playing with the bubbles and stood.

Eliza: "He lives in Honeysuckle Close, love. I shouldn't lose any sleep over it."

Tom: "Am I from his patch?"

I've decided I don't much care for Charlie.

Eliza, grabbing a towel: "If you think it might benefit your friendship, then yes."

Tom: "Cooool!"

Eliza: "You can get in now."

Tom: "Have you tested it wiv your elbow?"

Eliza: "No, I've had my whole arms in it."

Tom: "Righto."

Tom launched himself into the tub and emerged with a massive cloud of bubbles on his head. Eliza put the lid down on the toilet and sat down.

Tom: "Mum."

Eliza: "Yes, Tom."

Tom: "What's it like to be an adult?"

Erm.

Eliza: "You just Google stuff, really."

Tom: "And pay bills?"

Eliza: "Yes, and pay bills."

Tom: "When I grow up I want to be that man from Mister Chef."

Eliza: "John Torode?"

Tom: "No. The fruit and veg one. I definitely think he's from my patch and he likes a nice pudding."

Tom started searching around.

Tom: "Where's me bath cookery fings?"

Eliza: "Sorry, I'll get them."

Eliza leant over to the bathroom cabinet and lobbed out a cup, a funnel and a teapot.

Tom: "Go out for a few minutes and I'll make you something."

Bossy.

Eliza left the door ajar and went to finish packing her clothes for the weekend, keeping an ear out to Tom's bath-time whistling. A few minutes later there was a holler from the bathroom.

Tom. "Muuummm! I've made something for you."

Eliza, wandering back in: "Is it a nice cup of tea?"

Tom: "No, it's a strawberry coulis."

Oh.

Eliza pretended to gulp down strawberry coulis, whilst Tom made a Mohican out of bubbles on his head.

Tom: "Where are you going for your weekend away?"

Eliza: "Down south, Hampshire way."

Tom: "Hampshire? Isn't that where trolls live?"

Eliza: "Just the one, Tom."

Tom nodded and smiled.

Tom: "Mum, I've been finkin' about life and stuff."

Ooh, he's started to question his existence and the purpose of it all.

He's very young to be venturing into such realms. It took me until Lewis left for me to wonder what it was all about.

Eliza: "Oh, what sort of things? Why we're here? The vacuity of material goods? How the pure love of another human being can lift a person from utter desolation and a life lacking in purpose to a feeling of sheer joy and belonging, yet simultaneously wondering why the emotion exists when love can break your heart? Those sort of things?"

Tom stopped fashioning his bubble Mohican and stared at her.

Tom: "No mum, I'm seven."

Of course you are.

Eliza: "What are you thinking about then, Tom?"

Tom: "Wouldn't it be brilliant if the world was made of jelly?"

I let him make major decisions about my life.

I probably need to review that.

Eliza: "Yes love. It would make desserts much easier. You could just eat a field."

Tom looked at Eliza, seriously.

Tom: "Mum?"

Tom: "Why *are* we here?"

Eliza: "To wash your hair. Come on."

Eliza motioned for Tom to slide under the bubbles.

Tom, under a pile of bubbles: "I meant what's our purpose?"

I know what you meant.

Tom sat back up to let Eliza put on the shampoo.

Eliza: "Can we leave that for another couple of decades, please love?"

Tom: "Ok mum. I'll stick to thinking about jelly."

Eliza: "Good plan."

Mentor in Life Feature letter: *Dear Eli, I never knew you fell apart when I left you. I'm so sorry. If it's any consolation, ~~Gerry~~ I don't think my partner treats me with the respect I deserve. I work long hours to try and keep her and our son with a roof over their heads but all she does is complain. Yours, I-wonder-where-it-all-went-wrong*

Dear I-know-exactly-where-it-all-went-wrong, It's not really any consolation because I don't care anymore. Perhaps, ~~Gerry~~ she doesn't give you the respect you feel you deserve because you credit yourself with too much importance. And by the way, you have two sons but don't worry, I keep the roof over his head.

Chapter Eight

Billington Gazette Headline: **Pilkington Man Missing Since he was Lost. Appeal Inside** (Pun Points - Four – Charlotte is not happy as the misplacement of humans is no laughing matter but as she was off sick on print day, Gaz let it run anyway).

It was seven o'clock the next morning and Eliza was roused from her sleep with the telephone ringing.

Eh? Oh my god, someone's come a cropper.

It'll be someone from the 1980's because it's the land line they've called.

Don't let it be any one I like.

She scrambled out of bed, staggered down the stairs and clumsily picked up the landline phone.

Eliza, tentatively: "Hello? Is this an old school friend?"

Lewis: "Eh? No, it's me. Good morning, Eli."

Eliza to you..

Actually, Ms Wakeley to you.

Eliza: "Are you dead?"

Lewis: "No, I'm talking on the phone to you."

Eliza, irritated: "Have you lost the ability to tell night from day?"

Lewis: "I appreciate it's a bit early but I was hoping to speak to Tom and ask him something; make up for my recent visitation haphazardness."

Ah, he's read the reply to his letter.

Lewis, continuing: "There's a band he said he liked coming to Billington. I wanted to see if he wants me to get tickets. We could go together; it'd be nice for me to get out of the house. They go on sale shortly so I need to be quick."

Eliza, sighing: "Oh, hang on then."

Eliza put her hand over the receiver and called upstairs. She was greeted by a bleary-eyed, puffy faced Tom with his bed hair standing on end, stood at the top.

Tom, rubbing his eyes: "Who is it, me old finger 'n thumb?"

Eliza, calling up: "Dad."

Tom: "Whose dad?"

Eliza: "Your dad."

Tom: "Is he brown bread? It's very early."

Eliza: "No, he's talking. Dead people don't talk."

Tom: "Charlie said that dead people sigh."

Smarty pants, Charlie from the hood.

Eliza: "It's called the last breath. I don't think dad's having one of those. If he is, he's having a lot of them."

Tom: "What does he want? We ain't heard from him for weeks."

Eliza, losing patience: "Can you just talk to him? I need a cup of tea and Norris is climbing up my leg."

Tom staggered down the stairs and took the receiver whilst Eliza picked up a nagging Norris and went to put the kettle on.

A couple of cups of tea and fed animals later, Eliza did a wind-up signal to Tom who was still on the phone.

Tom: "I'd better go or mum will start moaning."

Oh, how very dare you!

Eliza: "Ahem! I do not moan; I encourage whilst making you audibly aware of the time."

Eliza tapped her wrist at an imaginary watch.

Tom: "Uh oh, she's starting. Bye dad."

Don't create the misconception that I am like other mothers who holler to get their child to shift themselves.

I am different. I am earth mother. I smile fondly and ruffle my late child's hair as he sits in his pyjamas five minutes before we need to leave the house.

I chuckle at his joy at being one of life's slackers.

I do not let such frivolous things get under my skin.

Eliza glanced up at the clock.

Eliza: "Aaargh! Shift yourself! You and your gabbing at a ridiculous hour has us all behind. MOVE!!"

I'll ruffle his hair in a carefree manner when I get to Lydia's.

She started to go up the stairs and tripped over Ellington.

Eliza, scowling: "Must you sit right under my feet?!"

Eliza waved him out of the way.

Eliza, muttering: "If only I had the ability to stop time!"

Tom, using his best Darth Vader voice: "You have only begun to discover your power. Join me, and I will complete your training. With our combined strength, we can end this destructive conflict and bring order to the galaxy."

Eliza: "I'll join you after the weekend. Book me in."

Eliza ushered him back upstairs.

Eliza: "Just go and put some clothes on, please and don't forget to pack Cheddar Chicken."

Mentor in Life Feature letter: *Dear Eliza, I like songwriting. I've been posting my lyrics online on social media pages and have been receiving some positive feedback. I was really gaining confidence until one person wrote that it was a pile of rubbish and I shouldn't be bothering. They said I was a pathetic loser. My family have said to forget about it and focus on the positive comments but I can't. All I hear in my head are the insults. Please can you help? Should I just give up and try something else? Yours, Music-is-my-passion.*

Dear Follow-your-passion-and-truly-live, You have fallen victim to the online troll (and probably a real life one, at that). I too have been the subject of this form of bullying. I used to write a blog and whilst most people were supportive and kind; one person took a twisted pleasure in being hurtful. They'd hidden their identity and did not know me, yet personally attacked me; making incorrect assumptions and accusations, without a care as to the truth. I stopped writing my blog; such was the profound effect it had on me but, over time, I realised opinions of friends and family matter and not somebody who is nobody to me. It's made me stronger, actually, as I understand how cyber bullying makes people feel and have the empathy to answer your letter. I once heard a quote which I hope helps: "There is no gesture more devastating than the back turning away." Report it, block them and forget the words they utter. Be kind, be you and follow your song writing dreams – how about you do a Taylor Swift and use them in one of your songs; she gets loads of number ones.

Chapter Nine

Billington Gazette Headline: ***Pilkington Re-enactment and Theatrical Society (PRATS) Lose Replica Tank after Painting it with Camouflage Paint*** (Pun Points – Not Applicable – this is just stating facts. The PRATS are idiots.)

Eliza: "Are you sure we've done everything?"

Jude: "Doors and windows locked. Check. Ellington with your rather alarming neighbour. Check. Norris free run of the house, cat flap open and spare food with aforementioned neighbour. Check. Your loquacious cockney offspring delivered to your scary best friend. Check."

Loquacious? Is that an insult?

I'll Google that in the car.

Jude: "Now, will you please give me your cases?"

Jude went around to the back of his car and clicked the boot open whilst Eliza dragged her two suitcases to him. She peered in.

Eliza: "Blimey, you've got a lot of stuff in there! What's it all for?"

Jude: "It's in case of an emergency. There's a jack, tools, water, foot pump, blanket. The usual. What do you have in your car?"

I thought we lived in England not deepest Peru.

Eliza: "Erm... I have an emergency Curly Wurly."

Jude, sighing: "What would you do if you broke down in the middle of the night?"

Eliza: "I don't drive at night. I have a child who goes to bed before nine."

Jude: "What about when you pop to the shops in the evening? I always do mine after the ten o'clock news when it's quiet."

Here speaks a non-parent. The blessed adult who didn't succumb to sleepless nights and constant guilt.

A human with no fear of the future world and what it holds through the eyes of his child.

A human with the glorious luxury of selfishness.

A human with the ability to go to the supermarket at midnight if he so chooses.

A human with a beautiful face, devoid of bags and the onset of early aging.

A human with no fear of dropping dead one day leaving a child bereft without a parent.

A human who can book holidays any time of the year.

A human with the energy to join a gym.

Eliza: "When you have a child your days of popping anywhere are over. It's a scheduled, protracted affair of coat finding, shoe-lace tying and chivvying."

Jude: "Oh, fair enough. I'll get you a little toolbox of bits just in case. I don't like the thought of you trying to change a tyre with a Curly Wurly."

Or I could just call roadside recovery and eat it whilst I'm waiting for the tow truck.

He's being helpful. Be gracious.

Eliza: "As you wish, my lord."

She gave a sweeping gesture with her hand which led to her being given a bemused look as Jude heaved her cases in the boot.

Too gracious, perhaps.

Jude: "Crikey Eli, what have you got in here? We're only going away for a weekend."

Eliza: "I haven't been away for so long; I've forgotten what you do. I've packed a few bits, just in case. You never know what the weather's going to do, so I've brought a few spare items of clothing."

Jude: "Yes you do. It's been a mild spring but with a, higher than usual, amount of rain; you can look at the weather app on your phone."

Eliza: "Never trust an app. It's technology designed by humans. Humans are flawed and as such so is everything they make."

Ooh, that was very deep for a Saturday morning. I might have to make a meme of that and post it up as my status.

Jude ushered her towards the passenger seat.

Jude: "Come on, my little ray of sunshine, hop in the car or we'll never get there."

After closing Eliza's door, Jude ran around to the driver's seat, started up the engine and pulled away from Eliza's house. As he drove down the road he looked into his rear-view mirror, raised his eyebrows and promptly pulled over.

Jude: "Your neighbour is walking your dog whilst wearing, what I perceive to be, a World War II RAF pilot's uniform. Are you sure he's sane enough to be responsible for anything living?"

Eliza swung her head round to look.

Eliza: "Oh yes. Philip knows Ellington only comes to military commands so is going the full hog. Lydia told him about method acting and he appears to be embracing the task."

Philip and Ellington caught up with their parked car and Eliza stuck her head out of the passenger window.

Upon seeing Eliza, Ellington strained madly on the lead, nearly yanking Philip's arm out his socket. A puffing Philip stopped at the car.

Philip: "Bleedin' canine!"

He bobbed down and doffed his flying goggles which were perched on top of his helmet.

Philip: "Hello Eliza dear, I thought I'd do an early morning walk with your disruptive pooch as I need to attend to a game bird before lunch."

Jude leant across the car.

Jude: "Is that a World War II pilot's uniform, you're wearing?"

Philip: "It is indeed, my dear chap. Most impressive of you to know its origins. I pilfered it from the PRATS. They'll not notice; PRATS by name and prats by nature, that lot!"

Philip chortled.

Ellington started scrabbling at the passenger door and rearing up to get to Eliza.

Eliza: "Oooh, get down Ellington, you'll damage Jude's paintwork!"

Philip: "Can't be having marks on the chappie's car, we'll be on our way. See you tomorrow evening, have a lovely time. Don't worry about a thing."

He yanked a reluctant Ellington away from the car.

Philip, with authority: "ATTENTION! Right Flank...MARCH!"

Ellington immediately fell into step and they made off down the road.

Eliza and Jude sat in the stationary car, watching the vision of a slightly overweight, middle aged man in full pilot's uniform hollering orders to a highly strung border collie. Eliza and Jude watched the pair of them in silence until they'd turned out of sight, towards the park.

Jude: "This is your normality, isn't it?"

Eliza: "Eh? I don't know what you mean."

Jude shook his head slightly, straightened up and continued driving.

Jude: "You do realise he'll have a Spitfire in his front garden when we get back."

Eliza: "Don't be ridiculous, he hasn't got the room. He struggles enough with his rose bush; it's had to endure a severe pruning this season. Plus, he can't nick a plane."

Eliza pulled out her mobile and Googled, loquacious - talking or tending to talk much.

Oh, a fancy way of saying chatty. Not an insult. That's good.

Mentor in Life Feature letter: *Dear Eliza, All my mates are dating but I can't find a partner. I'm fit, funny and really good-looking. I'm also loaded; I don't know what the problem is. Should I try internet dating? Cheers, I'm-an-Adonis.*

Dear Are-you-really-an-Adonis? Have a quote by John Bright which seems apt: "He is a self-made man and worships his creator." Modesty is an endearing trait;

one which should be harnessed and displayed whenever possible. I read a book once, Observations From The Precipice, and it said online dating is the new black. There's a website I can recommend: www.multitudeofmates.com – go on there and see how you get on.

Chapter Ten

Billington Gazette Headline: ***Three Remain Dead After Outbreak of Legionnaires' Disease in Billington Undertakers*** (Pun Points – six, was seven but Charlotte docked a point for humorising death)

They drove for, what Eliza felt was, a lifetime; carving their way through varying scenes of English countryside as they travelled from motorway to B-road. Every time she saw a new place name she felt compelled to say it out loud to inform, an already knowing, Jude.

Eliza: "…Welcome to Evenminster, please drive carefully… So where are we staying again?"

Jude: "Watershed B and B. It was recommended by a friend of mine. She said it was very quaint."

Ping! Alert! Female mentioned in passing.

She? Who it this woman?

What did that self-help book I read 'Men are from Caves and Women are their Slaves' say about men and women? Men only see women as sexual opportunities and skivvies; there to cook whatever they' hunter-gathered that day. I wish I'd never read that book actually; it's upset my equilibrium and perhaps provided an unnecessary insight into the male psyche.

Be impassive. Not a jealous or unhinged in any way.

Eliza, in an overly light-hearted manner: "She? Who is this she? What's her name?"

Jude: "She's called Daphne."

He doesn't look like he'd go out with a Daphne. Daphne and Jude. No, that doesn't sound right.

That's probably why they split up.

It is also quite an era specific name. I have yet to meet a Daphne in her thirties.

Maybe he had an 'older woman' phase. Hmmm.

I can give him that, though. He probably needed to get it out of his system.

I can't complain; I would think after experiencing Daphne's bosoms mine would look marvellous in comparison. Positively buoyant.

Jude, continuing: "She works on the reception at Head Office. She's been there ever since I can remember."

Ah, my knowledge of names and their decade of origin is bang on.

Eliza: "Oh, so not a friend then. A work associate. Nothing too friendly and she's probably nearing retirement... You are leaving Evenminster, thank you for driving carefully..."

Move along, nothing to worry about. Not an ex with long legs and nymphomaniacal tendencies.

Not even the author of 'Men live in Caves and Women are their Slaves' would be perturbed by Daphne. Maybe there should be a Daphne caveat on the whole men only see women as sexual objects chapter.

Jude furrowed his brow slightly but said nothing more.

Eliza: "I need a wee."

Jude: "Another one?"

Eliza: "I have had a child and as such my bladder is somewhat unreliable. Tom had quite a big head for my delicate pelvis. When I pushed him out I think I left my lady organs hanging in the breeze."

Jude: "That's a nice image, thank you."

Pleasure.

Eliza gave Jude a sidelong glance but he kept his eyes on the road.

Jude: "Next services, ok?"

Eliza nodded.

I wonder if I should try and be demurer.

I bet Daphne is quite proper. I bet she buys everything in Marks and Spencer's.

What would her ideal holiday be? She's been to Watershed Bed and Breakfast, so I reckon she's a British Isles sort of woman.

I bet she likes a good barge. I can see her in her wedges and summer slacks, pulling up along the waterways and having a nice pub lunch.

I bet she's very deft with a lock.

Eliza: "... Historic Aramore, where the King Henry got poked with a pike... Does Daphne like boats? I bet she knows the canal system like the back of her hand."

Jude: "Pardon? What on earth are you blathering on about now?"

Blathering?!

Eliza, slightly higher octave than usual: "Musing, Jude. Musing. Not blathering. I do not blather. I just wondered where else Daphne took her holidays, that's all. Nothing to use the word blathering about."

Jude, exasperated: "How the devil would I know? She signs me in and provides me with a lanyard to get in the doors when I attend meetings. I have no knowledge of how she spends her recreational time."

Not strictly true...

Eliza: "Except for the discussion about Watershed and her recommendation, of course."

Jude: "Yes, Eliza. Except for passing chit chat and discussion regarding bed and breakfast recommendations."

He called me Eliza. I might be in trouble.

Eliza: "Does she shop at Marks and Spencer's? ... Marnforth. The home of suet..."

Jude: "Be quiet now, please. I'm trying to concentrate."

Oh, that's nice.

Eliza huffed loudly and Jude looked across with concern.

Jude pulled the car over in a lay by.

Uh oh. He's going to dump me on the side of the road and go on holiday without me.

Jude hauled the hand brake up and looked hard at Eliza.

Gulp.

Jude, quietly: "Is everything ok with you, Eli?"

Possibly not.

Eliza: "Don't leave me here. I haven't got suitable footwear on for a walk home."

Jude: "I'm struggling to keep up with your random utterings. Have I done something to upset you?"

Jude picked up Eliza's right hand and kissed it gently.

Jude: "I care for you so much, Eli. If I've done something wrong, please tell me."

Eliza's heart jumped and she looked him, lightly kissing the back of her hand.

You're perfect.

I'd marry you and have three more children.

No, actually, I can't have three more children. I'd have to carry my cervix around in my handbag.

Eliza: "You're perfect."

Thank you brain and mouth. Finally working in unison and for not saying the other bit I was thinking.

Jude stopped kissing and looked up.

Jude: "Really? Well I'm not, but as long as I haven't caused you to be upset. If I'm honest, I don't confess to understand the inner workings of a woman's brain and yours is certainly more convoluted than most. I am in unchartered waters."

Eliza: "You and me both. My brain is an entity in its own right. It bypasses any filter mechanism."

Eliza smiled at him and patted him with her spare hand.

Eliza: "It doesn't matter about my cervix."

You had to do it, didn't you, mouth?

Jude let go of Eliza's hand and looked at her, perplexed.

Eliza: "Forget I said that last bit."

Jude, nodding: "Ok. I think that's for the best. I'll find you the next services so you can urinate."

Wee not urinate. Horses urinate. Ladies wee.

Please brain. Just stop. Jude can't cope; I can't cope.

Just look at the countryside and think nothing.

Is that a field of Llamas?

Or are they Alpacas?

I wonder what the difference is.

That Llama slash Alpaca over there looks vaguely familiar.

Eliza craned her neck as they sped past.

Ah, gone. Never mind.

Ooh cows. Now what ones are they?

Friesians?

No, they're black and white, these are brown.

Maybe they're a nice Jersey.

You can't beat a nice Jersey cow. They have lovely milk.

Eliza: "Jersey cows make a lovely cup of tea."

Jude: "Do they now? How do their hooves hold the spoon?"

Ah you see, he can keep up with my random utterings. He didn't even blink.

Perfect. Just perfect.

Eliza beamed across at Jude and he looked back at her and smiled broadly.

Social Media Meme posted from the motorway services toilet cubicle: *Happiness is the settling of the soul into its most appropriate spot — Aristotle*

Chapter Eleven

Southern Daily Times Headline: ***Llama looks like Bin Laden – Picture Exclusive!***

Several toilet stops and motorway miles later Jude swung his car into the gravelled drive of Watershed Bed and Breakfast. There in front of them, nestled amongst rambling roses and honeysuckle stood a, quintessentially English, chocolate box cottage. Eliza sighed as she took in its two eyebrow windows nestled beneath a long-ago thatched roof. The cob walls were lime washed white with peeling pale blue window frames which held in tiny single glazed panes of glass.

Eliza: "Oh Jude, it's lovely!"

Jude: "It is very pretty, isn't it? Good old Daphne."

Jude pulled into a space under the dappled shade of a silver birch and yanked the cases out of the boot.

Jude: "C'mon, let's get ourselves settled."

Eliza beamed broadly and hugged one of his suitcase holding arms.

They wandered through an old quarry tiled floor porch into a small hallway whereby they were greeted by a buxom lady in an apron.

She held out a robust arm which Jude dropped the cases to shake.

Buxom hand shaker, booming: "Greetings travellers! I trust you had a magnificent journey. I'm Mrs Tookery, owner, proprietor and general dogsbody of this crumbling establishment! If there's anything you require during your stay, ask my husband!"

She guffawed at her well-rehearsed and well used greeting.

Jude: "Lovely to meet you, Mrs Tookery. We've booked; the name is Julian Hardy."

Mrs Tookery: "You have indeed. Sign in here please."

She turned her attention to Eliza.

Mrs Tookery: "It is splendid to meet you, Mrs Hardy."

Eliza gasped.

Eliza: "Oh no. I'm not Mrs. Well I am, but not his. Not yet. Or maybe never, I don't know. I can't be that presumptuous."

Just shut up.

Jude looked up at her from completing the form and smiled a crooked grin.

He thinks I'm an idiot.

Mrs Tookery raised her shoulders and winked.

Mrs Tookery: "Oooh! How naughty! I don't condone extramarital affairs, obviously. I was brought up to do the right thing but, as I say to Nigel, that's my husband, you can't judge. We let you all in. We are not enablers; we are in the hospitality trade and as such we turn a blind eye to everything. Well, as long as it doesn't affect the mattress. I've got the onset of arthritis; I can't be over exerting myself on housekeeping duties."

Mrs Tookery looked at Jude long and hard and he squirmed under her scrutiny,

Jude: "Ahem, I've completed the form. If you'd be so kind as to let us have our room key."

Mrs Tookery ignored his outstretched hand and smiled at him. She rested her ample bosom on folded arms.

Mrs Tookery: "You look like my Nigel; a dead ringer. It's really quite distracting. He'd not indulge in an illicit dalliance, though. I'd chop his bally knackers off, if he so much as sniffed at another woman."

Misinterpretation of situation alert. Rescue required.

Eliza: "No knackers are needing to be chopped off, Mrs Tookery. I am divorced and this is my new boyfriend."

There. I've set the record straight.

I may be a failure on the marriage front but I've bagged a good one now so I'm not a complete dead loss.

Mrs Tookery let out a sigh of relief and unfolded her arms.

Mrs Tookery: "Oh, thank heavens for that, dears. I can handle divorcees. That's just poor decision making, not a sin. We all have poor judgement from time to time. Even me! I bought geese the other year after reading a Daily Mail article about them making good guard dogs. You see, we'd had a bit of trouble with rowdy locals trespassing across our flower beds; they can't handle their home brew. Well, it was the worst decision of my life. The geese were utter bastards to the guests; wouldn't let them out of their cars! I'm surprised our Trip Advisor rating didn't plummet."

Eliza and Jude stood in silence staring at Mrs Tookery.

I thought I was mad.

Jude found his voice first.

Jude: "Hmm, righty-ho. Keys? Possibly?"

Mrs Tookery: "Of course, my dear. Forthwith. You must be gasping for a beverage. You will find tea, open brackets and coffee for those who wish, close brackets, making facilities in your room. Should you require, we also have on offer, a range of other liquid refreshment to suit your requirements if you, erm, require. We aim to please here at Watershed Bed and Breakfast and endeavour to make your stay with us a happy one."

Ah back on script. Wonderful.

Mrs Tookery held out a key on a yellow fob.

Mrs Tookery: "You are in our 'Van Gogh' room. We theme our rooms so our guests can indulge in our creative outpouring. We tried a 'Tracey Emin' room but our guests didn't take kindly to making their own bed so changed it into a Banksy room. Sleeping in the decorative equivalent of a disused underground station isn't to everyone's taste but that's art, isn't it dears? Subjective."

Jude almost snatched the key out of Mrs Tookery's large hand.

Jude: "Lovely. We look forward to experiencing your artistic flair... Eliza, go. Now, please."

With pleasure.

Mrs Tookery, shouting after them: "Up the stairs, on the right. Mind the threshold; it's got a dodgy board. That's number eight on Nigel's 'jobs to do' list!"

Eliza and Jude ran up the stairs, tripped over a raised plank in the doorway and fell into the Van Gogh room. They straightened up and looked around.

They were surrounded by a sea of mustard yellow on the walls. Stuck to the paintwork were random images of sunflowers. Eliza went over and inspected them and deduced they had been cut out myriad magazines, posters and what appeared to be gardening books. On an old scrubbed pine chest of drawers was a Victorian water bowl and matching jug, above it hung a print of 'Bedroom in Arles'. On each side of the bed sat matching scrubbed pine bedside units complete with bedside lights which were made out of adapted vases topped with a yellow lampshade. Stuck on the front of the lampshades were more sunflowers. The bed linen was swirls of blue with stars on it.

Jude, agog as he looked around: "Gosh."

Eliza, pointing to the bed: "What's going on with the duvet?"

Jude: "The Starry Night. June 1889. Van Gogh's view from his asylum in Provence."

Eliza: "Oh. That's nice."

Jude: "Shall we go out?"

Eliza: "Yes."

Eliza and Jude left their dumped cases just inside the doorway and backed out.

Social Media Meme: *Every artist was first an amateur. Ralph Waldo Emerson.*

Chapter Twelve

Southern Daily Times Headline: ***Spread Eagle After the Watershed***

The Spread Eagle Pub, Wachten was pipped to the post by local Bed and Breakfast, The Watershed, in this year's fiercely contested Art in the Community prize. Their interpretation of Monet's 1899 Water Lily Pond whereby they placed a replica wooden bridge in one of their guest rooms thus creating a path between the bed and sink impressed the judges enormously and secured them the top prize. Asked for a quote Mrs Joan Tookery, 65, said "That was my Nigel's idea, he really is quite progressive. We're thinking of starting a Crowdfunder to have him hung in the Tate."

Eliza: "I'll drive. You've done enough for one day."

Jude: "If you're sure. Thank you."

Jude tossed the car keys at her and they jumped into the car.

Eliza: "Let's go and explore!"

Eliza crunched the gears as she tried to find reverse.

Eliza: "Apologies. I need to lift your flange. You only have to press down a bit on mine."

Jude blinked.

Eliza found reverse and shot back on the gravelled drive, spitting gravel everywhere.

Eliza: "Ooh, different biting point on the old clutch."

Jude cleared his throat, nervously.

Jude: "I can drive you know Eli; it really is no bother."

Eliza: "I wouldn't hear of it. I'm adjusting that's all. Give me a mile and we'll be tickety-boo."

Jude audibly gulped and checked his seat belt.

Eliza: "Where shall we go?"

Jude: "I read about a waterfall. Shall we go there?"

Eliza: "Yep, get my person's spot on the sat nav."

Jude: "Eh?"

Eliza: "GPS."

Jude searched Eliza's face for clues as to whether she was joking or not. Having seen no flicker, he smiled with amusement.

Jude set the sat nav and they set off.

A couple of miles down the road, Eliza had grasped the ability to drive Jude's car. Having gained confidence she swung it around the country lanes. As they approached the brow of a hill, Jude let out a cry.

Jude, flapping his arms madly: "Aargh! Eli! Car!"

Eliza: "FLIP-FLOPS!"

Eliza swerved madly onto the wrong side of the road, past a car which was parked on a blind hill and cut in quickly ahead of an oncoming van. She stopped the car at the side of the road and stared in her rear-view mirror, puffing.

Eliza: "Jeezus! Unless a wasp has just flown in that driver's ear or they're having a stroke then there is no excuse for stopping abruptly on the brow of a hill."

She looked across at Jude who was breathing deeply.

Eliza: "Are you alright?"

Jude nodded whilst continuing to breathe deeply.

Eliza: "To the waterfall?"

Jude continued to nod.

Eliza: "Right you are. You just keep on with the inhaling thing. In for ten, hold for ten and breathe out for ten. Not too deep or you'll faint. I did that once and came to with Norris kneading my face. It wasn't very Zen."

Eliza started up the car again and once she'd gained momentum down the hill, she took it out of gear.

Jude, having regained his normal pallor, looked down at the out of gear stick and then at Eliza.

Jude: "What are you doing?"

Eliza: "Seeing how far I can freewheel without putting it in gear. My best Pilkington run was starting by the gate at the top of the hill, the one with a dubious hinge, and finally stopping by the telegraph pole opposite the Anchor pub. That was an epic day."

Jude: "Why?"

Eliza: "What do you mean, why?"

Jude: "Why do you freewheel?"

Eliza: "Because that's what you do down hills."

Jude: "Is it?"

Eliza: "Is it not?"

Jude: "No."

Eliza: "Oh."

I must check the Highway Code when I get Wi-Fi.

I'm sure he's mistaken but I'll not show him up as we're having a nice time.

They continued to drive in silence for another twenty minutes with the sat nav navigating them to the waterfall.

Jude, pointing: "There!"

Eliza: "Oh!"

Jude: "Shall we park up and have a look?"

Eliza: "Ok."

Eliza swung the car into a makeshift hard core car park beside the top of the waterfall and they got out.

They wandered the ten metres to the waterfall and peered over the edge of the bank to look at it.

Eliza: "It's a waterfall."

Jude: "Most sagacious of you."

Big word alert! Google meaning after the Highway Code query.

They stood there for a few moments and it started to spit with rain.

Jude: "Back in the car?"

Eliza nodded, then quickly pulled a departing Jude back.

Eliza: "Let's take a quick selfie before we leave so it looks like we're having a good time."

Jude gave her a quizzical look.

Jude: "We are having a good time, aren't we?"

Eliza: "Yes, yes. Smile!"

They both planted a fixed grin on their faces and Eliza took the picture.

Jude wandered back to the car and sat back in the passenger seat whilst Eliza checked the photo and tutted.

Eliza opened the driver's door and leant in.

Jude: "Everything alright?"

Eliza: "I looked a bit old; I think it's the light, so I want to delete it. Can we go back and get another one?"

Jude: "Really?"

Eliza: "Everyone does them these days. It's the new black."

I resisted for so long but I have been lured by the memes and inspirational quotes.

Jude: "Is it indeed? How about we buck the trend and just live in the moment?"

Eliza: "How frightfully radical of you. Ok."

He definitely doesn't post pictures of his dinner on social media.

Eliza flumped back into the driver's seat.

Eliza: "Where to now?"

Jude looked out of the window and peered at the sky.

Jude: "I think it's just a shower. Shall we wait here until it passes and then go for a walk?"

Eliza: "Ok, where to?"

Jude shrugged.

Jude: "Nowhere in particular, just a walk."

How romantic.

Eliza: "Ooh, as in a 'hold hands and scuff the leaves together whilst giggling at the innocent joy of it all' sort of walk?"

Jude ruffled his brow.

Jude: "Yes, I'm sure we can find some leaves where we can do that."

Eliza: "Ace. You're on."

Jude smiled broadly at Eliza and her heart skipped.

Eliza: "You're proper lovely."

Jude picked up her left hand and held it gently in both of his then bent his head down kissed the back of it.

Jude: "So are you."

Eliza sighed and felt a warm glow wash over her.

I am lucky.

The man of my dreams seems to like me as much as I like him. I wonder how often that happens.

I shall have to look up the percentage for that. I bet I'm a minority statistic.

Social Media Photo Post: *Jude and Me at a Waterfall. (Please note: I don't actually have seven chins; I was at the wrong angle.)*

Chapter Thirteen

Mouth of the Estuary FM playing in the car: *Welcome to MOTE FM weather. We're expecting the clouds to disperse and a clear afternoon, so use your time wisely and be a street walker.*

A few minutes later, after much cloud inspection, they felt it dry enough to leave the car.

Jude: "Ready for a stroll?"

Eliza: "Ready."

They jumped out of the car and looked around.

Jude: "Up or down?"

I can do hills. It's a chance to show off my ascending prowess.

Eliza: "Up."

Jude nodded, grabbed her hand and started off at a quick pace, up past the waterfall, towards a relatively untrodden path towards some woods.

Ooh, he's a bit quick on the steppage. I'm a bit puffed already.

Eliza clamped onto his hand with a vice-like grip and allowed him to practically pull her up.

Jude turned behind him.

Jude: "Are you ok, Eli? Is it a bit steep for you?"

He'll think I'm frail. I cannot admit I need a sit down.

Eliza: "Oh no, it's fine. I might stop and have a quick look at the view though; admire the waterfall from this vantage point."

Jude, smiling: "Ok, no problem."

Eliza stopped and breathed deeply whilst pretending to admire the splendour of the falling water as it splashed over the rocks below.

A couple of minutes later, Eliza had gathered herself enough to continue up the hill.

Eliza: "I've admired enough. Crack on."

Jude nodded, grabbed her hand again and continued his rapid trek up the ever-steepening hill.

I should have said down. Never say up again unless there's an engine involved.

Jude looked over his shoulder at her.

Jude: "Are you alright, Eli? You're puffing a lot. We can turn round if you like."

Eliza: "No, no. I'm fine. I always breathe like this when scaling a mountain. It keeps my lungs from collapsing from the altitude."

Jude, chortling: "We're nearly at the top, I reckon there will be a lovely view when we get there."

Knickers to the view. Keep on at this pace, I'll be having a lie down at the top.

Eliza: "I can hardly wait."

That bit is true. The sooner this hike is over the better.

Jude: "Shall we stop, so you can admire some more scenery for a minute?"

Eliza: "If you don't mind."

Jude stopped and Eliza stared blankly at a Douglas fir tree whilst catching her breath.

Eliza: "Shall I hug it? It looks an old one."

Jude: "If you feel the need."

Eliza: "It's grounding and makes you at one with nature."

Jude: "Fair enough, hug away then."

Eliza moved towards the tree and put her arms around it. She leant her face in, deeply inhaling its earthy smell and rested her cheek on its bark.

That's an odd sensation. A bit squelchy; not very bark-like.

Eliza moved her face back from the tree and realised she'd been leaning on a large lump of fungus.

Eliza flung herself back.

Eliza, waving her arms around: "Aargh! It's fusty! I've got a fusty face!"

Jude started laughing.

Jude: "It's grounding. It makes you at one with nature."

Eliza: "Shut up! Is it poisonous? I don't know my mushrooms."

Jude: "I'm sure it's fine. I'll just make sure I don't lick your face."

Eliza: "It's not funny; I could die."

Jude: "Stop being melodramatic and get up this hill with me."

I'm not hugging any more trees, it's too stressful.

Eliza and Jude traipsed up the remainder of the incline to be greeted by a plateau with a stone in the middle. Jude rushed over and took in the view from the stone.

Ah, lovely. Level ground.

Jude: "Come on! It's a wonderful view from here. You can see as far as the estuary."

Eliza trudged over and joined Jude by the stone.

Eliza: "Where?"

Jude pointed into the distance, towards a murky grey area. The rainclouds from earlier, still evident on the horizon.

Eliza: "Nice."

Jude pointed towards the opposite side of the precipice to a grassy gradient with trees at the bottom.

Jude: "It looks clearer down that side of the hill. Shall we go down that way? It looks like there's another woods at the bottom, you could cuddle some more trees."

Eliza followed Jude's gaze down the hill, past the small woodland at the bottom towards a wooden cabin in a clearing.

Meh, trees.

However, I do spot a building with seats outside.

This indicates it might be a tea shop.

A tea shop means cake.

Eliza: "Yep. Let's go. I'll race you to the bottom."

Eliza set off down the hill at a blistering pace.

Jude: "Hold on, Eli! It's steep, you might lose your..."

Jude didn't get to finish his sentence.

Instead, he was left open-mouthed and helpless as a cantering Eliza gained momentum down the hill, her legs buckling as she tried to slow down.

Eliza: "AAARGH!! Me legs!! I can't flip-flopping stop 'em!"

Jude: "Hang on, Eli! I'm coming!"

Jude started off behind her in an attempt to catch her up.

Jude raced down the hill and watched as a galloping Eliza merged into the woodland at the bottom of the hill.

Jude shouted to the sky as he ran.

Jude: "Please, let her be alright!"

Jude reached the bottom whereupon, past the first row of trees, he was met by a deep stream.

Jude, panicking: "Eli?! Where are you? ELIZA?!"

There was a splashing noise to his right and he looked over to be greeted by a sodden Eliza who was emerging from the stream; mud and leaves dripping from the tendrils of her hair.

Jude raced to her.

Jude: "Oh, my heavens! Is anything broken?"

Only my spirit.

Eliza: "I'm cold."

My brain feels odd.

I must take my clothes off.

I read it somewhere.

If you fall into freezing cold water you must remove them.

Eliza hauled her coat off.

Jude, alarmed: "What are you doing?"

Eliza didn't answer, instead she took her shoes off.

I must remove everything.

My brain is telling me to.

Jude: "Shoes?! Talk to me. Let me help."

Eliza spoke in a monotone.

Eliza: "I must remove them. I must remove everything. They told me to."

Jude looked confused and looked around.

Jude: "Who told you to?"

Eliza: "The falling in cold water people."

A look of dawning crossed a concerned Jude's face.

Jude: "Oh my goodness, you're at risk of hyperthermia. Get them off! Get them off!"

Jude rushed to her and urgently started peeling her clothes off.

Jude: "Put my dry clothes on. Quick!"

He started to remove his coat when a booming voice came from behind him. Meanwhile, Eliza inelegantly stepped out of her pants and threw them over her shoulder.

Booming voice: "You've been rumbled, me lad! Avert your eyes, Betty; there's a couple cavorting in the copse. The female is naked."

A baffled Jude turned to find a puce faced, hoary man in full walking gear brandishing his two walking sticks at him. A similarly clad elderly woman, presumably Betty, quickly directed her gaze towards a nearby Ash tree.

Booming voice belonging to livid walker: "I find your carry on quite objectionable, young man! This is a decent woodland. There's flora and fauna in abundance and not to mention squirrels. We don't need your kind upsetting the habitat. I've got a good mind to alert the local constabulary."

Jude, angrily: "If you wouldn't mind, *sir*, not jumping to conclusions. My girlfriend has just fallen into the stream and is at risk of hyperthermia. Time is of the essence and I need to put her into some dry clothing before she becomes ill."

Betty stopped staring at the tree and rushed forward.

Betty: "You silly man, Stanley. The girl is sopping wet."

Betty removed her coat and proffered it towards a shivering Eliza.

Good Samaritan, Betty: "Here you are, dear. Have this; it's padded."

Silly man, Stanley: "I bought you that for your birthday."

Betty to Eliza and Jude, sniffing: "I don't like it. You're a much better cause. Here you are dear, pop your little arms through there."

Silly man, Stanley, muttering: "That cost me ninety pounds in Millets."

Betty: "I would have preferred that sewing box I saw on the QVC channel. I dropped enough hints."

Jude stepped in.

Jude: "It's most kind of you, Betty, but Eli can use mine."

A half-clad Eliza bedecked in nothing but an elderly woman's purple walking jacket, piped up.

Eliza: "I quite like hers."

Betty: "You see, she likes it. There. It's found a good home. I'm warm enough in my fleece, it's got a double layer. Come on, Stanley. Leave these young ones to it."

Betty nodded good day to them and started off back into the woods. Stanley reluctantly followed on behind.

Betty, shouting over her departing shoulder: "You can keep the hanky in the pocket, dear. Wipe the mud off your face with it."

Eliza and Jude stared at each other for a moment before Jude sprung back into action.

Jude: "Right, let's gather your clothes up and get you somewhere warm. Do you feel a bit better?"

Warmer. Yes warmer.

My brain is defogging.

I see cake. I see a tea pot.

Eliza: "Tea shop. Cake. There's a cabin in the woods. I need tea."

Jude, full of concern: "Ok. Wait."

Jude ran in the direction of where Betty and Stanley went and came back a minute or so later to find Eliza in exactly the same stock still position he left her in.

Jude: "I caught up with Betty and her husband and asked where the tea room is and whilst I was at it, I got her address so we can return the coat."

I like the coat.

It was a gift from a stranger.

The coat is warm.

I might start shopping at Millets.

Eliza: "Do we have to give it back? It's a memory from our weekend away."

Jude: "Let's get a postcard, instead."

Eliza tutted.

Jude started collecting Eliza's strewn clothes.

Eliza: "Don't forget my pants. They might upset the habitat."

Jude smiled.

Jude: "You're feeling better, thank goodness. Come on, hop on my back, I'll piggyback you to the tea rooms but, for goodness sake, pull the coat down to cover your nether regions or we really will get arrested."

Social Media Meme: *Do Not Go Where The Path May Lead. Go Instead Where There is no Path and Leave a Trail. Ralph Waldo Emerson*

Chapter Fourteen

Ye Olde Wood Tea Shoppe sandwich of the day: **Hand chopped shallots nestled on a bed of locally crafted goat's cheese expertly drizzled with homemade sun-dried tomato chutney, lightly warmed to create a crisp outer layer.**

Jude gingerly deposited a bare-bottomed Eliza on to the ground.

He pointed towards a picnic bench situated outside the tea rooms and threw her wet clothes onto it.

Jude: "Slide in there and keep your legs together. I don't want you getting a chill."

Eliza saluted.

Eliza: "Yes sir! Legs shut, sir!"

A couple, who were sat with two young children on a nearby picnic table, stopped chatting and stared at each other.

The woman motioned for her partner to hastily drink up.

Jude rushed into the tearooms and came back shortly after with a steaming mug of tea and a slice of Victoria sponge.

He smiled and nodded by way of greeting at the departing family and the woman sneered at him.

Jude balked and passed the tea to Eliza.

Jude: "Some people are very rude... They had cheese and onion toasties but I thought you'd prefer cake. Drink this and we'll get you back to the B and B as quickly as we can."

A grateful Eliza seized upon the tea and glugged down a mouthful.

Jude: "Would you like a fork for your cake?"

Eliza shook her head, picked up the lump of sponge and rammed it into her mud plastered face.

Jude, kindly: "Bless you, Eli. The state of you."

I know, attractive aren't I?

He pulled a pile of serviettes out from his pocket, licked one and started wiping some of the mud off from her cheek.

He gently tucked a dirty, wet tendril behind her ear.

I'd say thank you but I feel I may have misjudged the size of my mouth.

This cake is a bit dry.

I wonder how long it's been sitting in the woodland.

I'm not making enough spit to swallow it.

When I write my book 'The Survivors Guide to Cake', for this place I shall write the comment: "Good in a stream emergency as raises one's spirits but be sure to enquire how long they've left it unattended in the serve-over prior to purchase."

It's not shifting, I'll have to add tea.

Eliza slugged back a mouthful of tea to add to the full mouth of cake and Jude backed off.

Jude: "Crikey, I know I said we needed to get you back to the B and B quickly but steady on Eli, you'll choke."

Shush, I'm concentrating.

That's a bit down. Good.

Argh. It's stuck!

Eliza chewed quickly, loudly swallowed her mouthful and slurped the rest of her tea.

She dramatically thumped the mug on the table and exhaled loudly.

Jude looked on, shocked.

Jude: "We'll hold off reserving a table the Ritz, if that's ok with you."

Ignore, he's making reference to your manners.

I'm sat dripping wet on a dank, wooden bench naked, save for a geriatric woman's coat with half the woodland flora and fauna up my every orifice. I'm only grateful a squirrel hasn't made an appearance out of my fanny.

Now is not the time for manners.

Plus, the Ritz probably don't serve sawdust for cake.

Eliza: "I had killer cake syndrome."

Jude: "Hmm?"

Eliza: "When it gets stuck betwixt your mouth and stomach; around about where your clacker is. I get it quite often with chips. Not the thin ones, a whole one of them can slide down like a dream. The fat ones; steak cut are bastards for it. That's called 'killer chip syndrome', obviously. Only a fool would mix them up."

Jude: "Clacker?"

Eliza wafted her hand across her neck.

Eliza: "The hangy down bit in your throat."

Jude: "Your uvula."

Oh, that's sounds a bit dubious.

Isn't that my lady regions?

Eliza: "No, it doesn't get stuck that far down."

Jude, stood: "I think you might be in shock. Let's get back into the warm. The tea lady said there's a road just down there and we can get a taxi back to the Watershed."

Social Media Meme: *It is not the mountain we conquer, but ourselves. Sir Edmund Hillary*

Chapter Fifteen

Watershed notice stuck on bath tiles: **Please adhere to our green policy and only use the bathing products you need. We can decant what you don't use for the next guest.**

An hour later, Eliza was submerged in the bath in Watershed's Van Gogh room. She had lobbed in all the free toiletries and all that was visible from the sea of bubbles was her nose.

Jude had dropped her off and stayed in the taxi to go and fetch his car which was still parked up by the waterfall.

She pulled herself out of the water, reached for her mobile phone and texted Lydia.

Eliza's text: "How's Tom? I've had an eventful day; I hugged a mushroom tree, climbed a mountain, ran ninety miles an hour down a mountain, fell in a stream, took all my clothes off, mooned at an old man, ate killer cake which got stuck in my vulva and tonight I will be sleeping in Vincent Van Gogh's imagination. xx"

Eliza threw the phone away from the bath and immersed herself back into the water.

A few minutes later her mobile phone pinged in response. Eliza yanked herself out of the bath, wrapped a bright yellow towel around herself and picked up her mobile phone.

Lydia's text: "Tom's lovely, he's taught me how to make a soufflé. Have you been drinking? xx"

Eliza's text: "No, but I intend to. Tell Tom I love him and will see him tomorrow. xx"

Lydia's text: "He says he loves you right back. He's pulling me away; I have to attend to his chocolate soil. Have a wonderful time with Jude. xx"

Eliza pulled open her full suitcase and delved in for some clothes.

I wonder what we're going to do next.

If we're going out, I need going out clothes.

Eliza placed a going out set of clothes on the bed.

But if we're flopping, I need flopping clothes.

She proceeded to lay out another outfit.

Ooh, what if he wants to get saucy?

I need something flattering.

She laid out her best pants and bra set.

Hmmm.

Whilst she was pondering there was a light tap on the door and Jude came back in.

Jude: "Ah, hello! Are you feeling better? Crikey, that's a lot of clothes."

Eliza: "What are we going to do next? I need befitting attire."

Jude surveyed the assembled garb on the bed. He pointed to her laid out underwear set.

Jude, smiling: "I like that set best."

Eliza gave him a sideways glance.

Jude tugged on her towel and she let it drop to the floor, leaving her bare-skinned.

Jude: "Actually, that's what I like best."

He pulled her towards him, wrapped her in his arms and started kissing her.

A couple of minutes later he gently let her go and swept the clothes off the bed. He pulled back Van Gogh's starry night duvet and lifted her up.

Uh oh. Dark bed linen alert.

Eliza: "Hold on, don't throw me seductively on there; it's got dark pillow cases."

Jude, still holding a naked Eliza: "Eh?"

Eliza: "I can't sleep or fraternise in them. I'd not settle. I'd worry that I may dribble and leave a mark. Go and see if they have any white pillowcases in the airing cupboard – and get a pale sheet whilst you're at it."

Jude, straining slightly as still holding a naked Eliza: "What? Now?"

Eliza: "Yes, please. If you don't mind."

Jude unceremoniously plonked Eliza down and huffed, indicating that he did mind a bit, to be honest.

Jude: "Fair enough. Hang on."

Jude left the room, leaving a naked Eliza stood around waiting.

I'll just busy myself folding up my clothes that he threw on the deck.

They're clean and now they are strewn over a painter's carpet.

A few minutes later, Jude came back into the room to be greeted by a bent over Eliza's bare bottom as she was picking up the remainder of her clothes.

Jude: "Ooff, good heavens!"

Eliza straightened up, hastily.

Eliza, rapidly changing the subject: "Did you get some?"

Jude: "Yes, Mrs Tookery wasn't best pleased, though. She thought we were casting aspersions on their creative efforts. She told me she wouldn't tell Nigel in case he took offence at us compromising the room's integrity and spat in our soup. Apparently, it's part of his artistic nature."

Eliza: "What? Getting a two-star food hygiene rating?"

Jude changed the sheet and lobbed a couple of white cotton pillowcases at her.

Jude: "Come on, swap yours, dribble-chops."

Eliza: "Aren't you going to change yours?"

Jude, grinning: "No. I can keep my drool in."

Eliza: "She'll know it's me then. You have to change yours too, that way it won't be just my soup that gets spat in."

Jude: "Really?"

Eliza: "Really."

Jude: "Did you bang your head when you fell in the water?"

Eliza: "Just do it so can we crack on with some nooky."

Jude started pulling off the bed linen his side.

Jude: "Such an enchanting turn of phrase you have, dear Eliza."

Eliza: "I know. I'm a proper lady. A stark naked one at that."

Jude: "Would it make you feel better if I disrobed?"

Eliza: "Absolutely. Do it. Do it now."

****

Later, they were laid in bed together; Eliza was snuggled up in Jude's arms with her head resting on his bared chest.

Eliza, wistfully: "Don't ever let me go."

Jude: "I'm afraid I have to."

What?! Oh god, I'm rubbish in bed. I'm not up to par. Maybe I should be a bit more adventurous… I might get some tips from Lydia.

He's married? No, I'd know that. Old big mouth Charlotte-long-hair would have told me.

Eliza, croakily: "Really?"

Don't beg it's unbecoming but keep it as a fall-back position if all else fails.

Jude: "You need the toilet all the time."

Jude grinned, cheekily, and kissed her gently on the top of her head.

Eliza huffed a sigh of relief and they laid in happy silence for a few more minutes.

Eliza: "Guess what this is."

She started flexing her buttocks in turn.

Jude: "Guess what, what is?"

Eliza: "It's a tune."

Jude: "I can't hear anything."

Eliza continued flexing her buttocks.

Eliza: "It's my bottom. Concentrate."

Jude: "You're playing name that tune with your bottom?"

Eliza: "Yes. Guess."

Jude: "Can't you sing it, instead?"

Eliza: "I can't sing, I don't remember words very well. I was slung out of the Brownies for miming to the National Anthem."

Jude: "This comes as no surprise."

Eliza: "To this day, I still don't know the words. It's the reason why I've never become an Olympian. I'd look foolish on the rostrum."

Jude, grinning: "You're not normal."

Eliza: "Whatever, just guess. It's taking its toll on my glutes."

Jude moved his hand down to the base of her spine.

Eliza: "I'll do the chorus."

Jude concentrated for a few seconds

Jude: "Ok... Shake your Tail Feather by Ray Charles."

Eliza lifted her head off his chest and stared at him.

Jude: "What?!"

Eliza, tutting: "It's, She'll be Coming Round the Mountain."

Jude: "That was my second guess."

Eliza: "Shall I do another one?"

Jude: "I'd rather you didn't. How about we go and sample Watershed's cuisine? I'm starving."

Eliza: "Yes, definitely."

Social Media Meme: *He has Van Gogh's ear for music - Billy Wilder*

Chapter Sixteen

Watershed Evening Menu: **Ask Nigel**

Eliza and Jude strolled, hand in hand to the dining room and Mrs Tookery bustled over.

Mrs Tookery: "Bed linen to your satisfaction?"

She's peeved. Ingratiate yourself.

Eliza: "Ah yes, thank you. It was most kind of you. I had a childhood calamity with dark blue sheets and the trauma has left its mark. Nearly lost a leg. I tried hypnosis but the flashbacks live on. I'm so grateful for you obliging; therapy costs a packet these days."

Jude pumped her hand by way of silent gesture for her to stop talking.

Mrs Tookery, somewhat stupefied: "Oh, well I see."

Mrs Tookery brushed down some imaginary crumbs from her skirt and continued.

Mrs Tookery: "We, at Watershed Bed and Breakfast, endeavour to make all our guests, even the loopy ones, feel at ease. We are an open border. Well, we have fences, but you could step over those, really. Nigel had to buy fence panels which would fit in the back of the car. We can't be having expenditure on delivery charges – running a profitable business is a knife edge. Should I say 'knife edge', dear? It won't set you off on an episode, will it?"

Eliza: "No, it's just sheets."

I'm also a bit off water courses now.

Eliza: "...And rivers at the bottom of big hills. I fell in one today. I think that'll stay with me for the duration."

Mrs Tookery looked at Jude with raised eyebrows.

Jude: "Yes, she's right. Eli fell in a big stream at the bottom of the waterfall."

Mrs Tookery, tutting: "I told you to mind the brook."

Eliza and Jude in unison: "When?"

Mrs Tookery, indignantly: "It is in the welcome pack."

Eliza: "Oh, we haven't read that."

Mrs Tookery folded her arms under her ample bosom and harrumphed.

Jude looked over Mrs Tookery's shoulder to a near empty dining room.

Jude: "Any chance of a table, please?"

Mrs Tookery: "Have you booked?"

Jude: "Er, no."

Mrs Tookery: "I see. Let me consult the diary."

She pulled a dog-eared notepad from her cardigan pocket and flicked through a few random pages.

Mrs Tookery: "At what time?"

Jude: "Now?"

Mrs Tookery pulled a pencil out of her other cardigan pocket, licked the end of it and sucked in her breath.

Mrs Tookery: "Hmmm. Yes, that's fine. We can accommodate you. Nigel and I are very like that, accommodating. It's our business!"

She ushered them over to a scrubbed pine table with two mismatched chairs by a window.

Eliza flumped down in one.

I'm exhausted.

How did Daphne put up with Mrs Tookery's never ending drivel?

That's probably why she bought the barge.

Mrs Tookery's enough to put you off human interaction for life.

Mrs Tookery: "My Nigel will take the orders - my veins are playing up. I'll go and fetch him."

A couple of minutes later, a bald, lanky man in his early seventies, hampered by a pronounced stoop, staggered over to their table. He wore a food-stained nylon shirt paired with safari shorts; hems of which hung above two porcelain white knobbly knees and a road map of varicose veins.

Eliza and Jude, in disbelief: "Nigel?!"

Possibly Nigel: "Yes. At your service."

He's as bald as a badger!

He looks nothing like Jude!

Jude let out an involuntary gasp and put his right hand on his full head of hair.

Eliza, patting Jude's other hand: "It's ok, it hasn't slipped off. It's all still there."

Jude, with relief: "Just checking."

Eliza and Jude, unashamedly, stared at him.

Mrs Tookery bustled over to them and took in their gawping faces.

Mrs Tookery: "I know, I told you, didn't I? It's the most astonishing likeness. I can't wait to tell Winnie down the post office."

They are polar opposites.

I wouldn't play She'd Be Coming Round the Mountain with my bare buttocks to that man, I can assure you.

Eliza to Mrs Tookery: "They could be twins."

Jude was still blinking and staring at his doppelganger.

Jude, quietly: "Indeed. It's like looking in a mirror."

Mrs Tookery excused herself and went off out to the reception area.

Nigel: "Can I interest you in our specials menu?"

Eliza: "Go on then."

Nigel: "There's soup of the da…"

Eliza and Jude, exclaiming: "NO!"

Nigel, flinching: "Oh, most categorical of you both. How about beef? I got some cheap from the meat van at the market; I could do with using it up."

Eliza: "What are you going to do with the beef?"

His rheumy eyes flickered with confusion.

Nigel: "I generally cook it."

I meant a beef bourguignon, burgers, meatballs or whatever but I don't care anymore.

Eliza: "Yes, use up some of the beef on me."

Jude: "I'll have beef surprise too, please."

Nigel: "Most obliged. Has my wife taken your drinks order?"

Eliza and Jude shook their heads.

Nigel, grimaced with annoyance.

Nigel: "She's the ruddy bane of my life - I have to do it all. The jobs list she's given me, takes up two pages of A3 paper; I never get time to watch the snooker. What do you want?"

Another residence to rest my weary head for the night.

Eliza and Jude ordered their drinks and Nigel shuffled off to the kitchen.

Eliza picked up her spoon and started looking into it.

Jude "Is it dirty? Do you need a clean one?"

Eliza: "No it's fine. I'm looking at my spoon face. I do it before every meal if the spoon reflection allows it."

Jude: "Did they teach you that at Swiss finishing school?"

Eliza grinned at him and put down the spoon.

Eliza: "Do you want to have a word with good old Daphne when you're next up at Head Office?"

Jude: "Mmm. I might disregard future holiday establishment suggestions."

Eliza: "We'll not go on her barge."

Jude frowned at Eliza.

He doesn't know about her barge. Only my brain and I know about that.

Eliza waved Jude on.

Eliza: "Ignore. Move on."

Social Media Meme: *A recipe has no soul. You, as the cook, must bring soul to the recipe – Thomas Keller*

Chapter Seventeen

Sandwich Board outside the Red Lion: **On Tonight! Back from the brink of bankruptcy, we welcome popular band The Descant Dudes. All Welcome (except their creditors - we're a family pub & could do without a punch up)**

Later that evening, Eliza and Jude decided to venture into the nearby village and found themselves wandering by a pub which was advertising a local band.

Jude: "Do you fancy giving it a whirl?"

Eliza: "Yep. I can take anything on after the work out my jaw got chewing that beef.

Jude, rubbing his cheek: "It was a bit of an undertaking."

They strode into the pub to see a disparate bunch of individuals with various instruments distributed around a make-shift stage area.

Jude fetched their drinks whilst Eliza found a table.

They began supping their drinks when an almighty commotion started from the stage. The Descant Dudes had begun their set.

Blimey, what a racket!

Eliza and Jude looked on in silence as the band knocked out an indistinguishable tune.

Jude, hollering over the noise: "Would you like to dance?"

Calm down, man; display a complete lack confidence like the rest of humanity.

Eliza: "I'll pass, if that's ok."

Jude: "I do love to dance. I might just do it on my own."

Jude went to get up.

I like to skip but I wouldn't consider doing it in public.

Eliza shook her head at him and motioned for him to return to his seat. Jude sat back down again, sighing regretfully.

Was I being controlling then?

Nah, it's normal to be riddled with insecurity and fearful of creating a public outcry.

After a few minutes, The Descant Dudes came up for air and grabbed their drinks.

Eliza, turning to Jude: "Well, that was a bit different."

Jude: "Indeed, the tuba is a very under-utilised instrument."

The band wheeled out a xylophone and a dishevelled, middle-aged man started whacking it with mallets.

Crikey, he's going for it.

I wonder if he's on drugs.

He's probably too old to take drugs. He looks like he has an allotment.

He is quite unrepentant with the bashing of those keys.

He's probably got his strength from pulling out his marrows.

He needn't really bother playing with such zest, there's only about six of us here and two of them are serving behind the bar.

All of a sudden he thwacked the mallet with such force, he lost his grip and it flew across the pub, just missing the left ear of an incoming customer.

The unimpressed customer bent over, picked up the mallet and brandished it at the, somewhat concerned, xylophone player.

Jude: "I reckon that's our cue to drink up and leave, don't you?"

Eliza: "Definitely. He should stick to his marrows."

Jude nodded without the faintest idea what she was talking about and led her out of the pub.

****

That night an unsettled Eliza looked across the bed at a snoozing Jude.

He's got a lovely face even when he's comatose.

He's so peaceful.

I wish I was as peaceful.

I can't settle.

It's an unknown bed.

When did this happen to me?

In my teens and twenties I was able to fall asleep on a bus, sitting upright.

Now, I need my own pillows and a familiar mattress.

I don't want to be awake on my own.

I'll wiggle about a bit in the hope Jude wakes up.

Eliza fidgeted about a bit.

Nothing.

She plumped her pillows up.

Still nothing.

She did an almighty yank of the duvet and completely exposed Jude, who sat bolt upright with surprise.

Oh that did it.

Jude, bleary-eyed: "WHA...?!"

Eliza, soothingly: "It's ok, the duvet fell off. Let me put it back over you."

Eliza hastily threw the duvet back over Jude.

Jude, coming to: "Are you ok? You're very alert for..."

He peered at his watch.

Jude: "... two in the morning."

Eliza: "I can't settle. Will you play eye-spy with me, please?"

Jude dragged himself up in bed and went to turn the sunflower bedecked bedside lamp on.

Eliza: "No! I'll wake up too much. We'll play in the dark and you'll just have to remember what's in the room."

Jude, from the darkness: "You've woken me up to play eye-spy in the dark?"

Eliza: "Technically, I've not woken you up. The duvet falling off and the wind blasting across your naked willy, did that."

Jude, indicating he didn't believe a word of it: "Mmm."

But he acceded.

Jude: "I spy with my eye... "

Eliza: "Your little eye."

Jude: "Yes, my *little* eye. Something beginning with b."

Eliza: "Bed."

Jude: "Spot on."

Eliza: "That was too easy. Do another one."

Jude: "I spy with my little eye, something beginning with s."

Eliza: "Sink?"

Jude: "No."

Eliza: "Sunflowers?"

Jude: "No."

Eliza: "Suitcases?"

Jude, yawning: "Nope."

Eliza: "I give up."

Jude: "Sleep."

Eliza: "You can't see sleep. You go to sleep."

Jude: "Ah, marvellous idea; I shall do."

He leant over, kissed her on the elbow and snuggled back down.

Jude: "Night Eli."

Tut. I didn't get to have a go.

What did my hippy books say to do when you can't sleep?

Clear your mind, breathe in for ten, hold for ten and out for... oh it's out already... out for two.

I'll imagine I'm on a boat, drifting on the open seas. I am lying down with the sun on my.... zzzz.

A few hours elapsed.

Eliza: "Wha...?! Whassat noise?!"

Eliza's eyes sprung open and she waited.

Then it came...

SNNNAAAAARRRRKKKKK!

Oh. My. God. It's Jude! He's snoring like a wart hog!

Eliza rolled over and looked hard in the dark at him with pursed lips.

Jude's throat: "SNNNAAAAARRRRKKKKK!"

If I punch him now I could pretend I did it in my sleep.

I can't man-handle him. It's wrong. This is the man of my dreams.

Maybe I'll just suffocate him with a pillow instead.

I wonder how many women kill their partners as a result of their snoring.

I'd put on Jude's epitaph 'We laughed and we cried but he snored, so he died.'

I hope I get a female judge – she'd be very lenient with the sentencing. She'd probably send me on holiday to a spa retreat so I could recharge my batteries, she'd be that understanding.

Article Googled at five in the morning: *Evidence of compassion shown when sentencing murderers and whether suffocation due to lack of sleep is admissible in court.*

Chapter Eighteen

Billington Gazette Headline: ***Farmer Glynn from Pilkington on the Moors said his doomed sheep was alive hours before it died. Full interview on page 5.*** (Pun Points – Not Applicable – we're reporting on a deceased sheep here people).

It was Thursday and Eliza was sat in the Merrythought Café waiting for Lydia.

Dave sashayed over.

Dave: "You're not dining alone, are you?"

I'm not a sitting on my own, dining for one sort of person.

Eliza: "No, I'm waiting for Lydia."

Dave: "May I sit with you whilst you wait?"

Eliza: "Erm, ok, if you want."

Dave pulled the chair out opposite Eliza and sat down.

He's staring at me.

That is quite awkward.

He's sighing quite heavily.

Eliza: "What are you doing, Dave?"

Dave: "Imagining this was my life."

Eliza: "Sitting in your café is your life, Dave."

Dave: "No, with you. Sharing thoughts and dreams."

Belinda strutted past and Eliza shot her a look.

Belinda: "Is he bothering you?"

Not bothering, just somewhat unsettling me.

Eliza: "No, no. I was just wondering if you needed help, you know, carrying stuff. Dave could help you."

Belinda: "Dave, stop perving at her. She'll get you arrested for harassment."

Dave quickly gathered himself and stopped staring at a discomforted Eliza.

Dave: "Sorry, no offence inten... uh oh."

Dave quickly got up as he spotted a Lycra bedecked Lydia, complete with turquoise legwarmers, stride the café door. He scuttled off quickly out to the kitchen.

Blimey.

Eliza, shouting over to Lydia: "Go on then; Flashdance over to the table!"

Lydia pranced over, did an over-zealous pirouette, apologised to the customer she nearly knocked out with her elbow and sat down.

Eliza: "You look like Jane Fonda."

Lydia, puffed: "Before or after the surgery?"

Eliza: "After."

Lydia nodded with satisfaction.

Lydia: "Sorry I'm late, Eli."

Eliza: "It's alright. Were you at the gym?"

Lydia: "No! Don't be daft. I have no wish to feel inadequate in a gym full of people who know how to use the equipment. I was shopping for blindfolds."

Lydia wafted her hand at a passing Belinda.

Lydia: "Tea and two crumpets with lashings of butter, please."

Eliza: "What are you doing? You never have butter."

Lydia, grabbing a departing Belinda's arm: "And a slice of cake. I don't care which one."

Belinda nodded and went off to the kitchen.

Eliza stared at Lydia.

Lydia: "It's about control. I'm rebelling – I had a pork pie for breakfast! Tony says it's all gone southwards with me; he says he remembers me when I was taut and nubile."

Eliza: "That's a bit harsh. You were together the first-time years ago. You've both aged since."

His face looks like it needs a foot pump.

Saying that, who am I to judge? Mine now has the ability to retain pillow folds until after lunchtime.

Lydia: "Tell me about it. I swear you can hear his balls knocking together when he walks."

Eliza: "… Sorry, shopping for blindfolds?"

Lydia: "Yes. He makes me do things."

Lydia pulled a face.

Lydia: "Disgusting things."

Eliza: "Urgh, what sort of things?"

Naked and blindfolded, hanging off the doorframe sort of things?

Lydia: "I walked into the bathroom the other day and he was bent over and said 'come over here and do what my mama used to.'"

Eliza: "Oh dear."

This could open up a whole world of something I don't think I wish to learn about.

Lydia: "Indeed, oh dear."

Eliza: "What did he want you to do?"

I'm almost too afraid to hear.

Lydia: "I'm appalled, darling."

Lydia shook her head with dismay.

Lydia: "He wanted me to cut his toe nails; he'd pulled a muscle putting his socks on."

Oh the relief. I can clear my image of his mother now.

Eliza: "Did you oblige?"

Dave sauntered over with the laden tray and went to put the crumpets down.

Lydia: "No! I most certainly did not. I tend to other areas; feet are not one of them. I'm attempting to spice things up in the bedroom department. I'm hoping if I blindfold myself so I can't see his saggy balls in my face I might get more in the momen... What the fuc...!"

Dave dropped the tray with a clatter and looked on in horror as the crumpets flung across the table and slid butter-side down on to Lydia's brand-new leggings.

Lydia: "DAVE!! You cretin!"

Dave leant over, picked up the crumpets and began fervently wiping the butter further into Lydia's Lycra.

Dave, muttering: "I'm so sorry."

Lydia, shrieking: "Get your hands away from me! You're ruining my garb!"

Belinda stalked over.

Belinda: "Is this man annoying you?"

Lydia: "Yes, he bloody is!"

Belinda: "Do you want to make a formal complaint? I've got me pad handy."

Eliza: "That won't be necessary, Belinda. He's no more annoying than usual. Stand easy."

Belinda tutted as she put her pencil and pad back in her apron pocket.

Dave to Belinda: "Pick up that tray and replace the order whilst I collect the smashed plates."

Dave picked up the smashed crockery and straightened up, uttering "straighten-up-the-mast" as he did so; Lydia shot Eliza a look and Eliza raised her eyebrows in acknowledgement.

Lydia: "Dave, can you stop bending over and making a getting up noise; it's making me re-evaluate my future."

Dave, put the plate fragments into his apron pocket.

Dave: "I'm very apologetic regarding the droppages, even to you, Lydia."

Eliza: "Have you got a grip issue?"

Dave: "No, I have a very reliable right hand. It's the subject matter; it unnerves me. I wasn't expecting to hear you utter such things whilst I was serving crumpets."

Belinda came back with a fresh tray and caught the end of the conversation.

Belinda, looking at Eliza and Lydia in turn: "What things did you say? Wank? Shitter? Fuckwagon?"

Dave, Eliza, Lydia and the surrounding tables gawped, open mouthed, at Belinda.

Lydia found her voice first.

Lydia: "I believe the utterance 'saggy balls' was what got him."

Belinda shrugged and scrunched her nose up at Dave.

Belinda: "Meh. Lightweight."

Dave, stuttering: "P...put the t...tray down and move away from the table, Belinda."

Belinda smiled and dawdled off.

Dave took a hanky out of his pocket and wiped his brow.

Dave: "I shall leave you to your order. I feel a bit hot so if you need anything else, please hail Belinda. I'm off to sit out the back for a few minutes."

Lydia rammed the slice of cake in her mouth and grinned at Eliza.

Eliza: "Don't you think this is somewhat cutting your nose off to spite your face? You never had buttered crumpets and cake for breakfast before."

Lydia, still munching: "I like the fact Tony believes I'm sweating on a treadmill but I'm eating a slice of Victoria Sandwich."

Belinda on the way past with another customer's order.

Belinda: "It's Madeira."

Lydia: "Whatever. It's calorific and that's what counts."

Belinda on the way back from attending to another customer's order.

Belinda: "You could cart your ancient bones around that new sports equipment in Pilkington Park."

Lydia spat out her mouthful of cake.

Eliza, nodding: "Oh, you're right. I saw Charlotte-long-hair talking about writing an article on it. The Parish Council set it up with the local funds."

Eliza turning her attention back to Lydia.

Eliza: "Shall we go?"

Lydia, stuffing the cake back in: "What now?"

Eliza: "You are dressed for speed."

Lydia: "Tut, alright then. Let me finish my crumpets and cake first. I should have taken pretend fitness up years ago; I'm a convert."

Mentor in Life Feature letter: *Dear Eliza, I'm all alone as my daughter has recently left home. Children grow up so fast, yet I realise I've dedicated my whole life to bringing her up. I had so many dreams before she was born. Now my life feels empty. Have I fulfilled my life's purpose? What's your advice, please? Yours, I-just-don't-know-what-to-do-with-myself*

Dear Dusty Springfield, They don't grow up fast enough, quite frankly. I've been living off a diminished wage for nearly a decade; it's a wonder I'm not a sex worker. Make a list of things you've always aspired to and make them happen. As the, somewhat protracted, quote goes: "Life is like a book. Some chapters are sad, some are happy and some are exciting but if you never turn the page, you will never know what the next chapter has in store for you." Bringing up your daughter was the bulk of the book, but turn the page as the next chapters are all your new dreams.

Chapter Nineteen

Billington Gazette Headline: ***Survey Reveals a Complete Social Meltdown in Billington Could Cause Uncertainty for Home Owners*** (Pun Points – Not Applicable – this is an investigation by Mandy, concerned about an equity dip in her house. This will be her evidence to show her neighbour who keeps using his circular saw at nine o'clock on a Sunday morning).

Half an hour later, Eliza and Lydia parked their cars in the Anchor pub car park in Pilkington, got out and wandered over to the park together.

They were greeted by myriad people hanging off pieces of newly installed exercise equipment.

Lydia: "Blimey, this is *the* place to be!"

Eliza: "Apparently so."

Lydia: "I only have to look at gym equipment and I feel fitter. What shall we try first?"

Eliza surveyed the equipment,

Eliza, pointing: "That one over there."

They strode past a middle-aged man trying earnestly to do the monkey bars and put their handbags down next to a piece of apparatus nearby.

Lydia: "What is it?"

Eliza: "Dunno; it looks a bit cross-trainery. There's instructions on this board. Get on and I'll read out what you have to move."

Lydia did a couple of star jumps and clambered on.

Eliza, reading the board: "...Hold the hand grips, firmly..."

Lydia, looking around: "There aren't any."

Eliza looked up at Lydia and then back to the instruction board.

Eliza: "You're back to front."

Lydia: "Oh."

Lydia scrambled off, turned round and grabbed the handle bars.

Eliza, nodding: "Now pull, left and right and wheel your legs about."

Lydia proceeded to follow the instructions for approximately thirty seconds and stopped.

Lydia: "Christ, I'm knackered. Next."

Lydia climbed off, put her hands on hips and exhaled, loudly.

Eliza: "I think you're meant to do it a bit longer than that."

Lydia: "You do it then, Kelly Holmes."

Eliza climbed aboard and started feverishly pedalling and pulling the arm levers.

Ooh, this is a bit of an endeavour.

It's upsetting my innards.

Eliza rapidly dismounted the machine.

Lydia: "See, I told you."

Eliza: "It makes you want to wee. Surely that's not its intention. What a silly design."

Lydia: "Next!"

They picked up their handbags and plonked them next to another piece of apparatus. They watched as an elderly woman deftly swung her legs back and forth, rhythmically.

If an ancient woman can do this, we've got it in the bag.

Aged swingy leg woman: "I won't be long, dears. I'm trying to get my new hips working."

And she's got replacement hips.

A few minutes later, the elderly woman hopped of the equipment and skipped over to another piece.

Eliza and Lydia did rock, paper, scissors - Eliza lost so went on first.

Eliza tried to copy the grace and speed of the new hips lady as per their visual tuition but failed miserably; her left leg swinging wildly and the right one almost static.

Maybe I've got one leg longer than the other.

Yes, that's it.

I'm not unfit. I've got leg length problems.

Eliza: "I've only got one leg, your turn."

Eliza scrabbled off and passed an imaginary baton to Lydia, which she grabbed.

Lydia did a couple of ostentatious stretches and stepped on the machine.

She started swaying her legs, wildly.

Eliza: "Oh, well done. Both your legs work!"

Lydia, shouting above the leg swishing: "I like this one, but it's splitting my Capability Brown a bit too much for comfort. I might split my legging stitches; though they are badly stained now thanks to Dave's dodgy hand control."

A man, who was stood behind Eliza waiting his turn, coughed, awkwardly.

Eliza, to Lydia: "Get off now, you're creating a queue!"

Lydia, still in full leg flow: "Righty-ho!"

Lydia abruptly stopped oscillating her legs and went to move off the apparatus and fell flat on her face.

The man behind Eliza, guffawed uncontrollably and went to pick her up.

Laughing man, grabbing one of Lydia's elbows: "Come on, Mad Lizzie. Up you get."

Lydia, face down: "Gerroff, unknown person!"

She looked up and stopped berating. A huge smile swept across her face.

Lydia, beaming: "Daniel?!"

Perhaps Daniel: "Yes, that's right. You remembered!"

Lydia allowed herself to be steadied and brushed herself down.

Lydia: "I remember any man who I've seen naked. It's one of my life skills."

Who is this marvellous naked person? He looks like Idris Elba.

Eliza, cleared her throat.

Lydia: "Oh, how rude of me! Eliza this is Daniel, Daniel, Eliza."

Daniel stuck his hand out and Eliza shook it.

Ooh, that's a rather masterful grip.

Lydia: "He was my life model when I did the drawing classes, back along. He helped me master proportion."

Lydia smiled, coquettishly at Daniel.

Lydia: "And from memory, there was quite a lot to master."

I can imagine, if his biceps are anything to go by.

Daniel winked at her and gestured to the cardio walker.

Daniel: "Are you done? I'm timing myself; I've got to get back to work."

Eliza and Lydia motioned for him to get on which he did, gracefully.

Where's my popcorn?

Eliza and Lydia unashamedly gawped at him as he enthusiastically swept his legs back and forth.

Lydia, whispering to Eliza: "I bet his balls don't knock together when he walks."

I bet.

Eliza shook her head.

Eliza, whispering back: "His balls are way too fit. I bet they do a workout on their own."

Lydia, whispering back: "I'd like to see that. A blindfold would not be a requirement."

Daniel jumped off the machine, checked his watch and threw himself into a series of squat thrusts.

Lydia: "Oh my god. It's too much; we need to move on or I won't be responsible for my actions."

Indeed. I might join you.

Eliza: "Ok, get yourself and your leg warmers over to that up-in-the-air bar."

They picked up their handbags and Eliza ushered Lydia away from the fitness spectacle that was Daniel as they went over towards the chin-up bar.

They placed their handbags down beside the bar.

Eliza: "You can go first. Up you jump."

Lydia proceeded to leap about helplessly in an attempt to grab the bar.

Lydia: "Is that the exercise?"

Eliza read the board.

Eliza: "No. You need to hold on to the bar and pull yourself up."

A smiling Daniel joined them.

Daniel: "Would you like some assistance?"

Lydia: "I can't reach the bar."

Daniel: "May I lift you?"

Lydia, with delight: "You may."

Daniel: "Hold your core stiff and stretch up."

Lydia visibly quivered as he gently put his arms around her waist and lifted her up towards the bar.

Daniel: "Well, grip it then! Don't just put your arms in the air!"

Lydia: "Oh, soz!"

Lydia grabbed onto the bar and Daniel let go of his grip and she promptly fell to the ground.

Daniel bent over and hauled her up.

Daniel, laughing: "You need to work on your upper body strength."

He checked his watch and tutted.

Daniel: "I've got to go; I'll be late back."

Lydia, crestfallen: "Oh, ok."

Daniel: "We'll have to catch up sometime, if you want?"

Lydia, without hesitation: "I want."

Eliza shot her eyebrows up and stared at Lydia.

Mind meld with me, Lydia.

Remember you have a boyfriend.

Lydia caught her cautionary glare.

Lydia: "I mean, I want to get fit so any pointers would be most gratefully received."

Lydia shot a look at Eliza which said, "there, happy now?"

Daniel: "Cool. I'm here most days so see you around."

He winked as he departed and they watched him leave the park.

Lydia patted her chest and puffed.

Lydia: "I felt like Baby in Dirty Dancing then. Ooh, he's got a strong grip."

Eliza: "Come on, I've had enough. Shall we go to the Anchor for a drink?"

Lydia: "God, yeah. I'm parched."

They picked up their handbags and were greeted by Valerie, from the Gazette, who was sat on the end of the sit up bars. On her lap was a Tupperware tub which contained two rounds of ham and pickle sandwiches and various picnic snacks.

Voluptuous Valerie, shaking her head: "You'll not get fit with that attitude, ladies!"

Lydia, somewhat indignant: "Sat on your bum eating sandwiches won't either."

Uh oh, Lydia doesn't know I know her.

Eliza, slightly hysterically: "Lydia, this is Vol... Valerie. She works with me at the Gazette."

Lydia: "Oh."

Eliza: "What are you doing here, Valerie?"

Voluptuous Valerie: "I was sent here to see if it's worth doing an article on. It seems very popular; I think we should cover it. It appears that the parish council have made a good decision regarding public funds on this occasion. Better than that ridiculous sculpture along the dual carriageway. I shall put in a request for Gavin to take some pictures. Why are you here? Aren't you working from home today?"

Eliza: "Oh, oh yes, I am. I wondered about it too, so I was doing some research."

Liar, liar - unfit pants on fire.

Voluptuous Valerie, ramming a triangle of sandwich in her mouth: "Most diligent of you, Eliza. You remind me of our Lorraine, we didn't think she'd amount to much either but look at her now - she's top of ambient commodities at Foodcutters in Aberystwyth."

Lydia: "I'm bored now. Can we go?"

Most definitely. I need to pour a gin and consider my air of underachievement.

Eliza: "Yes, let's write up my notes in the pub."

They bid their farewells and left Valerie stuffing a scotch egg into her face whilst sat on the fitness equipment.

Social Media Meme: *You never realise how long a minute is until you exercise.*

Chapter Twenty

Billington Gazette Headline: ***Pilkington Park's new Exercise Equipment Gets Off on the Wrong Footing with Reports of Several Twisted Ankles** (*Pun Points - seven)

Billington Hospital's Accident and Emergency department have reported a surge in strains due to incorrect use of the exercise equipment installed in Pilkington on the Moors village park. The council state all health and safety measures meet current legislation and its people's stupidity that's the problem.

Francesca put the duster down and turned the bank of overhead lights out in FunkyFurn's warehouse. The only light being emitted was from the dim bulbs in the various display rooms.

She wandered into the 'Art Deco' room and gently ran her fingers along the Bauhaus style chair. She switched off the glass side lamp and moved on to the next room.

She walked into the 'Mid Century' room and sighed deeply. This was her favourite display. She pulled up a G Plan chair and sat quietly at the dining table.

She sat there, in the half-light, contemplating.

Suddenly, the silence was broken by a clattering of the main shutter being hauled up and the bank of lights being switched on.

Francesca sat bolt upright and squinted to adjust to the bright light.

Booming voice from within FunkyFurn: "Where the hell are you? We'll be late."

Francesca stood hastily and called out.

Francesca: "Kenneth! I'm here, in the mid-century room."

Kenneth's footsteps could be heard striding expeditiously to where she was.

Kenneth stood at the entrance of the display room, hands on hips.

Kenneth: "What are you doing, woman?"

Francesca: "Saying good-bye."

Kenneth, looking around: "Who to?"

Francesca: "FunkyFurn, of course."

Kenneth sneered at her.

Kenneth: "Stop being sentimental. It's a shop, full of dross from dead people. It's served its purpose and it's sold for a good price."

Francesca: "I love this place. It's not dross, it's people's lives."

Kenneth shook his head in disgust.

Kenneth: "Good job I got rid of it. It's never good to become too attached to anything."

Francesca sighed and nodded.

Francesca, standing up: "I suppose you're right. I'm just being daft."

Kenneth walked over and held his arms out to her and Francesca folded into his embrace.

She looked up at him.

Francesca: "It's good to become attached to people, though, isn't it?"

Kenneth looked down at her and shrugged, noncommittally.

Francesca continued to look up at him. Willing him to say something to acknowledge her statement.

Kenneth let go of her and looked around.

Kenneth: "Haven't you switched all the side lamps off yet?"

Francesca: "I was doing it when you came in."

Kenneth: "No you weren't, you were sat day-dreaming. You need to hurry up or we'll be late for dinner. I don't like tardiness, you know that."

Francesca: "Sorry Kenneth, I'll do it quickly. Will you help me?"

Kenneth stiffened.

Kenneth: "No. It is your job. You don't have a dog and bark yourself, do you?"

Francesca flinched at his remark.

Francesca: "Well, we are a bit more than employee and employer, aren't we?"

Kenneth's eyes bore into her.

Kenneth: "And what, little lady, makes you think that?"

Francesca straightened up.

Francesca, boldly: "We are together; we are equals. I was hoping we could take our relationship to the next level and go public now. You're no longer with Dorothy."

Upon hearing her name, a mask of anger spread across Kenneth's face. He glared at Francesca and moved within an inch of her face.

Kenneth, seething: "Do not say my wife's name."

Francesca stepped back with surprise. A fear enveloped her as she pressed herself against the 1950s radiogram. Kenneth leant in further.

Kenneth, snarling in her face: "Let me make myself abundantly clear, Francesca. I would never, as you quaintly put it, go public with you. Would you like to know why?"

Francesca nodded, mutely; every muscle in her body taut with anxiety.

Kenneth: "I am a man of substance. But you?!"

He looked at her derisively.

Kenneth: "What sort of woman has an affair with a married man?"

Francesca opened her mouth to protest at his blatant double-standard but he placed his forefinger over it. She started shaking uncontrollably under his touch.

Kenneth: "I think you've said enough, don't you?"

Kenneth stepped back and she visibly sank as he moved away from her.

Kenneth chuckled as he looked at her and shook his head.

Kenneth: "The takeover of this place will be complete in a couple of weeks so you just keep looking pretty for the customers and polishing the pots. I can ask if the new owners will keep you on, seeing as you like it so much."

Francesca started sobbing and reached out to him.

Francesca: "But Kenneth...!"

Kenneth brusquely brushed her hands away.

Kenneth: "I haven't got time for this. Forget dinner, I'll go on my own. Look at the state of you; you'd be terrible company, anyway."

Francesca stood in shock as Kenneth turned on his heel and stalked back out of the warehouse.

Kenneth, shouting over his departing shoulder: "Lock up and don't forget to set the alarm, there's a good girl."

Mentor in Life Feature letter: *Dear Eliza, I'm in a terrible state. I thought my best friend was having it off with my boyfriend and, even though I never said anything to her, I secretly started to hate her. It turns out she wasn't and he was cheating on me with some old slapper called Megan. I feel awful for thinking such things about my best friend. Am I an awful person? Yours, I-got-it-all-wrong*

Dear We-all-get-it-a-bit-wrong-sometimes, A couple of years ago, I ran a short-lived venture which sold pre-loved furniture with my best friend. Someone was stealing from the till and I assumed it was her. I was completely wrong and it was a woman who wore pearls and a twin-set. I, too, felt awful but it's a lesson not to pre-judge people. Just because my friend looks the type to pilfer doesn't necessarily mean she would. Likewise, just because you invest in tweed doesn't negate you from thieving tendencies. Have this quote by the Greek philosopher, Thales: "The most difficult thing in life is to know yourself." Good advice for us all, don't you agree?

Chapter Twenty-one

Billington Gazette Headline: ***Deal with Billington Market Traders Stalls After Wholesale Disagreement*** (Pun Points - six)

It was Saturday afternoon and Eliza was absent-mindedly gazing out of her kitchen window, when she saw something scuttle across the garden path towards the house.

She dropped her cup of tea, with a clatter, onto the kitchen worktop.

Oh my god! I think that's either a very big mouse or a rat.

She peered to where she saw it scamper and there, poking out from underneath the azalea bush, was a long, pink, ringed tail.

Oh no. I can't allow that. It might eat the buds.

Do rats eat buds? They eat anything, they're vermin.

It'd definitely poo on the buds.

Eliza, hollered to Tom but there was no response.

He's got the music channel on really loud.

He needs to turn it down; it'll affect his forming eardrums.

Eliza strode into the lounge whereupon she found Tom manically gyrating his bottom around. Ellington was sat bolt upright in his basket; watching with alarm.

Upon seeing Eliza, Ellington slunk out, eagerly, from his bed and sat in front of her for a mollifying stroke.

Eliza obliged and gawped at Tom.

Eliza: "What are you doing?"

Tom swung round, whilst maintaining his dance routine.

Tom, puffing: "I'm shaking what my mamma gave me."

Eliza: "Oh."

Tom swung round and bashed his leg on the coffee table. He rubbed his ankle, feverishly, whilst continuing to dance.

Tom, puffing: "Grandma says I get my sense of rhythm from you."

Oh, charming.

Eliza went over to the remote control and turned down the music to a more tolerable level.

Eliza: "Can you stop channelling Beyoncé for a minute, please. There's a rat in the garden I need to attend to."

Tom promptly stopped moving.

Tom: "Awesome! I'll get me wellies."

Eliza: "I was going to suggest you stay in here and not let Ellington or Norris out."

Tom, moaning: "Aww, I wanna come; I've never seen a real rat before. I need to tell Charlie about it."

I bet he's seen plenty of rats in his hood.

Eliza, tutting: "Oh, come on then."

They put on their wellies and went out into the back garden. The rat's tail still evident from under the azalea by the back door.

Eliza looked at Tom.

Eliza: "What should I use?"

Tom: "A gun?"

Eliza looked at him, agape.

Eliza: "Funnily enough, I don't have access to one of those."

Tom shrugged and she looked around with her hands on her hips.

Eliza: "Get me a broom, please. There's one in the shed."

Tom: "Don't let it move before I get back, 'kay?"

Eliza nodded and waved him off.

Eliza grabbed the broom off a returning Tom and started brandishing it around in the vicinity of the rat.

Eliza, menacingly: "Come on, out you come! Let me at you...you Rolandy rat thing!"

Tom, clapping: "That's it, mum! You tell it!"

The rat, obediently, scuttled out from the bush and stopped, stock still and looked up at them with its beady little eyes.

Eliza dropped the broom.

Eliza: "Arrrgh! It's come out!"

Tom: "Good rat!"

Eliza: "What do I do?"

Tom, patting Eliza's arm: "Stay strong, me old finger and thumb! Don't let the rat win! Try and stare it out. I do that with Freya; she always walks away."

There was a slam of a door and brisk trudging over to where they were stood. It was Philip.

Philip: "Hello, dear Eliza. I saw you wildly, flailing around. Is everything alright? Has a bee gone up your blouse? I'd happily offer my services to remove it."

Eliza took her gaze off the rat and faced Philip.

Eliza: "There's rat near my kitchen, what am I going to do?"

Philip, raising an eyebrow: "Don't you like rats?"

Eliza: "The whole bubonic plague thing, put me off a bit."

Philip nodded.

Philip: "I would put the rodent's emergence down to the amount of rain we've had recently. When I went to The Anchor last night, the river was up past the reeds; any higher and I would have sat supping my beer in a rowing boat. Would you be so kind as to hold these?"

He pulled off a pair of binoculars from round his neck and thrust them into Eliza's hand, before marching over to Eliza's shed and coming back with a spade.

Without further ado, Philip held the spade above his head and flung it down with force; whacking the rat, squarely, on the head.

What the?!....

Tom, cheering: "Yay!!"

Philip bent down and inspected his damage.

Philip, joyously: "That got the bugger!"

Tom, excitedly: "Cooool! He thwacked a rat dead! Can I take it to school for show and tell?"

Eliza, somewhat stunned by what she'd just witnessed, shook her head, fervently.

Bloody hell! It's proper dead!

Eliza, to Philip: "You killed it! It goes against my hippy doctrines! I'm sanctimoniously pure these days!"

Philip tsked, loudly.

Philip: "What were you going to do, then? Stun it by chucking a crystal at it? I don't subscribe to such balderdash."

A delighted Tom and shocked Eliza watched in silence as a whistling Philip picked the deceased rat up by the tail. Swinging it around in time to his trilled tune, Philip, nonchalantly, lobbed it in to Eliza's wheelie bin.

Tom, in awe: "I can't wait to tell Charlie!"

Oh my god! I'll have to chant for a week and re-arrange my whole house to cleanse the effect of that!

It is also dead in my bin.

It's not even double-bagged and it's not collection day until next week.

Philip wandered back and motioned to Eliza to return his binoculars.

Philip: "I must get on, my dear. I'm on tit watch."

Eliza: "Oh."

A few moments later, Eliza's mobile rang; it was Jude.

Eliza: "Afternoon."

Jude: "Afternoon. What are you up to?"

Eliza: "Not a lot. I've just put my broom away; Philip killed a rat with a spade. In a minute, I'm off to have a chat with the ether about it; try and make amends."

There was a pause on the end of the line.

Jude: "That's nice... Would you like to watch a film together, this afternoon?"

Eliza: "But the sun's shining."

There was another pause on the end of the line.

Jude: "And?"

Eliza: "You can't watch a film when the sun's out; it's wrong. Watching television during the day is purely for knackered out parents with pre-school children. Television companies do it so you can prop the child up against a cushion and can get on with the vacuuming or having a mental breakdown... Or when you're ill; you can watch TV when you're ill, that's perfectly acceptable. I think it might be the law, actually."

There was a further pause on the line before he replied.

Jude: "I'll take that as a no, then."

Eliza: "I think we've got an iffy line. There's a time lag."

Jude: "It's me assimilating the information you furnish me with."

Eliza: "Fair enough. But I'd like to see you, even though you have a slow brain."

Jude: "I'd like to see you, too. Shall I pop by in half an hour?"

Eliza: "Yes, please."

That'll give me time to waft an incense stick about a bit and wish Roland a good passage to rat heaven.

Mentor in Life Feature letter: *Dear Eliza, My wife's cooking is ~~shit~~, rubbish. She burns everything. She gets upset when I point out to her that even the dog won't eat her bangers. What should I do? Regards, I'm-starving-hungry*

Dear I'm-starving-hungry, If you can't say something nice, say something funny. Rather than say her sausages damage your dentures, how about saying they make great kindling. It's positive, creative and will cut down on the heating bills. A survey said that sausages aren't very good for you so she's probably thinking of your health. However, we live in a society where all are equal so perhaps you'd like to recalibrate yourself to the 21st Century and do the cooking instead. How's that for a radical idea?

Chapter Twenty-two

Billington Gazette Headline: **PHARTS (Pilkington Heritage and Relic Treasury Society) Blown Away by Ancient Butt** (Pun Points – Eight)

It was Saturday afternoon and rivulets of water ran down the cottage's window pane.

Jude: "So it's ok to watch a film, now?"

Eliza: "Yes, it's raining."

Jude: "Where's Tom?"

Eliza: "He rung my mum to tell her about the rat and she offered to take him to a play-barn for the afternoon."

Jude: "We can watch an adult rated one, then."

Eliza, scrunched her nose up.

Eliza: "Not porn! I've just had my lunch."

Jude looked at her startled.

Jude: "No, not porn! I was thinking of something that didn't have either Bob the Builder or a grown man singing in rhyme in it."

Jude scrolled around, looking at film titles.

Jude: "Anything in particular?"

Eliza: "You choose; I'm easy."

Jude opted for one and pressed play.

Eliza: "Except for that one."

Jude tutted, stopped playing the film and started scrolling through the list of choices.

Jude, hovering over a potential option: "That one?"

Eliza: "Nah. It looks a bit gory."

Jude continued down the list.

Jude: "That one's not gory."

Eliza: "Do people get shot?"

Jude: "Only a couple."

Eliza: "No, then."

Jude, huffing: "You choose one."

Eliza: "No, no. You can. I'm not bossy like that. I'm an easy-going girlfriend."

Jude smiled.

Jude: "Are you, indeed? In that case, you'll be happy to watch this one."

He pressed play on an ambiguously entitled film, The Conflagrant.

A few minutes later Eliza tugged at Jude's arm. He responded by putting it around her and snuggling her in the crook of his elbow.

Eliza, pointing at the screen: "No, who's he?"

Jude: "The tall one?"

Eliza: "Yes."

Jude: "He's the one the film is about."

Eliza: "Is he the good guy?"

Jude: "Well, we don't know yet, but probably."

He's just saved a giraffe and a leopard. He must be the good guy; baddies don't bother with zoo animals.

A few minutes later, during a fight scene the, now most definitely the good guy, was getting a pummelling.

Eliza: "Does the good guy get killed?"

Jude: "I presume not as there's a sequel."

No point watching this bit then.

A few minutes later, Eliza pointed to an elderly man who was speaking.

Eliza: "Is that the man in charge of the False Memory Group?"

I'm not sure if I remembered that correctly.

Jude sighed.

Jude: "No, they all got shot. He's the one in charge of the assignment."

What assignment?

Eliza: "Why haven't we seen him before?"

Jude pulled his arm out from beneath her and looked at her, somewhat bewildered.

Jude: "We have, he was the one at the beginning, telling the good guy what his mission was."

Eliza: "Oh, I wasn't paying attention then."

Jude shook his head and settled back down to watch the film.

Fifteen minutes later, Eliza pointed at the screen.

Eliza: "Why has the good guy got fire coming out of his feet?"

Jude, patiently: "He's turned into a superhero. There was that scene earlier where he thought he was drinking a cup of tea but it was actually a highly toxic chemical."

No tea I've ever drunk has made my feet go on fire.

Green tea makes me burp but I don't think that's a super power.

How frightfully implausible.

A few minutes later, the good guy slash superhero was stood on the edge of a building; mulling over whether to jump off.

Eliza: "Why's he attempting to jump off there?"

Jude: "Because he's running away from the men with machetes."

Eliza: "He'll break his neck. There's stairs right beside him; he'd be better off running down them. The street's below and he can blend in with the crowd."

Jude: "He won't be able to blend into the crowd. He's wearing a bright yellow suit and a helmet. Anyway, it's not as exciting if he just walks down some steps. Jumping across a precipice is much more enthralling."

Is it now?

He's no superhero, he's an idiot.

He's wearing a ridiculous outfit which has no pockets for essentials.

Any self-respecting superhero has somewhere to put their keys and a tissue. Neville would have told you that.

Eliza: "How about he uses his magic feet? He could singe the machete men."

Jude: "They'd die too quickly if he did that. They need to stay alive for the sequel."

Eliza watched as the superhero escaped the machete wielding baddies only to accidently set fire to a row of shops and a disused warehouse with his fire breathing feet.

Eliza: "He can't work his feet very well; one of those shops sold designer settees. The insurance to replace that stock will be extortionate."

Jude: "He's only just got his super power. He's not familiar with the strength of it."

Eliza: "He should wear L-plates on his shoes."

Actually, that wouldn't work. People would think he had two left feet.

Jude sighed.

Jude: "Can we just watch it, please?"

Eliza, huffing: "Yes, alright."

Several minutes later, it cut to a scene where an elegant woman was laid, provocatively, across a bed. Eliza watched as the superhero emerged from the bathroom naked, save for a towel and his helmet.

What on earth does he look like?!

Eliza: "Why's he still wearing his helmet?"

Jude: "She can't know his identity."

Eliza: "He's ruined a lot of shops and set light to that random man with the beard. He's bound to get arrested at some point. If there's a police line-up she'll have to identify him by his willy. Think of the other men they'd have to hire for the identity parade; poor buggers. That's very unthoughtful."

Jude: "She's fallen in love with him, she wouldn't identify him anyway."

Eliza: "You can't fall in love with a man with a helmet and flaming feet. She must have had some right duff relationships to think that's the best she can get."

Jude: "And that 'random man with the beard' was the instigator of the chemical tea. He was the villain."

Eliza: "Oh. Good job he's dead, then."

Jude: "Indeed."

Eliza stretched and stood.

Eliza: "Would you like a cup of tea? I'll leave the toxic matter out of it. I could do without your feet setting alight; it'd upset the animals."

Jude: "Yes please. I'll pause the movie for you."

Eliza: "Don't bother, it's a rubbish film. You keep talking through it so haven't got the faintest idea what's going on."

I think I would have found porn more palatable.

Mentor in Life Feature letter: *My Dear Eliza, You're now in a position of sway. When are you going to get the council to listen about the bleedin' pot holes outside my house? Write a damning article on it and put it on the front page. With anticipation, your neighbour.*

Dear my neighbour, I merely answer life queries but shall do my utmost to get the editorial team to broach the matter with their contacts within the council. (The pot holes are encroaching on my bit of road now, so I shall expedite the request.) Anticipation duly noted, your neighbour.

Chapter Twenty-three

Billington Gazette Headline: ***Cat Branded a Troublemaker After Getting Stuck in 5 Trees in 3 Days*** (Pun Points – Not Applicable – a recalcitrant cat is no cause for humour.)

Later that evening, a drenched Tom and Christine Turner rang Eliza's doorbell.

Eliza opened the door to be greeted by her concerned mother.

Eliza: "Crikey! Come in, come in!"

Eliza's mother: "Oh Sparrow, it's raining cats and dogs out here! The river has burst its banks; it's all across the main street. I nearly flooded the car. If it goes any higher your lane will be in trouble."

Eliza looked at Jude.

Jude: "It's never been up this high, according to Billington records, so hopefully it'll subside."

Eliza's mother: "I hope so, Jude. I won't come in. I want to get home in case the water rises, further."

Jude: "I ought to call Gaz to come and take some photos for next week's edition. It doesn't seem fair on a Saturday night, though. I've got my camera in the back of the car; I'll nip down to the park and capture some images. I'll follow you out, Mrs Turner, to make sure you make it to higher water, safely."

Eliza's mother, tittering: "Oh, call me Christine; I insist."

Blimey, no one ever calls mum Christine. I don't even think dad does.

Call me Christine: "Are you sure about following me out? Thank you."

Eliza bid Jude and her mother a safe farewell and went off to dry off a soaked Tom.

Tom: "What's for tea? All that playing has proper worn me out."

Eliza: "I've gone retro. Crispy pancakes with potato waffles followed by Arctic roll."

Tom: "Any veg?"

Eliza: "Nah, we'll pretend we've had our five a day."

Tom: "Awesome!"

Eliza went and put the dinner on and her mobile rang from the lounge; it was Jude.

Eliza: "Hi, are you alright? Did my mum get out ok?"

Jude: "Hi, it was touch and go, to be honest. The banks have completely gone. I'm going to stay around by the main street to guide people away from the area. I'm a bit concerned, Eli."

Eliza: "Why?"

Jude: "It's still raining and the drains can't cope. It could go up to yours. Do you have any sandbags?"

Eliza: "No, but the PRATS probably have. They did a World War I re-enactment the other month; they made trenches. I'll run round to Philip's; he'll have a relevant telephone number."

Tom: "Mum!! There's a funny smell in the kitchen!"

Eliza: "Flip-flops! I'm burning the retro dinner. Take care, speak to you later."

Jude: "OK, I won't come back tonight, I'll update the social media pages and download the photos that I get, is that alright?"

Eliza, hurriedly: "Yes, yes, do what you want. Bye."

Eliza flung her phone down and dashed back to the kitchen.

After rescuing what she could, Eliza served up her offering to Tom who inspected it with dismay."

Tom: "You'd not get past the first round of Mister Chef with that effort."

Eliza: "Write a letter of complaint to the management."

Tom "I can't, I'm not good with spelling. Mr Potatohead-Arranger is not happy about it."

Eliza: "Ah well, it would appear your voice will go unheard. Bad luck."

Tom: "Harsh mummy."

Eliza: "Who's Mr Potatohead-Arranger?"

Tom stabbed his fork into a crispy pancake, chewed off the burnt bits and spat them back onto the plate.

Tom: "You know I got a new teacher 'cos the other one left with stress?"

Eliza: "Yes, Mr Archer."

Tom: "Charlie and me don't call 'im that. We call him Mr Potatohead-Arranger."

Eliza: "Charlie and *I* don't call him that."

Tom: "See everyone calls him it. He rearranges the face on Mr Potatohead so he's well scary. Last week he put an arm in his nose hole. That's just wrong."

Eliza: "Maybe Mr Archer is trying to be funny. Cut up your pancake, please."

Tom ignored her and continued eating around the fork.

Tom, seriously: "Scaring children so they have nightmares about potato heads coming after them with nose arms, is not funny."

Eliza: "No, you're right. Would you like me to have a word?"

Tom: "No, I'll handle it. Charlie and I are finking of hiding Mr Potatohead's body bits in the lost property box; no one ever looks in there."

Mentor in Life Feature letter: *Dear Eliza, My girlfriend asks what I'm thinking, like, all the time and when I tell her, she gets upset. She asked the other day when we'd just had you-know-what and when I told her I was thinking about how to reach the loose tile on the roof, she elbowed me in the knackers. Please help. Regards, I-want-my-balls-in-tact*

Dear Mr I-want-my-balls-in-tact, This is a common malady amongst men. I have learnt over the years; you are very often thinking about power tools or nothing. This unpalatable truth should be withheld under scrutiny as it only serves to confirm the fact not many of you are attuned to the verbal assurances required by female partners. If you don't want to lie and say you were thinking of asking her to marry you then stay mysterious. Women like mysterious.

Chapter Twenty-four

Billington Gazette Headline: ***Twins Reunite After Twenty Years in Billington's Supermarket*** (Pun Points – six)

A naked Francesca laid beside a slumbering Kenneth. She smiled as she took in his profile, illuminated by the moonlight drifting through the bedroom window. She leant over and gently stroked his angular nose.

Kenneth opened his eyes and flicked her hand away.

Kenneth: "What are you doing?"

Francesca: "Being affectionate."

Kenneth grunted and closed his eyes again.

Francesca: "I'm glad we sorted out that…er…misunderstanding."

Kenneth re-opened his eyes and sighed.

Kenneth: "What misunderstanding?"

Francesca: "The one we had in FunkyFurn."

Kenneth snorted.

Kenneth: "There wasn't any misunderstanding on my part."

Francesca's eyes, searched his.

Francesca: "But you sent me flowers by way of an apology."

Kenneth pulled himself onto an elbow.

Kenneth: "No, I sent flowers as I know that's what highly strung women want when they let their emotions get the better of them."

He looked at his watch and swung his legs out bed.

Kenneth: "I need to go. I've got matters to attend to."

Francesca looked across at her alarm clock.

Francesca: "At 11 o'clock at night?!"

Kenneth didn't reply and pulled his trousers on.

Kenneth: "I'll be in touch. I have space in my diary next Wednesday."

Francesca pulled herself out of the covers and sat upright.

Francesca: "Do you love me?"

Kenneth ignored her question and buttoned up his shirt.

Francesca folded her arms across her naked breasts.

Francesca: "I asked you a question."

Anger flickered across Kenneth's eyes before his base instinct hastily reminded him what a pleasant time Francesca afforded his more carnal desires.

Kenneth breathed in deeply.

Kenneth: "I have a much affection for our time together. I would not wish for it to be curtailed."

Francesca stared at him, contemplating, then dropped her arms onto the bedcover; realising this was a good as she was going to get.

Francesca, sighing: "I'll see you next Wednesday, then."

Kenneth exhaled and nodded; relieved at the outcome. He could do without histrionics post coition.

Kenneth: "I'll see myself out."

Francesca heard the front door close and as she slid back under the covers, the silence in the room allowed her thoughts to spill forth.

If only she hadn't brought up the flowers. She knew she shouldn't have.

And what was she thinking, asking if him if he loved her? It was her fault he left; why did she have to push him?

She buried her head into the pillow and thumped it with pent up anger.

She needed to show him that they were a team.

She needed to make him care for her as much as she did him.

She pulled the covers up and started to cry herself to sleep... once again.

****

It was four o'clock on Sunday morning.

Eliza was fast asleep when she was awoken by Ellington jumping on her bed.

Ellington roughly jabbed his paw in her face.

Eliza: "What the...?! Gerroff!"

Eliza sat up and turned on the light.

Ellington, satisfied he'd woken Eliza up, jumped off the bed and started bouncing, up and down by her bedroom door, looking out of the door, then back at her, in turn.

Eliza, rubbing her eyes: "What's the matter with you?"

Ellington started whimpering and leapt on her bed again. He then scraped his paw down her pyjama'd body.

Bounding off again, he resumed his demented display.

Eliza: "You're trying to tell me something in dog language. I don't speak dog. Is it a thief? Oh god, I hope it's not a thief."

Hang on, Tom!

Make sure he's safe.

Eliza shot out of bed and ran across the landing to check Tom's ajar door. She put her ear to the door and heard his slumbering snores.

He's safe. Panic over.

By this time, Ellington had gone half way down the stairs and was doggy mind-melding with her to follow him.

Eliza, whispering: "Hang on."

Eliza ran back into her room and came back with a coat hanger.

Eliza to Ellington: "Just in case I need to disarm an intruder."

She followed Ellington, who was still positioned on the middle stair, down into the hallway.

She was just about to step onto the bottom stair when her bare foot squelched into the carpet.

Eliza: "Urgh, what the blithering...?"

Ellington, you dirty dawg!

She switched on the hall light to be greeted by two feet of water which had ingressed through the front door.

Eliza: "Oh, flipping flip-flops! We've flooded!"

Alliteration. Gaz would be proud.

Now is not the time to wander off, brain.

Ellington was stood with her on the second to bottom step and looking up at her, earnestly.

Eliza: "Well done, Lassie."

Think.

Do I wake Tom?

No, let him sleep and try and assess the damage. I can do without both of us getting hysterical.

I need something on my feet. Wellies, ideally, but they are out by the back door.

Eliza to Ellington: "Seeing as you're such a clever dog, any chance of you fetching my wellies?"

Ellington continued to look at Eliza and the water in turn.

No, fair enough.

Eliza ran back upstairs and put the coat hanger down and looked around.

What have I got?

She came down a couple of minutes later holding a pedal bin from the bathroom which she'd tipped out onto the bathroom floor and a charity bag which she'd hastily emptied out onto her bedroom carpet.

On the second to bottom step she was greeted by Ellington who was on sentry duty. She put her left foot in the pedal bin and her right into the charity bag which she then wrapped around her leg and tied up by her knee.

Ellington's ears dipped down as he cowered at the sight.

Eliza: "What? I'm being resourceful. There might be sewage in that water. I don't want poo feet. There's no superhero with poo feet. Wait there; I'll come and get you in a minute."

She clunked down the bottom couple of stairs and waded through the water.

Oh god, there's holes in my charity bag foot.

It's too late now. Don't think about it; just get to your wellies and assess the damage.

Eliza slopped through the water into the kitchen, which, too was under a foot or so of water.

She turned on the light and was greeted by Norris who was sat bolt upright on the hob, sitting in the pan she'd cooked the potato waffles in. He mewed when he saw her; a look of disgust on his face.

It pays to not wash up, on occasion.

Eliza: "Thank goodness you're safe. Hang on I'm coming. It's a bit slow with a pedal bin as a boot."

Eliza made it across the kitchen and to her wellies; the top of which were peeking over the flood water.

She grabbed them and plonked them onto the work surface.

Oh, think of the germs.

I'll have to anti-bac that.

Eliza hauled herself out of her pedal bin boot and sat on the work surface. She then untied her charity bag from her leg and let it drop into the murky flood water which was swishing around her kitchen.

She spun round and washed her feet, hastily, in the kitchen sink.

She leant over and picked up a tea-towel and dried them before putting on her wellies.

Right. That's that bit done.

Let's have a look at the damage.

Eliza splashed through to the lounge and saw that Ellington's bed was underwater, as was Norris'. Eliza tutted as she looked at the sofa, immersed in the flood water.

That's going to honk.

She spotted her mobile where she had flung it the evening before when she burnt the dinner and picked it up off the arm of the sofa.

She glanced at it and saw that she'd missed several calls and had received a load of text messages.

Oooh, get me, all popular.

She looked at the text messages and saw they were from Jude and Lydia.

She read the most recent one first: Lydia's.

Lydia's text message: "Where in buggering balls are you? Why aren't you picking up your phone? Pilkington is flooded. Are you alright? I hear my old house is under two feet. xx"

When did she send that?

Oh, 11.50pm last night.

Eliza's text message: "Sorry for not replying, I was asleep. I was awoken by Ellington who notified me that his bed was submerged. I'm ok. Will try and rescue stuff in case it gets any higher. xx"

She scrolled down to the next message: Jude's

Jude's text message: "Hope you and Tom are alright. There have been many cars which have conked out in the flood water. Did you get your sandbags? xx"

Oh yes, sandbags.

I forgot about them.

She replied to Jude.

Eliza's text message: "Tom and I are fine. We are flooded, though. I've had to wear a pedal bin as a boot and my charity bag one leaked so I probably ingested poop through my feet pores. Forgot about sandbags as I was chatting about a teacher who puts incorrect body parts into Mr Potatohead's orifices. Will call you in the morning. xx"

Eliza also text her landlord to inform him and set about moving items which could be in danger, to higher surfaces.

As Eliza was completing her task in the lounge she heard a commotion coming down the stairs, then a clattering of lots of feet running back up the stairs.

Tom.

Eliza waded through to the bottom of the stairs and called up.

Eliza: "We've been flooded, Tom. We're all ok."

Tom emerged from the bathroom with the shower curtain in his hand, which he'd ripped from the pole.

Tom: "Oh, that's alright then. I got a paw in me face, I shot out of me Uncle Ned."

He pointed behind him.

Tom: "You've made a right mess in there. Whatcha done wiv the bin?"

Eliza: "I used it as a makeshift welly."

Tom scrunched his nose up to signify he thought that was a somewhat, daft idea.

He toddled down the stairs and before he hit the water fluffed out the shower curtain and stepped into the middle. He motioned to Ellington to get in, which he dutifully did. Tom then pulled the edges up around the pair of them and jumped in to the water.

Eliza: "Oh, what a marvellous idea."

Tom: "Common sense, innit? I'm not walking in that. It's got germs and feasties in it. They teached us it in class."

Eliza: "Taught. And I think you mean faeces. It does beat a pedal bin."

Tom: "You haven't inherited my brains but, never mind, you are a good mum. Did you hop? What did you put your other foot in?"

Eliza: "I used the charity bag which I had upstairs full of your old bits that you no longer wanted."

Tom: "My old art tablecloth was in there. That's waterproof, you could have used that."

Eliza: "Yes, yes, Einstein. I was half asleep and wasn't thinking straight. I need to make sure I move everything to higher ground. Are you going to help or just highlight my emergency boot flaws?"

Tom shuffled through the water with Ellington in his shower curtain sack into the lounge.

Tom: "Is the TV ok?"

Eliza: "Yes, I think so."

Tom: "Good. Can I watch something?"

Eliza, incredulous: "No! The plugs are under water and you'll blow it or us up. We are having a slight emergency situation here, Tom."

Tom: "Ok, ok. Chill."

Tom looked down into his shower sack at Ellington.

Tom to Ellington: "Mummy's not good in water but at least she kept her clothes on this time."

Eliza's mobile rang; it was Jude.

Eliza: "Hello, you're up early."

Jude: "I received your text. I kept my phone on audible, in case you wanted me."

Eliza: "I always want you. We're flooded."

Jude: "So I read. How badly?"

Eliza: "Nearly to the top of my welly, badly. I've text the landlord. It's going to proper pong when it dries out."

Jude: "It will be a few weeks at least before you will be able to move back in."

Eliza: "What?! I'll have to move out? That didn't even cross my mind."

Jude: "Of course. You can't live with flood damage, especially with a child. It will require refurbishment."

Eliza: "Oh."

Jude: "Eli."

Eliza: "Yes."

Jude: "I was wondering. You can say no, if you want..."

Eliza: "What."

Jude: "Well, if you and Tom, obviously, that goes without saying... Well, if you wanted..."

He coughed nervously.

Oh, spit it out man. I'm stood in a foot of water here with a child and dog in a shower curtain and a pissed off Persian perched in my potato waffle pan.

Eliza, slightly impatiently: "Yes, what?"

Jude, all in one breath: "Well, would you like to move in with me?"

Ohh, I can hear the blood rushing in my ears.

Don't drop the phone.

Do. Not. Drop. The. Phone.

Eliza, breathlessly: "As in together?"

Jude: "Erm, yes."

Eliza: "As in, you and me?"

Jude: "Yes. And Tom."

Eliza: "Oh, yes, and him."

Jude, gently: "Would you like to?"

Eliza: "You really want to? Are you sure? I am a bit mental. I don't think dangerously so. I don't kill people. I'm just a bit..."

Jude interjected.

Jude: "Eli, stop. You're wonderful."

Eliza: "Am I?"

Jude: "Yes."

Eliza: "I'm not really."

Jude: "You're my wonderful."

I might faint.

I mustn't, I'd drown in poo water.

Eliza: "Let me talk to Tom about it and I'll call you back. Is that alright?"

Jude: "Of course. I'll be over shortly to give you a hand. See you in a bit."

Eliza: "Ok, bye."

She put the phone on the highest shelf of the bookcase and sighed.

Tom: "Are you alright, me old china? You look a bit peaky."

Eliza: "Do you want to move in with Jude?"

Tom: "When?"

Eliza: "He didn't say. I presume straight away. Our cottage will need renovating after the water damage."

Tom: "Ok. I like him, he's got a really big telly. And he cooks better than you."

Oh thank you.

Eliza: "Well that's settled then. Off to Jude's we go."

Social Media Meme: *Let us be grateful to the people who make us happy; they are the charming gardeners who make our souls blossom. Marcel Proust*

Chapter Twenty-five

Billington Gazette Headline: ***Cracks Form After Explosive Council Planning Meeting - Councillors Request Back Up*** (Pun Points – six)

Eliza and Lydia walked gingerly across the ice-rink like flooring that was installed at the Merrythought Café and flopped down at an empty table.

Dave cautiously looked on and nudged Belinda to go over to them.

Dave to Belinda: "Now remember, politely take their order and surreptitiously glean the nature of their topic. If it's racy, I'll use the plastic crockery."

Belinda: "Yeah, yeah. I gotcha."

Belinda mooched over to Eliza and Lydia's table.

Belinda: "Alright. How's it going? Old misery chops wants me to ask what the topic of conversation will be today."

Eliza and Lydia looked up at her with surprise.

Lydia, curtly: "Tell him from us, it's none of his business. He provides the beverages and larded cuisine; that is all."

Belinda, hollering to Dave: "The one with the bad extensions says, 'keep yer beak out!'"

Lydia involuntarily clamped her hands around her head, shocked.

Dave beckoned to Belinda to come back to him and she dawdled back to where he was standing.

Belinda: "What?"

Dave: "Did you tell them why I was enquiring?"

Belinda: "Oh, nah. I forgot that bit."

Dave, tutting: "Well, tell them!!"

Dave directed Belinda to go back and explain.

Belinda wandered back to Eliza and Lydia's table.

Belinda, sighing: "He wants me to tell you, you're costing him a fortune in broken crockery."

Lydia: "Oh, are we now?!"

Belinda: "Yeah, he said any more filthy talk and you're both barred."

Lydia: "How dare he! We're leaving. Come on Eli."

Eliza sighed and went to reach for her coat as Lydia stood, indignantly, and scraped her chair back on the highly polished floor.

Lydia: "Oh, and for your information, my extensions cost a bloody fortune. I'll have you know; they came from a twelve-year-old Tibetan tribal girl who lived on a diet of yak milk. I don't suppose your hair has ever drunk yaks' milk."

Dave looked on in horror and came scuttling over.

Dave: "What's happened? Why are you leaving?! Belinda, what have you been saying?!"

Belinda shrugged.

Belinda: "Nuffin, just words. Like what you said."

Lydia to Dave: "Barred, are we?!"

Dave ushered Lydia and Eliza to sit back down.

Dave, sternly: "Belinda?!"

Belinda: "What?! I was using my initiative and offering a workplace solution."

Dave: "My café is not the place for you to start using your initiative. Stick to toast proffering if you don't mind."

Belinda: "Tut. I'm undervalued. I've a good mind to go to ACAS."

Dave, huffing: "Just go and serve customers please Belinda, and see if you can do it without offending them."

Belinda pulled a face at him and stalked off.

Dave turned his attention back to Eliza and Lydia.

Dave: "I'm so sorry. She's doing a business course at college; it's got a lot to answer for. She's been a nightmare since she read the chapter on employment rights. Now, what can I get you?"

Eliza and Lydia placed their orders and he left them to it.

He gave Belinda a 'when I get my hands on you' look as he trudged past her towards the kitchen.

Eliza: "Right, tell me your news. I have some."

Lydia: "Ok. It turns out, Tony's infantile."

Eliza, shrugging: "Most men are."

Lydia: "Really?"

Eliza: "Yes, not many men really grow up."

Lydia: "Yes, but when their balls drop, they should be able to reproduce. I think Tony should have told me."

Eliza: "He probably doesn't realise he is."

Lydia: "He does, he had the test."

Eliza: "There's a test? Is it a bit like a MENSA one? What constitutes a fail?"

Lydia: "Not enough swimmers, I think."

Eliza: "If they can do the crawl, they're a grown-up? I never knew that was the benchmark for adulthood. Do they have to be able to do a width or a length?"

Lydia: "Well, a length I'd say and then up your pipes."

Huh?

Eliza: "Sorry, up your pipes?"

Dave came along with their teas and started to place them on the table.

Lydia: "Yes, the sperm has to go up your pipes."

Eliza, shrieking: "Sperm?!"

Dave fumbled about with the teapot and threw it onto the table, quickly followed by the cups.

He stared long and hard at Eliza, who shrugged and grinned up at him.

Lydia: "Yes, as I say, he's infantile."

Dave, cheerlessly: "Infertile."

Lydia: "Oh, yeah. That. Same thing."

Dave shook his head and mumbled 'stupid woman' under his breath as he departed.

Eliza: "Ohh, he can't have children; not he is one. Got you. Shall I be mother?"

Lydia nodded so Eliza poured the tea.

Eliza: "Well, that's alright, isn't it? You've got Freya. You've never said you wanted more children."

Lydia: "Well, I'd like the choice. The opportunity has been stripped away from me. I think I know what may have caused it."

Eliza: "What's that then?"

All the testosterone has gone to his vocal chords, probably.

Lydia: "I was looking through his personal papers and he has a monthly direct debit for those little blue things."

Looking through his personal papers? Reminder to self to broach that at some point.

Eliza, none the wiser: "He pays maintenance to the Smurfs?"

Shagging a Smurf has definitely got to be a sexual low. I'm not surprised his bits gave up.

Lydia: "They aren't real, Eli."

I know. I just don't know what you're talking about.

I'm playing for time whilst my brain catches up.

Eliza continued to stare blankly at Lydia.

Lydia: "Viagra, darling. He takes Viagra."

Eliza: "Oh! He's got a subscription?! I've got one of them for that upcycle magazine. My mum bought me a year's worth one Christmas and it's so good at explaining how to wax a difficult stool, I've kept it on. I don't suppose his mother gave it to him as a present, though. That'd be a bit weird... They might have a close relationship."

Lydia: "Put a croissant in your mouth and stop talking for a minute."

Eliza obliged.

Lydia: "I didn't actually mean all of it in one go... They can make you infertile, apparently."

Eliza raised her eyebrows in acknowledgment whilst brushing flakes of croissant from around her mouth.

She glugged from her tea and swallowed the remainder of her croissant.

Eliza: "It's probably a blessing. He'd be a very old father. I imagine he'd be rubbish in the parents' sack race on sports day. He'd probably lie down in it and have a nap. Either that or plant some potatoes in it."

Lydia nodded.

Lydia "You're right. I'll not address the situation. Oh yes, I read your MILF letter.. Did you really think I was stealing from the shop?"

Eliza: "Yes, I'm so sorry. The thought did cross my mind."

Lydia, shrugging: "You're forgiven, darling. If skiving is thieving, then I did indeed steal from the business."

Eliza: "Thank you. Can we talk about my news now?"

Lydia: "Yes, ok."

Lydia shovelled a buttered muffin in her mouth.

Eliza: "Jude's asked us to move in with him!"

Lydia promptly spat the half-chewed muffin across the table. A passing Belinda curled her lip.

Belinda to Lydia: "Animal."

Lydia waved her off and beamed at Eliza.

Lydia: "Oooh! This is huge! When?! What?! How?!"

Eliza: "The night the cottage flooded. I was stood in my wellies and Tom was stood in the shower curtain."

Lydia: "Ok. When do you move in?"

Eliza: "This weekend."

Lydia clapped her hands together.

Lydia: "He'll be asking you to marry him next. What will you say?"

Eliza: "Well, he probably won't."

Will he? Ooh, he might. Should I wear white? Nah, that's stretching it a bit.

I quite like dusky pink. A simple A-line with kitten heels. Saying that, you can't beat a Grecian with a nice floppy sleeve.

We wouldn't be able to have soup for starter at the wedding breakfast if I had floppy sleeves. I can't do my first dance with soup sleeves... it'd have to be the dusky pink...

Lydia, poking Eliza: "Eli! Eli! Come back to me!"

Eliza broke away from her wedding musings.

Eliza: "Sorry, as I say, I hadn't really given it a thought, we'll see. I might say yes, if he asks."

Lydia: "Well, I'm delighted! Is Tom happy?"

Eliza: "He's more than happy; he likes his big TV and they talk about mechanical things together. Plus, he has one more person to try his culinary delights on."

Lydia: "Great! Do you need help? I don't think Tony's back is up to it but Freya and I can."

Eliza: "No, you're fine but thanks. We'll meet up again next week and I'll fill you in on it all."

Eliza and Lydia raised their teacups and chinked them together.

Mentor in Life Feature letter: *Dear Eliza, I flit from relationship to relationship as I don't want to be without a boyfriend. Being in with a man, defines me and makes me feel better about myself. My friends say I'm a bit of a goer and need to pack it in but I'm scared to be on my own. Please offer some words of assistance. I'm worried as I'm on first name terms with the staff at the GUM clinic. Much love, I've-had-plenty-of-stds-but-I've-never-had-crabs.*

Reply: Dear I've-had-plenty-of-stds-but-I've-never-had-crabs, What's a Queen without a King? Historically speaking, more powerful. Take your last course of antibiotics and place your crown firmly on your head. Be Royal. Be Regal. (You don't have to learn German or hire servants though, I'm talking metaphorically.)

Chapter Twenty-six

Billington Gazette Headline: ***Pilkington Floods cause Chaos but Local Retailers Buoyant after Dinghy Orders Flow in*** (Pun Points – Not Applicable – factual consumerism article by Mandy).

Jude held the lead of a straining Ellington and Tom hugged a scrabbling Norris as they watched Eliza wedge the final case into Jude's car.

Eliza, with hands on hips: "I think that's all that we'd need, immediately."

Jude was blinking at his laden car.

Jude: "You did leave the kitchen sink, didn't you?"

Eliza: "Oh ha-de-ha. I've only packed the essentials."

Jude: "Remind me never to go camping with you."

Eliza: "You're ok, I never want to go camping with you."

Jude, with surprise: "Oh!"

Eliza, patting his hand: "Not in a, I-don't-want-to-go-on-holiday type of way, as in, I never want to go camping ever again. I went to a festival the other year; thirty odd years getting my life together and I ended up in a field full of drunk people with the imminent threat of trench foot. The bogs were miles away and highly dubious, so I bought one of those portable pipe things to wee in. It's never taken me so long to relax my pelvic floor... and the bugs! Oh, my god, you'd have thought I was on safari in the Serengeti. The only good thing about it was the boho clothing I bought for it; though it costs a fortune to look that poor."

Jude: "I thought you were at one with nature."

Eliza, seriously: "On my terms, Jude."

Their attention was distracted by Philip blustering out of his front door.

Philip: "Hello, what's going on here?! Where are you off to?"

Eliza: "I'm moving out."

Philip looked crestfallen.

He reached out and grabbed Eliza's hands.

Philip: "I do hope my treasure hunting in your overgrown patch didn't have any bearing on your decision, my dear Eliza."

Eliza extracted her hands from his clammy grip.

Eliza: "No Philip, the fact you regularly trespass into my garden and nearly put your spade through an unexploded bomb has nothing to do with it."

Tom, adjusting a squirming Norris: "We're going to mummy's boyfriend."

Tom pointed Norris at Jude.

Philip, beaming at Eliza: "Well done you! But I'll miss you, dreadfully. I don't mind admitting I found it very therapeutic, looking at you out of my bathroom window, pruning your bush."

Eliza and Jude paled and stared at him.

Philip continued, oblivious.

Philip: "I did wonder if you might have been a bit over zealous; I think natural is best but I do concede it does look good as a duck."

He's talking about my box hedge.

It's not a duck it's a replica of Norris.

Philip, continuing: "Topiary is an acquired taste. Where did you learn it?"

Eliza: "YouTube. A man did his into the shape of an elephant. That was far too advanced so I decided to keep to domestic pets."

Philip: "I might continue with the shaping until the next tenant takes up residence."

Jude: "Oh, she'll be back."

Philip: "Will she?"

Eliza: "Will I?!"

I thought it was permanent.

Jude cocked his head slightly at Eliza, with confusion.

Jude: "Er, yes. It's just whilst the cottage is being renovated after the flood."

He looks scared.

Eliza, quickly: "Yes, yes of course it is. I knew that!"

He didn't say it wasn't permanent.

But, then again, he didn't say it was.

A look for relief flooded across Jude's face and he continued.

I'll pretend I didn't just witness that expression.

Jude: "Did yours get damaged, Philip?"

Philip: "Of course not! I've got military training. I filled a load of bin bags with the contents of my larder and duct taped them to my exterior doors. I've had to chuck the flour but the rest was recoverable."

Bleurgh.

Eliza: "It's been floating in poo!"

Philip: "Correction – the external bags were floating in excrement. Only a few splashes went inside where the tape peeled off. Anyway, a bit of shit never hurt anyone."

Eliza: "Language, Philip!"

Philip, to Tom: "Sorry, dear boy. I forget about young ears."

Tom shrugged.

Eliza: "The renovations should be under way this week. Hopefully, there won't be too much disruption to you."

Philip: "I'll keep you briefed on progress."

Eliza: "Thank you."

A restless Ellington strained on his leash to nibble Norris' tail.

Tom: "Oi, gerroff! Mum, can I drop the cat?"

Eliza: "No, we need to get him in the car."

Jude: "We must be off. I need to allocate space for this lot!"

Philip: "Of course, good luck young man! See you soon. Oh, and don't forget to get on to the council about those bloody-buggering potholes."

Philip turned to go back into his cottage.

Philip, muttering: "He's a brave man... Though, she does have all the attributes to gratify a man..."

Jude and Eliza in unison: "WE CAN STILL HEAR YOU!"

A departing Philip raised his hand by way of apology and disappeared back into his cottage.

Mentor in Life Feature letter: *Dear Eliza, My mates' girlfriends say I invade their space. I'm only being friendly and mucking about. One hit me the other day when I pinched her arse. You girls are right funny creatures. One minute you want us to be all over you then you call us ~~fucking~~ weirdos when we touch you. What's your take on it? Cheers, women-really-are-from-Mars.*

Dear Women-aren't-actually-from-Mars-we-just-like-good-manners, My advice would be to leave at approximately three feet between you and any woman for, at least, the next ten years. I shall leave you with this thought: If you put your ear up to a stranger's cheek you can hear them say, "Piss off!"

Chapter Twenty-seven

Billington Gazette Headline: ***Join our 'Save the Ducks' Campaign* - Pilkington's potholes are so deep; ducks are losing their chicks in them. Locals are mounting an around the clock vigil. We urge the council to take action.** (Pun Points – Not Applicable - Distressed ducks is a serious issue.)

Jude: "Look, it's not my fault you have to go on the training course. You might enjoy it."

Eliza: "Meh."

Jude: "Think of it as a team building exercise."

Eliza: "I don't like exercise, you know that."

Jude: "Just do me a favour and do your best, ok?"

Eliza: "Yes, yes."

Jude smiled across the car at a stony-faced Eliza who was strapped into the passenger seat.

Jude: "Are you going to get out? They'll be leaving soon."

Eliza: "Why can't you come?"

Jude: "I'm not the one who runs amok when the editor's away! Head Office were not impressed, Eli. We might not get another chance if we run another edition with dubious content."

Eliza sighed.

Eliza: "Ok. I'm ready."

Jude: "Atta girl. See you later. Now don't worry, the school's been informed I'm picking Tom up and we'll make you dinner."

Eliza nodded with resignation, left the car and walked across the car park towards the mini-bus, which was sat, engine running. She stepped aboard and was greeted by Gaz who was waiting for her.

Gaz: "Abouts time, laydee. Tickets please!"

Eliza, flatly: "I don't have a ticket."

Gaz: "It's an expression, innit?"

Eliza turned round to wave good-bye to Jude but he'd already left his car and was striding towards the office.

Oh, no wave then. Tut.

Gaz: "Are you's ready for a bit of blue-sky thinking?"

No.

Eliza: "Absolutely."

Charlotte clapped her hands together.

Charlotte-long-hair: "Spit spot! We can't be late; that'd really put the cat amongst the applecarts. Oh, that's an interesting cardigan, Eliza. Did you knit it?"

Interesting, when referring to an article of clothing, is not a compliment.

Voluptuous Valerie: "I think it looks lovely, Eliza. Is it designer? My favourite designer is OSFA."

Erm...

There's no need to tell her what OSFA actually means, she's being nice about your clothes.

Eliza: "Thank you, Valerie."

Eliza scrunched her nose up at Charlotte who sneered and waved at the driver of the mini bus to set off.

Charlotte-long-hair: "FYI, to give you the heads up..."

She's doing it again...

Eliza: "They're synonyms. It negates the use of an acronym."

Charlotte-long-hair: "What?!"

Eliza: "Oh, nothing. Do carry on; it was just FYI."

I realise annoying her is my new hobby.

Charlotte muttered something under her breath and continued.

Charlotte-long-hair: "Anyway, I've been designated team leader, obvs, so any queries about the time-table or lunch menu you should address me."

Eliza, dryly: "Marvellous."

Charlotte caught Eliza's tone and shook her head.

Charlotte-long-hair "Sarcasm won't get you anywhere in life, Eliza."

Eliza: "It got me runner-up in the 2019 European Sarcasm Finals."

Charlotte-long-hair: "Really?"

You're not real.

Eliza: "No."

Though, if there was a European Gullible Final you'd probably win.

As the journey progressed the group sat in silence on the way to the training venue only to be broken by a head-phoned Valerie suddenly singing, 'I want to sex you up!' to the silent bus.

Eliza looked around but no one else appeared to have noticed.

Okaaay, just me then.

I'm bored.

What do I always suggest to Tom when he moans in the car? Look out of the window. Yes, I'll do that.

A couple of minutes later Eliza involuntarily piped up.

Eliza: "Train! I win!"

Charlotte looked across at her and raised her eyebrows.

Eliza: "Sorry, force of habit."

Charlotte-long-hair: "Bless, you're more at home with the company of toddlers, aren't you?"

Shut up. He's nearly eight now, actually.

Charlotte took her mobile out and leant across to show it to Mandy.

Charlotte-long-hair: "I ran twenty kilometres last night."

We're English, use miles. Though, it doesn't sound so impressive saying 12.42 miles.

How do I know that twenty miles equals that?

Let's see if I can do another... thirty kilometres... easy 18.64.

Goodness. I need to Google if that's right.

Eliza scrabbled into her bag to retrieve her phone.

Blimey, I am right. It must be a hidden talent I've got.

I could go on Mastermind.

Mandy ignored a phone proffering Charlotte, pulled a magazine out of her handbag and started flicking through the pages. Charlotte turned her attention to Eliza, instead.

Charlotte-long-hair: "Would you like to see my app?"

Eliza: "No thanks. I'm happy to take your word for it."

Charlotte-long-hair: "My cardiovascular fitness is better than that of an Olympic athlete. It's probably because I'm part Scandinavian."

Shut up you tiresome old fit-bag.

Eliza: "That's nice. I read an article that said every mile you jog it adds a year…"

Scandinavian legged Charlotte-long-hair: "Really? To your life?"

Eliza: "No, to your face; it's all the running into the elements so you might want to try power walking instead."

Charlotte shot Eliza a filthy look to which Eliza shrugged.

Mandy stifled a giggle and smiled at Eliza.

Mandy the greyhound: "Would you like to read my mag, Eliza?"

Eliza: "That'd be great, thank you."

Mandy got up and stretched her wiry body towards Eliza, offering the magazine.

As Eliza went to grab it, her attention was distracted.

'Allo, what's that?

Ohh, she's got a pierced nipple.

I can't unsee that. I fear I may talk to it instead of her face for the rest of my Billington Gazette life now I know it exists.

It looks very prominent.

Eliza grabbed the magazine and thanked the nipple.

Mandy, following Eliza's gaze: "You're looking at me tit, aren't you?"

Charlotte looked across and curled her lip at Eliza.

Eliza: "Er, well. Um."

Eliza vaguely pointed at her piercing.

Well, this is awkward.

Mandy the Greyhound: "It's alright; it's me piercing, I get you; you ain't no sapphic. I was meant to have them both done but I fainted after the first one went in. The bloke what done it had his knee on me chest when he tried to get the piercing gun in; he'd never seen such a thick nipple in all his life. It's my Kev's fault; he thought it would be erogenous. He thought he'd be able to hang off 'em. He can't; it's bleedin' agony. I can't even sleep on me front nowadays."

Charlotte squirmed, awkwardly.

Charlotte-long-hair, in a sing-song voice: "Too much information!!"

Mandy ignored her and continued.

Mandy the Greyhound: "Do you wanna look?"

I do and I don't.

Eliza: "You're ok; I can see enough. Thanks, though."

Gaz sat bolt upright and leant over.

Gaz: "I'll have a squizz!"

Charlotte held her hands up and flapped about.

Charlotte-long-hair: "You most certainly will not! Mandy, you and your metal bosom, sit down!"

Mandy and Gaz tutted and returned to their seats.

The rest of the journey to the training venue went by in near silence, broken only by the random lines of song which burst forth from Valerie, courtesy of her mp3 player.

Mentor in Life Feature letter: *Dear Eli, My boyfriend has the biggest manhood I have ever seen. It makes my eyes water. I could use it as a clothes dryer it's that much of a whopper. It's a bastard to contain. What should I do? Best Regards, Don't-swing-round-it'll-have-my-eye-out.*

Dear Don't-swing-round-it'll-have-my-eye-out, I sympathise. My boyfriend has a huge penis and whilst it's magnificent to behold in an aloft state, it's not without its perils. My best friend and I used to refer to him as The Mighty Sword, but of course we never told him that. As Nelson Mandela once said: "May your choices reflect your hopes, not your fears."

Chapter Twenty-eight

Billington Gazette Headline: ***Diminutive Owner of Billington Bakery Belittled by Buyers*** (Pun Points – seven plus extra for alliteration)

The assembled staff from the Billington Gazette sat in a semi-circle of tables facing the projector screen waiting for the course presenter to appear.

A greasy-haired middle-aged man bustled in a few minutes later and glared at the group.

Obviously quite unhappy with his lot, course presenter: "I'm late but that's life; an ongoing dirge of chores and rigmarole."

Well, aren't you a little ray of sunshine?

He looked down at the notes that had been left on a table for him.

Miserable course presenter: "Ah, you're that bunch from the paper who keep ballsing things up."

Charlotte gasped and shot her hand in the air.

The course presenter looked over his shoulder to see if there was anyone behind him.

Confused miserable course presenter: "Is that hand for me?"

Charlotte-long-hair: "Yes. May I speak?"

Back to just being miserable course presenter: "We aren't at school; you don't need to put your hand up. What do you want to say?"

Charlotte-long-hair: "Anything you've heard regarding errors have been grossly misquoted and, as the famous phrase says, Venice wasn't built in a day. We requested this course in order to expand our knowledge to ensure we continue to bring top quality content to the Billington readership. Isn't that right?"

Charlotte looked around, expansively, at her work colleagues for support but none was forthcoming.

Charlotte stared at Eliza.

Charlotte-long-hair: "Isn't that right, Eliza?"

Why pick on me?

Your version of events is more fictional than the Wizard of Oz.

Eliza, muttering: "It was something along those lines."

Charlotte nodded approvingly.

Disinterested course presenter: "Is that right? I was led to believe it was last chance saloon because some halfwit let something offensive run."

Charlotte shot a look at Gaz and he pointed at her.

Actually, quite correct with his version of events course presenter: "Anyway, I'm Doug. I'll hand out some labels; write your name on it and stick it on yourselves."

He looks so downcast; I wonder why he's so dejected.

Training can't be a bad job; meeting new people each day.

I wonder if he's just lonely.

I shall use some of my hippy learnings to cheer his day up. It said on page 43 of 'Making a Difference through Simple Gestures', a smile can transform someone's day.

As Doug got to Eliza, he handed her a label and she flashed one of her, what she presumed to be, winning smiles.

He dropped the label and took a step back, perturbed.

Disturbed Doug: "Do you need the ladies?"

Oh, charming.

Eliza: "No, I'm fine."

Try again.

Eliza shot him another toothy beam which sent him straight back to his table.

As they quietly wrote their names on the labels a massive fart broke forth from the direction of Valerie.

Voluptuous Valerie: "Oops, 'scuse me."

Doug gave her a dispirited look, turned his mouth an extra centimetre downwards and opened a window.

Doleful Doug: "Right then, let's get on with this. I've got a presentation I have to do, then you need to do some team building activities. Happy? Doesn't matter if you are or you aren't, to be honest, but it's in my script."

He glanced around the room and when his eyes alighted on Eliza, she shot him another manic grin. He pulled a face and busied himself with preparing his presentation slides.

Once he had run through his presentation, he told them to come up with a workplace problem and to work as a team to find a solution to resolve it; mapping out their thoughts and reasons for doing so as they went along. He then excused himself for half an hour.

Charlotte, inevitably, took charge.

Charlotte-long-hair: "Do any of you have any workplace problems to offer? We need to do some joined-up thinking."

If you didn't join up your thinking it would just be random words. Cursive thoughts are a given.

Charlotte-long-hair, continuing: "We must get our drawing board together."

Tut, she just can't help herself.

Eliza: "Act."

Charlotte-long-hair: "I don't think we need to take up performing arts. We just need to identify, scrutinise and resolve."

You silly woman.

Eliza: "We must get our *act* together."

Charlotte-long-hair: "Exactly. I have an idea which I want to cascade down to you."

Gaz: "Hold up. I's got perceptions that I want heard."

Gaz sprung forth and started regaling a ream of ideas.

Charlotte briefly paused as she digested his list.

Charlotte-long-hair, tutting: "Nope. Anyone else got anything to say?"

Well, after the cavalier manner with which you dismissed Gaz's surprisingly valid suggestions; I'll pass if it's all the same.

Gaz started with another list of thoughts.

Charlotte put her hands on her hips and scowled at him.

Charlotte-long-hair: "Can you just stop it now?"

Gaz: "Sorry Lotty, there ain't no off switch on awesome."

Charlotte-long-hair: "Shut up."

Valerie shot her hand in the air and Charlotte sighed, impatiently.

Charlotte-long-hair: "Yes?"

Voluptuous Valerie: "We have a problem with biscuit selection in the office."

Charlotte-long-hair, huffing: "Next."

Mandy the Greyhound, boldly: "I know a workplace problem we have and I can also see a solution."

Charlotte-long-hair, sarcastically: "Oh, marvellous! Speak then."

Mandy the Greyhound: "You. You don't listen to other people's opinions. The solution is for you to shut yer trap and let someone else get a look in."

Voluptuous Valerie guffawed and Gaz gave her a high five.

I must not giggle.

Nope, it's involuntary.

Charlotte was taken aback and glowered at Eliza.

Why pick on me? I didn't say it and I also didn't give Mandy a high five!

Charlotte-long-hair: "Are you laughing, Eliza?"

Eliza: "No. It's just my happy disposition."

Gaz winked at her.

Charlotte-long-hair, agitatedly: "For the record, I do listen to other people; I just happen to think their ideas aren't very good. I am a passionate person – I've got Italian blood. If I come across wrong, it's because of that."

You must have got your Italian blood via a transfusion.

The only Italian in you is the remains of last night's pizza.

Italian blooded Charlotte-long-hair: "Well, seeing as I *apparently* don't listen to anyone else; let's peel the onion and see what you've got, Eliza."

The beginnings of spaghetti Bolognese?

Tut, I'm going to have to come up with something.

Why focus on workplace problems?

What happened to focussing on the positives?

Think…

What do I see as a problem apart from everything about you?

Your lunches. They bother me.

I imagine myriad ways of killing you every time you eat an egg sandwich.

Eliza: "My workplace problem is I don't like the smell of egg sandwiches; they make me wretch and you eat them every Tuesday and Friday. My solution is for you to have ham and cucumber, instead."

Charlotte sighed heavily.

Charlotte-long-hair: "Is that the best you can do?"

Eliza: "Yep."

Charlotte-long-hair: "Then we shall run with my idea."

I thought we might.

Charlotte-long-hair, continuing: "The slowdown in newspaper sales is accelerating; we need a marketing campaign to raise paper sales of the Gazette as it's all going online these days. Other papers have 360-degree coverage to keep readers in the loop."

I wouldn't mind keeping you in a loop.

Charlotte-long-hair: "We need a loss leader."

We've already got a dead-loss one.

Voluptuous Valerie: "We can't drop the price of the paper; we barely cover costs as it is. What's our loss leader going to be?"

Charlotte-long-hair, snapping: "Well, I can't think of everything!"

Eliza: "How about we do a supplement? Something that people really want and would normally pay a lot more for. It could be a house or celebrity style magazine – We could call it Billington Style – showcasing the must-haves for the up-and-coming Billington resident. We could also charge for advertisements. It can be available every month. We just need to make sure the newspaper articles the week the supplement is attached are really good, so the readers keep coming back."

Gaz, Mandy and Valerie murmured and nodded in agreement at the idea.

Charlotte-long-hair, dismissively: "We'll park that idea for the moment."

I'll park you.

Doug wandered, listlessly, back into the room.

Doleful Doug: "Have you done it?"

Charlotte-long-hair: "We have. Well, nearly."

Doug: "You've had your time limit; if you haven't resolved the issue in the given time, you've failed."

Charlotte-long-hair, flustered: "Ok, ok. We have done it."

Doug looked around the room and Eliza flashed him her best smile. Doug frowned, nervously poked one of his little fingers in his left ear, rattled it around then took it out and inspected it before addressing Gaz.

Doleful Doug: "Charlotte appears to have an unyielding grasp of the mouthpiece; Gavin, your turn to speak. What's the team's problem, strategy and solution?"

Gaz stood and flexed his shoulder muscles.

Gaz: "Thank you for the opportunity to speak, Mr Trainer Man. You's identified the team's problem just then."

Gaz looked pointedly at Charlotte who squirmed under his gaze, then back at Doug.

Gaz, continuing: "It don't matter if you're the cleaner or the stand-in editor, you's all-important and the same; equals. You's all part of the cogs that make the wheel of the Billington Gazette run, innit? We looked under the bonnet and the strategy is to tell Lotty to lighten up a bit cos without us she'd not have any articles to put in. The solution is her letting me use her fancy pens when she's on holiday. Oh yeah, and respect. The solution is respect."

He did a peace out signal and stepped back from the table.

That and giving up egg sandwiches.

An awkward silence descended across the remaining group; no one daring to look at Charlotte.

Doug gathered himself and ushered for Gaz to sit down.

Situation salvager Doug: "Erm, yes. Indeed. A team has every voice heard. Right, I think that's all the content covered for this session. Time for lunch; follow me."

Doug slid his paperwork off his desk and scuttled out of the room.

Well, that all went rather well.

Lunch.

Gaz, Mandy, Valerie and Eliza all picked up their belongings and hurried after Doug to the office canteen, leaving a stupefied Charlotte staring at the space Gaz had just left.

****

Later that evening.

Jude: "How did it go, today?"

It was more Lord of the Flies than Little Women.

Eliza: "Fine."

Jude sighed with relief.

Jude: "Oh, that's marvellous. Head Office will be pleased."

I think that might be overstating it, somewhat.

Jude was holding the baking tray as Tom ladled the spaghetti out of the saucepan onto their plates when his mobile rang.

Eliza: "It's ok you two, I'll carry on plating up. Tom, you lay the table."

Tom: "Righto, chief."

Eliza and Tom started clattering about so Jude moved into another room to take the call.

When he came back in a few minutes later, Eliza and Tom were sat at the table waiting for him.

Eliza smiled and ushered for him to sit down.

Eliza: "Bon Appétit."

Jude sat down.

Jude, pre-occupied: "Yes, indeed…"

They all settled down and ate their dinner. Tom wolfed his down rapidly then excused himself and Cheddar Chicken from the table to watch Horrid Henry in the lounge.

Jude cleared his throat.

Jude: "Um, that call before dinner. It was from Douglas Nerwill, the course trainer."

Eliza: "Really? What did he want?"

Jude: "He's put in a complaint about you."

Eliza spat out her chip.

How bloody dare he!

Eliza: "What?! Why? What have I done?!"

Jude: "He says you were like something out of The Shining and it unnerved him. His actual words were 'I don't know how you can sleep with that; she looks like she might sever a testicle in the dead of night with her bare teeth and serve it up for breakfast'."

Eliza was incredulous.

Jude: "What were you doing to him, Eli?"

Eliza: "Well, I have never been so insulted in my life! I was smiling at him. Chapter 43 or was it 34, I can't remember now – 'Make a Miserable Bastard's Day by Proffering a Grin'. How flip-flopping ungrateful! I was cheering up his inner self."

Jude: "I believe his inner self is terrified of you."

Eliza: "Tut, there's no helping him. A smile costs nothing."

Jude: "That's not strictly true, the result of yours will probably lead to therapy."

Meh.

Jude: "I'll not pass his comments on. I told him I'll touch base offline with you."

Eliza: "Don't you start with the corporate speak. I've had a right bellyful of low hanging fruit and I'm up to here with helicopter views."

Eliza wafted a spaghetti laden fork over her head.

Eliza: "Charlotte suggested a post training course team building debrief but I'm busy that day."

Jude: "That's efficient. When is it?"

Eliza: "Oh, I don't know, she didn't say."

Uh oh.

Smile.

Smile the inner-self terrifying, therapy inducing smile.

Jude shook his head at her and continued eating his dinner.

Mentor in Life Feature letter: *Hello Poppet, we just wanted to tell you how clever we think you are; ameliorating Billington's citizens, one word of wisdom at a time. We're refurbing the restaurant and need you to settle an emulsion colour argument – I want Caramel Soil but Clive wants Burnt Broccoli. Your call. Love B & C xx*

Dear B & C, You are kind, thank you. My choice is Caramel Soil because who wants Burnt Broccoli with their dinner? See you soon, Love Eli xx

Chapter Twenty-nine

Billington Gazette Headline: ***Recent Blustery Weather Cause Wind Chimes to Fly Off the Shelves*** (Pun Points – six)

It was Thursday morning in the Merrythought Café.

Eliza: "Your hair looks lovely."

Lydia: "Well, after that comment from Belinda last week, I decided to get a cut and blow job."

Eliza: "Very nice. It suits you."

Lydia: "Thank you, darling. Did you get my Dear Eliza, big willy letter?"

Eliza: "Was that from you?!"

Lydia: "Of course, I did it for a bit of fun."

Eliza: "Ohh."

Lydia: "Why are you looking like that?"

Eliza: "No reason..."

I replied and put it in this week's newspaper.

Dave approached with his note pad.

Dave: "May I be so bold as to enquire the topic of today's conversation. Do I need to bring shatterproof crockery?"

Eliza: "No, we're pure today, thanks Dave."

Dave: "Oh splendid. What can I get you?"

Eliza: "I'll have tea and a couple of buttered muffins. Lydia, what do you want?"

Lydia: "I'll have the same but only one with butter. I'm only half rebelling today."

Dave nodded.

Dave: "No problem. Belinda will bring your order shortly."

Dave moved away from the table and Lydia bent over the Formica table towards Eliza.

Lydia: "Tony and I were talking the other night as we were still not getting anywhere down there."

She pointed to her crotch.

Lydia, sighing: "I tried putting the blindfold on him but it didn't work; he just put it on and went to sleep. Said it reminded him of a long-haul flight he once took to the United Arab Emirates."

Lydia, sighed expansively.

Lydia, quickly: "Anyway, he suggested a trompe l'oeil."

Eh? He wants to create an optical illusion using paint techniques? What does he want you to paint? A 3d BDSM chamber on your bedroom wall?

Lydia, coughing into her fist: "And he wants you to join in."

That's very kind of him.

Eliza: "Well, I could give it a bash. I can paint a chest of drawers."

Belinda wandered over to their table, unceremoniously plonked the muffins and tea down and mooched off.

Lydia's eyes widened.

Lydia: "You mean, you're willing to give it a go?"

Eliza, pouring their tea: "I don't see why not. Will he pay for my time? It might take a while to get it right."

Lydia looked shocked.

Lydia: "I thought you didn't agree to that sort of thing. You've changed; Jude must have loosened your morals."

Eliza: "What are you talking about? It's art and quite tricky to get right. People study for years to get the technique."

Lydia: "Well I never. I'm astonished. They always say it's the quiet ones... I'm not sure if I could go through with it. I've never thought of you in that way. It could ruin our friendship. I don't really want to see your... you know..."

Lydia pointed to Eliza's nether regions.

Lydia: "Bits."

Erm, something tells me we might not be on the same page here.

Eliza: "Trompe l'oeil. An optical illusion using paint techniques."

Lydia's jaw dropped.

Lydia, shaking her head: "Ohhhh, no that's not what he meant. He meant a threesome."

Eliza, shrieking: "A ménage a trois! He wants me and you to have sex with him?! Is he mad?!"

Eliza dropped her tea cup in surprise and it smashed on the Teflon-like tiles.

Dave hastily deposited the breakfasts he was carrying to the next table and rushed over whilst Eliza grabbed every serviette she could to start mopping up the table and her lap.

Eliza, very apologetically: "Sorry Dave, I'll pay for that."

Dave crouched down and picked up the smashed cup.

Dave, standing up: "It's ok, after all my recent breakages, I contacted the wholesaler and told them I'd bought a dodgy box. They've agreed to replace them with a new lot. As long as we look after the next batch I'll not be out of pocket. I shall fetch you a replacement cup of tea."

Eliza: "Thanks Dave."

Dave drifted back to the kitchen.

Lydia: "So anyway, I thought you'd say no so I suggested we try talking dirty instead. When I was Clarabelle, I was a natural. It was mind blowing, Eli. Tony's voice uttering complete filth; it's absolutely pelvic shattering. Keep it up and he might cancel his pill subscription!"

A voice that can break bones. I'm not sure that's a positive.

Eliza: "I'm not sure I could do it. I'd feel silly."

Lydia: "It's only because it's new. I bet it'd make Jude go weak at the knees. Have a go. Try it out on me."

Dave wandered back out of the kitchens, new cup and fresh tray of tea in hand.

Ok, I'll give it a bash. It can't harm.

Eliza, using her best sultry voice: "Let me take your trousers down you naughty, naughty boy."

With that Dave promptly dropped his tray and everything smashed on the floor, once again.

Dave, exclaiming: "Bollocks...!! Shit!"

Lydia burst out laughing.

Eliza clamped her hands over her mouth in horror.

Dave, shaking his hands and head fervently: "I can't cope. It's all getting too much for me."

Oh my god. I've broken Dave as well as his cups.

Belinda dawdled over.

Belinda: "You're a right bell end, Dave. I could sue you for failure to protect an employee from hazards within the workplace. Promote me to manager and stay out the back and I might reconsider. I've got a diploma now."

Dave pulled the tea towel out from his belt hook and handed it to Belinda.

Dave: "It's yours. I'm going home for a lie down."

Belinda, Lydia, Eliza and the rest of the café all gawped, silently, as he opened the till, peeled out a load of notes and after wedging them in his trouser pocket, watched as he picked his jacket off a coat stand and strode out of the café.

Belinda turned to Eliza and Lydia.

Belinda, confounded: "He's gone."

Eliza and Lydia: "He has."

Belinda, flatly: "I'm in charge."

Eliza and Lydia: "You are."

Belinda: "What do I do now?"

Lydia, shrugging: "Use your diploma, I suppose."

Belinda: "Oh."

Mentor in Life Feature letter: *Dear Eliza, I have the best boyfriend, like ever. He calls me his princess and buys me clothes and that. The problem is he writes in text speak, like all the time. It drives me mad. I am a sucker for grammar and full sentences. I got a grade 9 in my GCSE, so I find it like, well annoying. Shall I dump him? Lots of love, English-is-my-first-love-after-Justin-Bieber.*

Dear Have-English-as-your-first-love-above-Justin-Bieber, I too used to subscribe to the, if you can't win an argument, correct their grammar instead, school of thought. I actively stopped talking to people who used the sentence "C u L8er". However, years of chakra aligning and navel pondering has rubbed the edges off me a bit. Plus, when I ran a craft competition for the shop I used to own, I made a shocking comma error on several hundred leaflets which I posted door-to-door. Emblazoned across them in Helvetica 48 point was the phrase: "Come to our shop and paint children. Win a cake!" It wasn't my finest hour but it has lessened the annoyance of they're, their and there, as it proves we're only human.

Chapter Thirty

Billington Gazette Headline: ***Police Capture Local Photographer after Negative Exposure*** (Pun Points – six)

Eliza was stood at in the playground, waiting for Tom.

It's so quiet at pick up now Freya's changed schools. Lydia was the only person I spoke to at school. Maybe, I should try and find someone else to talk to.

Charlie's mother started wandering towards her.

Ooh, ten o'clock. Jenny from the block, approaching. She might be my friend.

She was beaten by an exuberant Tom and Charlie.

Jenny from the Block: "Hi, Charlie was wondering if Tom wanted to come for tea next Thursday."

Tom leapt in the air.

Tom: "Yes, please!!"

Eliza: "That'd be lovely, thank you."

Jenny from the Block turned her attention to Tom.

Jenny from the block: "Is there anything you don't like to eat, Tom?"

Tom: "Avocadoes. I can't bear 'em; they make me bilious."

Charlie's mother looked at Tom with surprise.

Jenny from the Block: "Oh. Right you are, I'll cross avocadoes off the list."

He sounds pretentious.

Jenny from the Block won't be my friend with an affected child. She's from the hood.

Eliza: "Sorry, it's my mum's fault. She puts him in front on reruns of MasterChef when he visits and they try out some of the recipes."

Tom: "How about tapas?"

Jenny from the Block looked non-plussed at the pair of them.

Jenny from the Block: "Will pizza do?"

Tom sighed.

Tom: "Yeah, I s'pose I can rough it. It's good for me to have a wide palate."

I must have a word with mum. He'll be a social outcast like me at this rate.

Eliza: "Ignore him. He is normal really."

Be my friend.

The other mother gave Eliza a sceptical nod and ushered her child away.

I can sense she does not believe me.

Tom to a rapidly departing school mother and child: "Please can you put them crinkly tomatoes on the top? My life has been transformed since I found sun dried tomatoes... Oh and olives! I like the black ones – as long as there ain't no stones in 'em."

Eliza put her hand out and covered over Tom's mouth.

Eliza, calling to their retreating backs: "Thursday then?"

The mother turned and nodded briefly.

Jenny from the Block: "Thursday."

Tom removed Eliza's hand from his mouth.

Tom, hollering after her: "And no avocado, there's a turtle dove!"

This time Jenny from the Block didn't turn round.

Eliza turned her attention to Tom.

Eliza: "Will you just stop talking please, Tom."

Tom: "For how long?"

Eliza: "Forever."

Tom: "Silly mummy. I can't manage two minutes, you know that. Grandma says I am a golden eagle with infinite knowledge; released into the world from society's conforming cage. She said I was born to spread that wisdom."

Eliza: "Did she now."

What had she been sniffing when that nugget came forth? Eagles aren't in cages for a start and I question their infinite knowledge. I've yet to see one on Mastermind.

Eliza: "Had grandma just made the Christmas cake with lots of cherry brandy when she told you that?"

Tom: "Yes! How did you know?! You are a side kick."

Eliza: "Psychic not side kick. No, Tom. I just know grandma's alcohol induced madness."

Tom: "What's alco-whole?"

Eliza: "It's a beverage that makes you talk twaddle."

Tom: "Ahh, tea makes you do that."

Shut up.

Eliza: "Walk on child."

They wandered out of the playground and as soon as they were out of sight of his classmates, Tom held Eliza's hand.

Eliza: "Did you have a good day?"

Tom shook his head.

Tom: "Not really. Mr Potatohead-Arranger told me off because I said the biggest mammal in the world was a frickin' elephant and I got ten out of forty in English. I'm a bit sad about it all."

Aww, I don't want my little boy to be made to feel inadequate. He's got the whole of his adult life to have his shortcomings highlighted.

It doesn't matter if he's an underachiever.

Eliza: "Don't worry about it, love. Clarke Kent isn't Superman but that's ok because the world needs Clarke Kent's. Without Clarke Kent's there'd be no Superman."

Tom: "What?"

Eliza: "Nothing. Just try harder, please."

Tom: "Righto."

****

Francesca bounded into the room and beamed at Kenneth who was sat in his favourite chair with his feet on a foot stool.

Kenneth: "You look happy with yourself."

Francesca held up the current edition of the Billington Gazette.

Francesca: "I'm so excited! Look what I've found!"

She threw the paper onto the dining room table and leafed through to the new periodic magazine section, Billington Style.

Francesca, gabbling: "Now FunkyFurn has sold, I thought we could set up another business. Look! They've got a new supplement, all about interesting local buildings. There's an article about an old pumping station which is up for auction; ten miles out of Billington. I've made an appointment for us to go and see the guy from the auction house tomorrow. We could renovate it and turn it into a wonderful wedding venue."

Kenneth: "We?"

Francesca: "Yes. You and me; together."

Kenneth, levelly: "Why would I want to invest in something with you?"

Francesca: "Because we're a team, silly."

Kenneth got up from his chair and kicked the foot stool to one side.

Kenneth: "Silly? Hmmm."

She might be decent in bed but she was getting far too carried away. This needed to be stopped.

The atmosphere in the room suddenly chilled. Kenneth shook his head and moved inches away from Francesca's face.

Kenneth, slowly and deliberately: "It is not I who is silly, Francesca. A team would intimate that we are of equal standing. Which of course, we're aren't."

Kenneth moved away from her and he sat back down in his chair.

Francesca's joy, felt just moments before, disintegrated into anguish.

Francesca, quietly: "Why are you being like this, Kenneth? I was so excited to show you."

Kenneth: "Indeed. Excited to spend *my* money on a dilapidated edifice. You've got ideas above your station, little missy. You work for me not with me."

He flicked an imaginary speck of dust off his shirt, echoing his dismissiveness of Francesca.

Francesca, sadly: "I thought you loved me. You acted like you did."

Kenneth snorted.

Kenneth: "A short lived fascination. I thought you were more interesting than you are. No harm done; lesson learnt."

Francesca looked physically wounded and clutched her stomach.

Kenneth's lip curled.

Kenneth: "Look at you."

He waved his hand at her.

Kenneth: "You're nothing; a sad, lonely spinster with unachievable dreams - living your life vicariously through the success of others, namely me."

Francesca started to cry.

Francesca, her eyes beseeching: "Oh Kenneth! How can you be so cruel?!"

Kenneth: "Cruel?! Don't be ridiculous. Telling you a few home truths is not cruel. It's for your own benefit. I hope one day you wake up and get a life."

Kenneth chuckled.

Kenneth: "Word of advice, don't aim too high, we wouldn't want you to fail now, would we?"

He took in Francesca; her soul breaking in front of him, tutted and waved her away.

Kenneth, curtly: "Unless you're going to cook my dinner, you can leave now."

Francesca pulled herself up, shook with indignation and through her tears started to shout.

Francesca, screeching: "Cook your dinner?! You've got a nerve, Kenneth Cuthbert. Is this how you treated Dorothy? No wonder she left you!"

Kenneth shot up from the chair and hissed at Francesca.

Kenneth, through gritted teeth: "Do. Not. Speak. Her. Name."

Francesca roughly wiped the tears from her cheeks and her mouth contorted into a miserable grin.

Francesca, chanting: "Dorothy... Dorothy... Dor..."

Kenneth roughly grabbed her arm.

Kenneth, gravely: "Be very careful, Francesca... I advise you to leave now or I can assure you, you will regret it."

Fear enveloped Francesca as she realised she'd overstepped the mark.

They stared at each other for a few moments. Hers defiant and his twinkling with menace.

Francesca dropped her eyes, tilted her chin in the air with false confidence and turned on her heel to leave.

Satisfied he'd made his point; Kenneth dropped his grasp. As she left the room, he picked up the Billington Gazette from the table and threw it at her.

Kenneth: "Take that pathetic rag with you. The day they run a decent story is the day I give up business."

Mentor in Life Feature letter: *My Dear Eliza, I extend my sincere apologies for any grievance I caused regarding my suggestion of indulging in trilateral intimacy. I appreciate, it's not for everyone. Apology over with, I write to ask if you could spare my dear Lydia on a Wednesday for the next few weeks as I need a lift to the physio. My sciatica is causing much discomfort in the bedroom. Yours, If-you-ever-change-your-mind-you-know-where-I-am*

Dear   I-won't-change-my-mind-but-thank-you-for-thinking-of-me, Apology accepted, let's never mention it again. I think you mean Thursday, but yes that's fine. I hope the physio remedies your getting up noise too.

Chapter Thirty-one

Billington Gazette Classified Job Section: ***The Head of Billington Secondary School Needs a Hand. Could you Step in?*** (Pun Points – five)

Jude came blustering through his front door and promptly tripped over Norris who had gone to greet him.

Jude: "Ooooff!!"

He dropped his bag in surprise and fell to his knees; Ellington bounded about his head and jabbed one of his front paws in Jude's eye.

Jude waved Ellington away; scrambled up to a squat position and rubbed his eye.

Jude, waving away two overzealous animals: "Wait!"

An unimpressed Norris mewed in disapproval and a stroke wanting Ellington bounced about, wildly on the spot.

Jude gathered himself and opened his arms to them.

Jude: "Sorry, I'm not used to creature welcome parties. Hello."

A forgiving Norris and Ellington threw themselves at him and left a couple of cuddles later.

Jude straightened up and looked down at the fur-riddled state of himself.

He wandered into the kitchen to find Eliza stood at the breakfast bar with her lap-top and Tom sat at the kitchen table watching YouTube clips on Eliza's mobile phone.

Jude walked over to Eliza and pecked her a kiss, hello. Eliza smiled and continued looking at her lap-top.

Tom: "Evenin'. Are you alright me old china?"

Jude: "Hello Tom. Apart from being physically assaulted by your pets, I'm fine, thank you."

Eliza: "You should feel honoured, Ellington never left his bed for anyone before."

Tom giggled at the mobile he was transfixed upon.

Jude to Tom: "What are you watching?"

Tom held up Eliza's mobile phone so he could see.

Jude: "Why's that man hitting his head with a watermelon?"

Tom: "He's fallen out of love with himself."

He looked at Eliza and she shrugged.

Jude: "How was school?"

Tom tutted slightly at the interruption, pressed pause on the clip and put down the phone.

Tom: "Alright. Mr Potatohead-Arranger told me off for telling Charlie about the time mum shut me in the dark cupboard. Ooh I was scared. Even Cheddar Chicken were quivering."

Eliza looked up from her lap-top and shook her head.

Eliza: "Cheddar Chicken was quivering."

Tom: "Did you feel it where you were?"

Eliza rolled her eyes.

Jude looked at Eliza with surprise.

Eliza: "Don't listen to him, he's not a credible witness."

Eliza turned her attention to Tom.

Eliza to Tom: "You were looking for your bicycle helmet under the stairs and Norris accidentally rubbed his face against the door and knocked it shut. You were too short to turn the light on, that's all."

Tom using his best Obi-Wan Kenobi voice: "Luke, you're going to find that many of the truths we cling to depend greatly on our own point of view."

Eliza: "Whatever."

Jude went over to Eliza.

Jude: "What are you up to?"

Eliza: "Answering a Dear Eliza letter. A woman has been with her partner for two years and still gets butterflies when he walks into a room. It must be lovely to be that in love."

Jude looked surprised at Eliza.

Eliza "What?"

Jude shook his head slightly and sighed.

Jude: "Nothing."

He gathered himself and looked directly at Eliza.

Jude: "I wonder if I may have a word about a Dear Eliza letter."

Eliza sensed the tone of his voice.

Uh oh, I think I might be in trouble.

Eliza: "Tom, can you get in that bath I ran for you, please. I'll be up in two minutes. Sing loudly so I know you're not drowning."

Tom: "I am an independent spirit. My free will says no."

Eliza: "Mothers negate all free will. Now get in the bath."

Tom: "The Resistance will not be intimidated by you."

Eliza gave Tom her sternest look and he gulped.

Tom: "I fancy a dip, actually."

Tom scraped his chair back, lobbed Eliza's mobile phone across the work surface and skedaddled upstairs to his waiting bath.

There was a pause as Jude waited for Tom ears not to be present.

He's frowning. I am definitely in trouble.

Jude: "You replied to a Dear Eliza letter from your ludicrous friend, Lydia, about big willies, didn't you?"

Eliza: "Ah, well. I didn't know it was from her. Is it illegal to put in letters from friends?"

Jude's voice went up an octave.

Jude: "That's not the issue. The issue is you replied, and I quote, 'my boyfriend has a huge penis and whilst it's magnificent to behold in an aloft state, it's not without its perils'."

Eliza: "Oh... sorry. I didn't think about that. I didn't name you."

Jude put his hands on his hips.

Jude: "Eli, everyone at the Gazette knows you're going out with me! I've had all and sundry hold a conversation with my crotch all day!"

Whoops.

Jude: "Do you have any idea how hard it is to maintain any air of authority when the person you're talking to conducts the whole conversation with their gaze firmly on your willy?"

Eliza: "I'm devoid of any willy-hood, so no. Sorry, it'll not happen again. I presume it won't be in this week's edition?"

Jude: "No Eli, one of the perks of being the editor is you can remove any references to the size of one's manhood before it makes the supermarkets."

No damage done then.

Eliza: "You want to look on the bright side; imagine the embarrassment if I'd replied you'd got a tiddler and I'd told everyone that."

Every cloud and all that.

Jude: "Well, there is that benefit, I suppose."

***

Later that evening, Tom, Eliza and Jude were watching a talent show on the television. Norris was curled up on Jude's lap and Ellington was slumbering, peacefully in his basket.

Tom shook his head, impatiently.

Tom: "Blah blah, she's dead; he's got a terrible illness. Enough with the back story and let's get on with the singing, shall we?"

Jude and Eliza looked at each other.

Jude: "You're responsible for that."

Oh, charming.

Jude's mobile pinged and he picked it up.

A couple of minutes later, he put it down and scratched his head.

Eliza: "Everything ok?"

Jude: "Hmmm. That was my brother, George."

Eliza: "You have a brother, George? I thought you only had a sister, Dorothy."

Jude: "We don't have much to do with him. He's a bit... alternative."

Ooh, I like alternative. It sounds hippy and intriguing.

I bet his meridians are marvellous.

Eliza: "Oh, what did he want?"

Jude: "He needs somewhere to stay for a bit; whilst his house is tidied up. Apparently, he's received a letter from the council."

Eliza: "Is his house messy?"

Jude: "I haven't been allowed over the threshold for nearly twenty years but suffice to say, I was quite relieved at the fact."

Eliza: "Is he married?"

Jude: "He's a bit of a loner. I can't remember the last time he had a partner. Dorothy might know more about that aspect of his life."

I expect he's so at one with the universe he doesn't need other people.

Eliza: "Does he look like you?"

Jude: "Erm, I would presume there's a family resemblance."

Eliza: "Then he must stay here."

I'd get to look at two Judes and one will help keep my life force in check.

Jude rubbed his chin, dubiously.

Eliza: "He's alright to be around Tom, isn't he?"

Jude: "Oh, of course. He was quite the joker when he was younger; Tom and George would probably get on like a house on fire."

Eliza: "Then that's settled. It can't take long to tidy up a house; I'll help on my days off."

Jude: "If you're sure, Eli."

Eliza: "Of course, I'm sure. Someone with your eyes and with a better sense of humour; it'll be great to have him around."

Jude blinked and raised an eyebrow.

Jude: "I'll forget I just heard that, shall I?"

Eliza: "Yes, okay."

Probably best.

Mentor in Life Feature letter: *Dear Eliza, Every day, on my way to work, I see a sad old lady sat on a bench. I want to stop and go and sit with her and ask what makes her so forlorn. It might make me late for work, though. Should I? Yours, wondering-if-I-can-help*

Dear wondering-if-I-can-help, I found myself in a similar situation whilst attending a training course recently. There was a right old misery chops and I made it my mission to make him smile. Apparently, my smile unnerved him to the point of complaint; so it would appear you can't save everyone. As that saying goes: "You can lead a horse to water but the reflection can ~~scare the shit~~ cause alarm to the uninitiated." My advice is – on your day off, go and seek her out and strike up a conversation. She might be lonely and you may be the only person she will speak to all day. Little gestures can make a person's day but also be prepared for the possibility that she may hit you with her umbrella and alert the police.

Chapter Thirty-two

Billington Gazette Headline: ***Mass Survey Reveals Surprising Mobile Phone Fears*** (Pun Points - Not Applicable – this was a serious fact-finding mission from Valerie.)

In the most in-depth survey we've ever carried out, we can reveal that a poll of 47 Billington residents feel the range of smart phone emoticons is out of control with 89% of responders suffering feelings of inadequacy by not knowing when to use a goat. A 100% of respondents, however, couldn't give a fig about 5G.

A few days later, Eliza was boiling the kettle for her first cup of tea, when a flustered Jude whisked into the kitchen.

Jude: "Eli, please can you sniff my crotch?"

And he seemed such a nice boy.

I've not even had my first cup of tea of the day yet.

Thank goodness Tom's still upstairs.

Eliza: "Must I?"

Jude: "I've an important meeting this morning and I don't have another pair of decent trousers clean."

Is it my fault and this is my forfeit for not being a fifties housewife? Sniffing your crotch before seven in the morning...

Eliza: "Can't you sniff them yourself?"

Please, if you wouldn't mind...

Jude: "I can't tell. They did have quite a disagreeable effluvium because I dropped Norris food on them. The stupid cat nudged my hand just as I was scooping his breakfast out of the tin. I've wiped them down but I can do without smelling of tuna all day. I'm attending a meeting regarding the deliberation of the new Billington highway layout."

Eliza visibly sagged with relief.

Eliza: "Oh. That's ok then. I thought you were being all sexually deviant. I don't mind sniffing your crotch for fish. Present your nether regions."

Jude jutted his slightly damp willy toward Eliza's face.

Eliza: "Hmmm, a bit of a waft but nothing a wet wipe won't cure."

Jude: "Thanks."

Eliza went over to her bag and pulled out a packet and lobbed them at him. Jude grabbed a couple and proceeded to wipe his trousers down.

Eliza gave a disapproving look at Norris, who was sat bolt upright in his basket with a beatific look on his face.

Eliza: "Naughty Norris, you didn't tell me you'd already had breakfast. You've had a double helping."

Norris mewed in response.

Eliza to Norris: "Well, you should care. You'll get fat."

Norris stretched his front legs out, stood and turned his back on Eliza.

Eliza to Norris: "You can ignore me all you want, chunky chops but less tea for you."

Jude was watching the exchange with fascination when a bleary-eyed Tom wandered into the kitchen.

Tom, running his hand through his mussed-up bed hair: "Where's me brekkie, me old finger 'n thumb?"

Eliza: "It's coming. I got waylaid with Jude's crotch."

Tom: "Can I have a drink, please? I'm parched, I woke up with Cheddar Chicken's leg in me chops."

Eliza: "Help yourself to some milk."

Tom wandered over to the fridge, pulled out the carton of milk and started glugging from the bottle.

Eliza's eyes widened with surprise.

Jude will think we're animals!

Eliza: "Tom! Why didn't you use a cup?!"

Tom, shrugging: "You said help yourself. You need to be more specific with your requests."

Tom shoved the milk carton back in the fridge, wiped his mouth with Cheddar Chicken then clambered on to a stool and perched at Jude's breakfast bar.

Tom: "Morning, Jude. Are your big boy balls ok? Did mummy hit you there? Charlie got hit with a tennis ball once, he were bent double all through history."

Jude ruffled his hair, awkwardly.

Jude: "Erm, morning. No, it's erm... I mean, they're... erm."

Come to his rescue.

Eliza: "Of course I didn't hit him there, Tom. I treat Jude's nether regions with the utmost respect. I nigh on praise them. Norris knocked cat food on them."

Tom: "Oh, that's alright then. Naughty Norris. Watcha up to today?"

Jude, relieved the subject had moved away from his testicles: "I'm off to a meeting about the new Billington road system."

Tom: "Cool! Mum, are you off to work with that annoying woman who thinks she's the bees-knees?"

Aargh!

Jude shot a disapproving look at Eliza.

Eliza, tittering: "Haha! You are funny, Tom. I have no idea what you're talking about! Aren't children funny, Jude? They come up with all sorts of ridiculous notions."

Tom looked intently at Eliza.

Tom: "That's your lying face."

Eliza: "Shut up."

Tom shook his head, slowly.

Tom: "You're lashing out because I've highlighted your indescriptions. Grandma told about me that."

Grandma has a lot to answer for.

Eliza: "You've highlighted my *indiscretions*."

Tom: "See, I'm always right."

Jude to Eliza: "I don't know why you don't like Charlotte. She's nice."

Nice. Meh.

Eliza: "Is she now?"

Eliza took out a bowl poured Tom's cereal into it.

Eliza, continuing: "She's a walking atlas. A patchwork of countries stitched together with egg sandwiches...

She also confuses her idioms and gives me too much filing. Where did you find her?"

Jude: "Billington public toilets."

Good lord!

Eliza's eyebrows shot in the air and she dropped the bowl of cereal, clumsily, in front of Tom.

Tom: "Oi! Steady on. I need it in me bowl!"

Eliza thrust a spoon at Tom and started slopping the milk over his cereal. Tom shook his head in disgust and took the milk carton off her.

Jude. My Jude. Indulging in illicit loitering sex with random toilet visitors?! Surely not.

Jude, continuing: "She was running the campaign to renovate the 1950's toilets - to upgrade them."

Oh, Fundraising. Phew.

Eliza: "Oh, thank heavens. I thought you met whilst you were looking for seedy no strings attached sex for a moment then."

Jude shot a look at an agog Tom and motioned to Eliza with wide eyes.

Oh, a child. My child.

Eliza: "Forget you heard that, Tom. That sort of slipped out. Unlike Jude's mighty sword in Billington's toilets."

Haha!

No, not haha, not appropriate at all. Shut up.

Tom: "Mum, I'm seven; this sort of stuff fascinates me and I have a duty to tell all my friends."

Eliza: "Oh, no you mustn't!"

Eliza did a 'fingers on lips' motion.

Tom: "I am a child. I have a very low secret-keeping threshold."

Eliza: "Do you want me to get you Portobello mushrooms, or not?"

Tom rolled his eyes and tutted.

Tom: "Ok. I not tell on you."

Bribery. The ultimate weapon.

Eliza nodded with satisfaction.

Jude: "Now then, you two, George is moving in later today. He should be here in time for tea."

Jude turned to a cereal munching Tom.

Jude: "He's very interesting, Tom. He likes Lego. He used to collect it. He is, erm, one of life's collectors."

Eliza: "Shall I make dinner? I can make a welcome tea for him."

Jude: "Oh, don't go to any trouble, Eli. He used to be a really faddy eater."

It's because he's new age. He probably lives on alfalfa seeds and lactose free brie.

Eliza: "It's because of his life-force leanings. He needs to keep his pipes clear of earthly debris. I shall make something interesting out of vegetables."

Jude checked his watch and stood, hastily.

Jude, perplexed but running late: "Ok, if you're sure. That'll be a lovely gesture. Thank you."

He pecked Eliza on the lips.

Jude: "Got to dash, I'll see you two later."

****

Later that morning, Eliza was just about to stride into the school playground when Tom tugged her arm.

Tom, gently: "You can leave me at the gate now mum. I can walk in on my own. I'm a big boy."

Eliza felt a jolt inside.

Eliza: "Ooh... erm... I'm not sure I'm emotionally ready for that, Tom. Can I leave you at the hall? Work up to the gate leaving thing?"

Tom let go of Eliza's hand and rubbed her arm.

Tom: "Be strong me old treacle. You can do it."

I feel all discombobulated.

Eliza: "Oh."

Tom: "Life changes, it takes courage to move on but I believe in you."

Eliza: "Is that one of grandma's pearls of wisdom?"

Tom: "Yup."

Thought so.

Eliza: "Ok, we'll do it today and see how I feel."

Tom nodded, sagely.

Tom: "Well done mummy. See you later. Have a good day."

Tom stopped rubbing Eliza's arm and ran into school, catching up with Charlie on the way in.

Eliza, shouting after him: "I'll get you those mushrooms in town later!"

But Tom was gone.

Eliza stood by the school gates feeling sad.

He didn't even look back.

Is this the future? My child teaching me how to be independent from him?

Eliza shook the dolefulness away and headed off to start her day.

Mentor in Life Feature letter: *Dear Eliza, I am in a relationship with a man who was married when we got together. He is no longer with his wife and I asked if we could take our relationship to the next level. He became very hostile and refused, which came as a great shock to me as I'd never seen this side of him, previously. He's always been so mild-mannered and kind. I want us to be a team but he seems to feel he needs to be in charge. How can I make him change his mind and persuade him I can make him happy? Regards, I-don't-want-to-be-just-his-mistress*

Dear I-don't-want-to-be-just-his-mistress, You can't make people fit what you want. He has shown his true colours. I offer these words of advice, which might help: If you find yourself in the wrong story, close the book and go back to the library for another one. (This time read the blurb on the back a bit better, though, and make sure he's not already betrothed.)

Chapter Thirty-three

Billington Gazette Headline: ***Billington Crime Statistics Released – Serious Crime Down but Murder on the Rise*** (Pun Points – Not Applicable – Under no circumstances can such matters be humorised. (As per Charlotte.))

Jude pressed the screen on his car dashboard and dialled Eliza and spoke via his hands-free.

Jude: "Hi Eli, I'm held up in traffic. Even more reason why the Billington Gazette should support the new flyover. Is George there?"

Eliza: "He is."

Jude: "Is he ok?"

Apart from looking like a bag of bones who's spent the past ten years living rough, foraging for food from bins, presumably without the benefit of any access to washing facilities, absolutely.

Eliza: "I believe so."

Jude: "I'm so sorry I'm going to be late, Eli. Start dinner without me. I'll get back as soon as I can."

Eliza: "Ok, drive safe. See you in a bit."

Eliza clicked off her phone and turned her attention back to the table to find Tom sat, arms folded staring stony-faced at George.

George: "What's this?"

He poked his finger into the quiche and Tom recoiled.

Eliza: "Vegetable quiche."

George: "Has it got eggs in it?"

Tom, levelly - arms still folded: "It's a quiche, George."

Eliza: "Don't you like quiche?"

George: "It's a bit eggy but I'll tolerate it."

Eliza: "Most magnanimous of you. I'll cut you a slice."

Because that's what most people do – not put fingers with rather dubious looking fingernails in the middle of it.

Eliza dropped a slice onto George's plate and he peered closely at it.

George: "What's that bit?"

Eliza peered at what he was suspiciously prodding.

Eliza: "Carrot."

George looked incredulous.

George: "In a quiche?!"

Eliza: "Yes."

George: "Is that a mushroom?"

Eliza: "Yes. Portobello."

Tom: "Mum, can you make him stop, I'm starving."

Eliza: "Sorry."

Eliza put a slice of quiche on Tom's plate.

George was still inspecting his quiche as Eliza shoved the salad bowl in front of him.

Eliza: "Salad, George?"

George: "Put it there, I'll choose what I want."

He then proceeded to pick bits of pepper out and put them on his plate.

Tom watched and sniffed, disapprovingly.

Tom, mid-forkful: "Peasant."

Eliza: "Tom!"

George: "Is there any meat at all in this meal?"

Eliza: "No. You're a vegetarian."

George: "Am I? Who said that?"

Erm, no-one actually. I assumed because Jude said you were alternative; I took it to mean bohemian and at one with nature. A lover of all things living. An assumption which I feel may be misguided.

Eliza: "My brain."

George stood and scraped his chair back.

George: "No matter. I've brought some haslet with me. I'll mix it in with this muck."

George left the room and came back a few moments later with three slices of haslet.

Where did he keep that? He couldn't have got further than the hall. He must have a meat stash in his coat pocket.

George: "Wanna try some, laddie?"

George proffered a slice to Tom who peered at it with interest.

Tom: "What meat is it?"

George: "Pork with spices and all things nices... And you know what they say about piggies? Nearest thing to humans you'll ever eat."

Tom's eyes widened and he went to take a slice.

Eliza batted his hand away.

Eliza: "No! No, he doesn't want any, thank you."

Tom looked crestfallen, huffed at Eliza and continued with his meal.

Just then, the front door opened and in bustled Jude. Ellington sat bolt upright, throwing a snoozing Norris off his back and got out of his basket to have a look. Norris did a grandiose stretch and followed him. Jude threw his belongings on the hall console table and rushed into the kitchen, animals in tow.

Jude: "Hello, hello! So sorry I'm late. Hello Geor….Good heavens, there's a bit of a niff in here! Ellington, have you been a dirty dog?"

Ellington went from wagging his tail to a slunk down position, ears back.

Tom pointed to George.

Tom: "Nah, That'll be 'im. He pen and inks."

Jude bent down and stroked a subdued Ellington who started wagging his tail again.

Jude, standing back up: "Blimey George, when did you last have a wash?"

George: "I don't recall. I have no requirement to conform to social encumbrance."

Jude: "You do whilst you're in my house, you blummin' honk. Can you go and have a bath, please?"

George tutted.

George: "I'll take my haslet with me. The rest isn't up to scratch so I'll leave that."

Oh charming.

They watched as George picked the slices of meat off his plate and put them in his pocket as he left the room.

I knew it! He keeps emergency meat in his clothes pockets!

Jude opened the window and sat down at the table, cutting himself a massive slice of quiche.

Jude: "Mmmm, this looks wonderful, Eli. Thank you."

He leant over and kissed her.

He's over compensating because of his rude brother.

How thoughtful.

Eliza: "How was your day?"

Jude: "Long. Sorry I wasn't here when George arrived. Has he been ok?"

Eliza: "He's nothing like you except for the eyes. I was hoping he'd be another you with hippy bits bolted on but he's not. He eats haslet because it's like spicy people."

Jude: "I did say he's a bit of a loner but he's pleasant enough, if a bit out of touch with society."

Tom: "He needs to learn how to use a knife and fork. Shall I teach 'im? I think we've still got my Winnie the Pooh set at home. Can we nip back and get 'em?"

Eliza: "It's fine, Tom. I'm sure he learnt, he's just a bit out of practice."

I don't suppose there's a knife and fork requirement when you eat food out of clothing.

Eliza's mobile phone pinged to indicate she'd received a text.

Eliza, reading: "That's Brian, he's coming to help me tomorrow. We thought we'd spend a few hours at George's clearing the decks."

The sooner we get started the sooner he can go back home.

I can prove to Jude what an industrious and giving girlfriend he has... so he realises he doesn't want to ever live without me and proposes.

Jude: "If you're sure, Eli? I can get a team of people in to do it."

Eliza: "I won't hear of it! Anyway, Brian loves a good clean. He's bought new Marigolds especially."

How hard can it be? I've watched those cleaning programmes. They have it all done and dusted by lunchtime.

Jude: "Thank you."

Tom: "Mum, why can't we eat people?"

Eliza: "Cannibalism is frowned upon Tom. I do believe it is illegal."

Tom: "Really? That is a shame."

Eliza: "Yes, isn't it? There'd certainly be some people on my lunch menu."

Charlotte, the smorgasbord of worldly body parts, for one.

Tom: "Yeah, and there's some right big 'uns out there. Think of the number of sandwiches they'd make!"

Eliza: "Quite. Who want's apple crumble?"

Jude and Tom shot their hands up.

They proceeded to finish their tea accompanied by the echoey tones of George singing an out of tune rendition of 'O Sole Mio whilst he took his first bath of the year.

Mentor in Life Feature letter: *Hello Sparrow, Your father and I were wondering if Tommy would like to come and stay with us for a few days now your house is under 3 feet of water. Love, mum x*

Hello Mum, this is a work's email, it's only meant to be used for problem letters. He's off on Easter holidays from tomorrow so I'm sure he'd love it. I'll ask later. Love, Eli x

Hello Sparrow, Sorry. I'll not write on it again. Love, mum x

Chapter Thirty-four

Billington Gazette Headline: ***Exclusive: New Roundabout in Billington Will be a Turning Point for the Town but Red Tape Holds up the Flyover*** (Pun Points – six)

The next morning Jude had left for work and Eliza walked into the house after dropping Tom off at school.

She was greeted by George stood at the breakfast bar, naked save for some very saggy boxer shorts, eating a lump of crust.

Oh dear.

Just then the front door bell rang and Ellington gave a perfunctory woof from his basket.

Saved by the bell.

Eliza ran over and pulled open the front door.

Eliza: "Brian!"

Brian: "Hello, poppet! Mwaw."

He air kissed her as he wandered into the house and bent over to stroke Ellington who had bounced over to say hello upon hearing Brian's voice.

As he stood, George silently walked down the hallway.

Brian: "Good lord! Hello!"

George grunted by way of greeting on the way up the stairs.

Brian, loudly whispering: "Who's the poster boy for rickets?"

Eliza: "That's George. He of the cluttered house."

Brian: "Well, if his pants are a gauge, I think I should have bought more gloves!"

Eliza: "Come on, let's get this over with. Which one do you want to be? Kim or Aggie?"

Brian: "Kim. I look good with a bun; it sets off my jawline."

Eliza nodded as they gathered together a haphazard array of cleaning products which Eliza had assembled and set off on their mission.

****

Brian: "Left! It's down this road here, apparently."

Eliza pulled the car into Magnolia Lane.

Eliza: "Which number?"

Brian looked at the scrap of paper and up again.

Brian: "Fourte... Oh no..."

Brian pointed to his right and Eliza looked to where he was pointing.

Please don't let it be this one.

Brian peered at the metal numbers screwed on a wonky rusty metal gate which was being held up with one hinge and nodded, gravely.

Oh dear.

Eliza pulled the car up outside and they both sat, motionless and took in the sight before them.

There, amongst the road full of pretty front-lawned houses, stood an ivy covered 1930's semi-detached house. Just visible amongst the overgrowth were two closed-curtained upstairs windows. Downstairs, ripped yellow nets hung at a once pretty bay window, now a sorry sight with peeling paint and a cracked left pane.

Eliza looked at Brian and they both gulped.

Brian: "How many bottles of bleach did we bring?"

Eliza: "Just the two."

Brian: "I think we might need a pallet load. Come on, poppet."

Brian patted Eliza on the hand and went to fetch the cleaning products from the boot. Whilst doing so the front door of the semi attached to the house of doom, opened and out sprung a highly strung middle-aged woman. She wiped her hands on a tea towel, hung it over her shoulder and went storming over to Brian.

Tea towel woman: "Ah! About bleedin' time! How many times have I had to call you? Hmmm? Hmmmm? I do not wish to keep leaving a messages on your blasted answerphone. I have onions to kibble."

Brian: "I beg your pardon?"

Tea towel woman peered at Brian.

Tea towel woman: "Oh, hang on, you're not who I asked for. You're not from the council, are you? You're from that posh nosh place in town. We went there for my Sharon's 30th, very nice - if a bit pricey. I said to my Willy, we could get the same from Iceland and put an extra sprig on top and get 20 for the same price... I didn't order you. What are you doing here? Has there been a mix up? I'm sure I pressed option three."

Brian: "I beg your pardon?"

He's stuck on loop. Rescue him.

Eliza skittled out of the car and pointed at George's ramshackle abode.

Eliza: "Hello, you live next door then. How long has it been like this?"

Brian looked at Eliza with gratitude.

Brian, muttering: "Thank you, poppet."

Tea towel woman: "Who are you? Are you option three? It's been like it too bloody long! We can't move because of it. It's affected the house prices and it's killed off my forsythia. My knees are dreadful – I should be in Alicante now, feet up, being tended to by my Willy but not even the estate agents in the high street will go near the place and they're willing to flog anything. Barbara had a sinkhole outside hers and still got the full asking price."

Brian: "Oh, I might be able to help you with Alicante. I think I have an accidental time share there."

Eliza: "I'm a relation, sort of, not really. More of a lover but not his, I hasten to add. His brother's. He keeps a lovely house; we're staying there because ours got flooded. It might be permanent, we don't know. I don't like to presume…"

Shut up with the deluge to unnecessary information to a complete stranger.

Eliza: "Anyway, we're here to give it a spruce up."

I'm trying to show him what a selfless, giving person I am by offering to help his meat smuggling brother out so that he'll ask me to marry him.

Tea towel woman looked around.

Tea towel woman: "Who? Not just you two, surely? A food bod and a brother lover?"

Eliza: "Yes, we'll have it tidied up in a jiffy."

Tea towel woman, huffing with hands on hips: "Well I admire your optimism. One should be grateful something is finally being done. Even if you just attend to the outside, it'll be a bonus, at least we can get a valuation done then."

Brian picked up the crate of cleaning products and made off towards the house and tea towel woman went back towards her front door.

Tea towel woman calling to Brian: "Oh, your chairs could do with a bit more padding, an' all. I know a man down the market who could help you with that. Got some lovely foam for my outdoor furniture from him, I did. I'll hook his number out for you."

Brian waved her off.

Brian: "Yes, yes. Goodbye."

He rolled his eyes at an approaching Eliza.

Brian: "Cheeky woman! I'll not tell Clive, those chairs cost him a fortune! He bought them off that chap who appeared on Dragon's Den. They're the only thing we've kept after the refurb."

They walked up the weed strewn path to the arched brick porch.

Brian: "Key?"

Eliza ferreted around in her hand bag and found the key fob George had given her that morning and she gave it to Brian.

Brian: "I'll go in first. Make sure there isn't a dead body in the hallway."

Eliza: "Thank you."

Brian tried the two keys and one turned the lock. He tried to push to front door open - it went a short way then was prevented from going any further.

Brian handed the cleaning crate to Eliza.

Brian: "Here, hold this. I'll give it a bit of oomph."

Brian shoved the door with his shoulder but it wouldn't move. He peered his head round the gap to look into the hallway and gasped.

Brian: "Ooof! Fuck me!"

Eliza: "Oh no! Is it a body?!"

Please don't say it's a body.

Brian: "It's worse than that, Eli."

What could be worse? Two bodies?

Half a body and we have to find the rest? He probably ate the rest because he ran out of haslet.

Eliza: "What is it? What is it?"

Brian pulled his head back through the gap and turned to her. His face a look of utter disgust.

Brian: "It's Spam."

Eliza: "What?! As in post? Is there a pile of it blocking the doorway?"

Brian: "No, Spam as in Spam, Spam, Spam, Spam, Spam...

Eliza: "Yes, yes. Alright. How much Spam?"

Brian turned back and put his head through the gap in the doorway again.

Brian: "Two, four, six.... Ten.... Eighteen.... Twenty-six.... Thirty-eight..."

He turned back to Eliza.

Brian: "About fifty odd tins of it. All of which are leaning up against the front door. We'll have to see if we can get in around the rear. He must have got out of the house via the back door."

They looked to the left of the house where there was a paint peeling side gate.

Eliza: "It looks like it needs a key. There's only two on this fob. Try that one."

Brian tried the random key but it didn't work.

Brian: "Maybe it just needs a shove."

He gave the gate a push with both hands and they went clean through two wooden panels.

Brian: "Ooh, whoopsie! Might need a spot of glue on there!"

He reached through one of the broken wood panels and unlatched the gate from the inside and shouldered it open.

Brian: "This is all very Harrison Ford for a weekday morning. Where's me whip when I need it?! Wait there, I'll check out the access."

A minute later, Brian reappeared, sucking his lips.

Brian: "We can get in but be warned, it's like Steptoe's yard in there."

Eliza, hesitantly, followed behind Brian, stepping over piles of wood which were scattered amongst the weeds. To the rear of the overgrown garden were rolls and rolls of barbed wire.

Eliza: "What on earth does he need all that barbed wire for, Brian? No one would want to be kept in here and no one in their right mind would want to break in."

Brian: "You're asking me? I know about petit fours, poppet, not fortifications of trench warfare. My natural habitat, this is not."

Eliza: "I know, Brian. Come on, let's get this done. Jude will be so grateful he'll propose and you can get some foam for your dragon chairs."

Brian nodded, unlocked the back door and led the way into the kitchen.

They stood in the kitchen; the sunny day seemingly at odds with the dismal sight they were welcomed with as shafts of light highlighted the dust dancing through the air.

Brian looked around and gasped.

Brian: "Look at the cooker, Eli!"

Aargh!! It's laden with grease. I can't even work out where the hobs are.

Brian: "I'm not touching it! And neither are you. Gloves or no gloves."

He went to move further into the kitchen and his feet made a squelching sound across the 40-year-old cracked lino.

Brian: "Oh dear god, I'm sticking to the floor!"

Eliza: "Oh Brian, this is awful! What are we going to do?"

Brian: "Assess the damage then get a skip."

Eliza nodded in agreement.

Brian held his hand out to Eliza and they moved from the kitchen to the Spam hallway.

Brian: "Ready to see what joy awaits us in the lounge?"

Eliza nodded.

Brian: "Ok."

He gingerly pushed the door open to the lounge.

Brian and Eliza, in unison: "What the...!!"

Stacked neatly in piles were hundreds of wrapped bars of ancient Knights Castille and Shield soap. Piled next to them were bottles and bottles of water, then beside them fifteen baseball bats and a row of batteries.

Brian: "Maybe he's inventing something."

Battery operated soap on a bat?

Eliza: "There's an unnerving number of bats for a person who doesn't own a baseball team."

Brian: "Mmmm. Somewhat concerning."

Brian pointed to a dusty timepiece on the shelf above an old three bar gas fire.

Brian: "That's a lovely clock on the mantelpiece, though. It reminds me of a piece I saw at the V and A. Clive and I went to London for the day the other year... or was it on Antiques Roadshow? Or it could have been at a car boot sale. Can't remember... What's all that over there?"

He wandered over to a pile of boxes which were assembled under the bay window.

Brian: "Well, I never!"

Eliza: "What are those little boxes of?"

Brian: "Condoms, Eli. Lots and lots of condoms."

Urgh! I've seen him in his pants, there's no way he needs them.

Brian inspected a few of the boxes.

Brian: "They went out of date in 2008."

Figures.

Eliza: "Maybe he did a smash and grab on Boots in the 1990s and he's been holed up with the stolen goods ever since. Explains the soap and condoms."

Brian: "Last time I checked, Boots didn't stock baseball bats and barbed wire."

Eliza: "Do you think I should remove myself and my son from his vicinity?"

Brian put the condom box back on the pile and wiped his hands on his trousers.

Brian: "I don't know, poppet. It's all a bit unusual, isn't it? To think he's from the same stock as your wonderful chappie, Jude. It beggars' belief. Saying that, I'm the opposite to my sister, Lisa. She looks shocking in a kaftan. Do we dare venture upstairs?"

Eliza: "How bad can it be?"

Brian gave her a look.

Eliza: "Forget I said that. Come on."

Eliza led the way and when she got to the top of the stairs, hesitantly pushed open the doors to the bathroom.

Overflowing out of the bath were piles of magazines.

Well, that explains why he doesn't succumb to the encumbrance of bathing society.

Brian, over Eliza's shoulder: "What joys await us in here? Oh, reading matter."

Brian gently elbowed past Eliza, peered in and rifled through some of the magazines.

Brian: "Oooh, now then... Some of these are quite old. I'm sure I saw something about these having a worth."

Brian continued to flick through the pile.

Brian: "A majority of them are in very good condition; I don't think they've been read. Any chance of you getting your friend, Henry, over to have a look? We could persuade hoarder matey boy to flog a few of them; it might help pay towards the skip hire."

Eliza: "That's a good idea, Brian. Hang on, I'll give Henry a call."

Eliza fished out her mobile and called Henry.

Eliza: "... Yes, Brian and I are here now... Yes, in Billington... Magnolia Lane. Can't miss it, it's the dilapidated semi... The one that looks condemned. Oh, lovely, Ok. See you shortly."

Eliza put her mobile back in her bag.

Eliza: "He's coming over now."

Brian: "Oh, splendid!"

Ten minutes later, Brian and Eliza were standing in one of the bedrooms marvelling at a pile of evaporated milk tins when there was a tentative knock on the front door.

Eliza: "That'll be Henry."

Eliza made off downstairs.

Brian: "Don't leave me alone, a skeletal arm could drop out of a wardrobe! I'm coming with you."

Social Media Meme: *And those who were seen dancing were thought to be insane by those who could not hear the music. Friedrich Nietzsche*

Chapter Thirty-five

Billington Gazette Headline: ***Local Crowdfunded Eco-Welly Inventor Steps up Bid to Become a Sole Trader*** (Pun Points – seven)

Eliza and Brian trotted downstairs, out of the kitchen door and shouted at Henry to follow them down past the side gate.

Henry blustered along a few moments later, calling over his shoulder.

Henry: "Yes, certainly madam! I'll be sure to tell them."

Eliza and Brian: "Kibbling woman."

Henry nodded.

Henry: "You're to start on the outside. You've spent too long shilly-shallying indoors, apparently. Hello."

Eliza and Brian bid him good morning and Eliza beckoned Henry to follow.

Henry, upon stepping into the kitchen: "My goodness me. This is simply awful. How long has it been derelict?"

Eliza: "Two days. The occupant is my boyfriend's brother and is living with us, currently. He insists on picking fault with my food so he needs to move back asap."

Brian: "And you want to earn proposal brownie points."

Eliza: "Yes... and them."

Henry: "Good lord! Someone lives here?!"

Brian: "Indeed. Do you want to have a gander at the magazines we found, Henry?"

Henry: "Yes, of course. May I look around the rest of the place? It's astonishing - like a time warp. My grandmother had a cooker like that."

Eliza: "Be my guest. There might be other stuff we can flog so we can mend that gate."

Eliza waved Henry through to the hallway. He stopped when he saw the Spam.

Henry looked at the pile then looked back at Eliza and Brian.

Henry, nonplussed: "It's half a hundred weight of Spam."

Eliza and Brian: "It is."

Henry: "Is it in date?"

Eliza: "Does it matter?"

He's in shock. A perfectly plausible reason for erroneous questioning.

Henry: "No, not really."

Eliza motioned him to go to the lounge - he duly did so and they trailed after him.

Henry: "Oh my!"

Eliza: "I know, there's an unnerving amount of bats and batteries."

Henry: "Eh? Oh sorry, I didn't notice those. Oh yes, that's somewhat threatening."

Henry stepped over the bats to the mantelpiece, picked up the clock and rubbed his chin.

Henry: "Well I never!"

Brian: "I like that. I said to you Eli, didn't I? That's very stylish. It's a golden nugget in amongst a pile of Knights Castille bars."

Henry scratched his head, deep in thought.

Henry: "This really is most interesting."

Brian: "I know, I agree. I'm sure I've seen a similar one on the Antiques Roadshow. Clive and I love that. Sundays aren't Sundays without the jaw dropping of pensioners who find out the casket they kept their car keys in is actually Napoleon's toothbrush holder."

Henry: "Would you allow me to take a photo to check it out, Eli?"

Eliza: "Oh, just take it with you, Henry. It's got to be safer than here. It looks like the ceiling could cave in at any moment."

Henry: "If you're sure. I'll do some research."

Henry's artefact trained eye scanned the room.

Henry: "There's nothing else here of any interest... Oh what's that by the window?"

Brian: "Condoms. Now, they are out of date."

Henry looked appalled and shook his head.

Eliza: "Maybe he thought he'd become a lothario but changed his mind. Same with the washing. Maybe he thought he'd have a wash so bought lots of soap then thought... nah... and take up rounders. He invested in bats but hurt his bowling arm...or perhaps he has a low boredom threshold."

Offering solutions for lunacy. That's right up your street isn't it, Eli? Just like the old days.

Henry looked blankly at Eliza for a moment.

Henry: "Where are the magazines?"

Brian: "In the bath tub. Follow me."

Henry followed Brian upstairs and proceeded to look through the magazines and the rest of the stashes. Meanwhile, Eliza pulled on her rubber gloves and half-heartedly started swishing a damp sponge over the few available surfaces.

It'd be best to clear the lot and start again.

I'll have a word with Jude later.

It's Jude's fault I'm dusting a box of out-of-date condoms.

It's because of his beautiful eyes. His beautiful face. His beautiful everything.

He's responsible for me being stood amongst this agglomeration of bizarre belongings amassed by his aberrant brother.

I say, even my thoughts are using big words these days. That's Jude's editorial influence.

He even makes my sentences better.

A few minutes later Henry and Brian came back downstairs.

Henry: "Some of the magazines are quite early and good condition. I'll look into the auction value for them and your friend can sell them via online sites."

Eliza: "Not my friend, Henry. I don't have friends who keep Spam in their hallway."

Henry, cheekily: "No, just ones who put granary loaves in commodes."

Mr Hicks.

Eliza: "Accepted. Though bread is the staff of life, I don't believe Spam is. Come on Brian, shall we pull a bit of ivy off the front of the house to cheer up old kibble chops so her knees can retire to Spain?"

Brian: "Yes, ok. I'll see if Jude's doolally brother collects knives so we can hack it down. If he doesn't, I'll be quite disappointed in him."

Henry: "Aichmomania."

Eliza: "Bless you."

Henry: "No, Eli. Collecting of knives. That's what it's called."

I knew that. Ahem.

Eli: "Ohh, that aichmomania. Sorry, I pronounce it slightly different to you."

I pronounce it as 'a person to be avoided'.

Brian pulled open several of the swelled drawers in the kitchen.

Brian: "Bingo! A draw full of hatchets! I knew you wouldn't let me down, crazy man. Come on Eli, let's get cracking. One for you... one for me... are you staying Henry?"

Henry: "I can help for a bit but I have to get back to the auction house for twelve."

Brian: "Pick your cleaver."

Henry picked a knife and they set off around the front of the house to make the outside look more presentable.

Social Media Meme: *Keep Calm and Hire a Sniper.*

Chapter Thirty-six

Billington Gazette Headline ***Faces Lift as Court Decides Claims Against Crooked Local Cosmetic Surgeon were not Puffed up and Practice is Dissolved*** (Pun Points – six)

Eliza pulled the car into Jude's driveway and sighed heavily.

Eliza: "I'm whacked! Do you want to come in for a cup of tea, Brian?"

Brian: "Yes please, I'm parched. I'm not used to such physical activity on a weekday. I won't stay long; I need a bath. I'm desperate to expunge the putrescence that has seeped through my pores."

They got out of the car and Eliza opened the door of Jude's house and walked into the hallway.

It was unusually quiet.

Where's Ellington?

Eliza, calling: "Ellington?! Norris?!"

Nothing.

How very odd.

Eliza, calling: "George?!"

Nothing.

Maybe he's taken Ellington on a walk. That's kind of him.

The least he can do, quite frankly, considering he knowingly let me go to his filth infested abode.

Eliza: "Right then Brian, let's get the kettle on."

Brian: "I'm going to freshen up. I need to decontaminate before my brew."

Brian excused himself to Jude's downstairs toilet and Eliza wandered into the kitchen and filled up the kettle from the sink and absentmindedly looked out of the window to the garden, beyond. Something caught her eye and she dropped the kettle into the washing up bowl.

What on earth?!

Eliza shot out the back door to find a pleased as punch Ellington bouncing about with something rather unpleasant in his mouth.

Eliza, urgently: "Ellington! What are you doing?! Drop!"

Ellington continued to bounce about, gleefully.

Err! What is that in his mouth?

Eliza, sternly now: "Drop! I mean, CEASE!"

Ellington dropped what he had in his mouth to the ground and bounded over to her.

George emerged from behind a large camellia.

George, tutting: "What are you doing, you silly woman? You've ruined it now."

Eliza, in confusion: "What?"

Pardon, not what, mummy.

Not now Tom-in-my-head, something odd is happening.

George: "He was just getting the hang of it."

Eliza walked over and inspected what Ellington had dropped.

248

Eliza, repulsed: "Uuurgh!! It's a squished squirrel! You dirty dog, Ellington!"

Ellington stopped bounding around, slunk down and hung his head in shame.

Eliza, turning to George: "How did he get hold of that?!"

George, very unhappy with the situation: "You coming here, upsetting the training. It's taken me bloody hours to get him to pick it up. Namby pamby hound. All he wanted was tennis balls and sticks."

Eliza, incredulously: "You actively encouraged my dog to find a dead squirrel?! Its innards are hanging out!"

George: "No, of course not. I found it for him."

Eliza, astonished: "Pardon?"

Well done, mummy.

George: "It's road kill. He's not up to finding it yet."

Come again.

Eliza: "I don't understand."

George: "Of course you don't. You're not prepared. The state of your fruit bowl tells me that."

Giving my dog road kill and dissing the amount of bananas I've bought, after the morning I've had...

I'm gonna blow...

Eliza, shrieking: "I suppose having two tonne of Spam and a draw full of cleavers shows preparedness, does it?! Cleavers don't open Spam, you stupid man! "

George shook his head and tutted.

George: "Spam comes with a ring pull."

He tapped his head with this forefinger.

Just then Brian stuck his head out of the kitchen door.

Brian: "Yoo hoo! I've made the tea!"

Eliza turned and waved at Brian.

Eliza to George, haughtily: "Do not train *my* dog again, please. He is a pure dog and I do not want him qualified to pick up dead things. He does not touch dead animals."

George: "Except to eat them."

Eliza: "What? I mean, pardon? What?"

You tried, mummy. You failed but you did try.

George: "He eats tinned dog food. That's dead animals."

Must you be so pedantic?

Eliza: "Whatever."

Eliza turned to go back into the house.

George: "Before you strop off, I've got something for you."

George rifled through his back pocket and pulled out a piece of paper.

George: "I've written a list of the items you can't get rid of."

Eliza reluctantly turned back, took the fat-splatted sheet of paper and read George's scrawl.

Barbed wire (both inside and out)
Evaporated milk
Batteries (all amperage)

Soap
Prophylactics
Tinned Meat
Bottled water (you can chuck the sparkling muck – I bought that in error)
All items that could be interpreted as a cudgel
Anything else I might have forgotten which is replicated and stored in considerable amounts

It's the world's worst shopping list.

Eliza: "What about the bath magazines? Can we sell them, please? They might pay for a skip."

George shrugged as he bent over and put the dead squirrel in his haslet pocket.

Eliza with her best telephone voice: "Good. I'll await the verdict from Henry as to the size of skippage we can acquire. Good day to you."

She whacked her thigh and Ellington scuttled along and walked to her flank, looking up at her with apologetic eyes.

George hollered after her.

George: "I meant to ask, before you set on me with your verbal tirade; I need a decent pillow. Can you sort one out when you make my bed? I like soft; duck down is fine."

So says the man who owns a mattress with myriad unidentifiable stains which documents a human's life from birth to death.

I suppose you'd like me to go and hook a fresh duck off Pilkington's pond and pluck it with my teeth for you. We're not living in a millennial version of Upstairs Downstairs.

Eliza held one of her departing arms up in the air.

Eliza: "I can't hear you! I've walked away!"

Eliza stalked into the kitchen and took the cup of tea Brian was proffering her.

Eliza: "Thanks Brian. I don't think I like him very much."

Brian, laughing: "What? The man who makes the Atkins diet look like a detox and keeps an entire year's rations for a 1950's housing estate in his living room? The same man who could have had all major service utilities cut off from his house in 1970 and he'd still not realise? That man? How frightfully judgemental of you, poppet!"

Brian ferreted through the cupboards and pulled out the biscuit tin.

Brian: "Wash your hands and have a Hobnob. Let's get his place a bit ship shape and ship him out so you can go back to your cosy little world."

Eliza nodded.

Eliza: "He's not good for my chakras."

Brian: "I know. I'm sure one of mine dropped out when I fell through that bleedin' rotten gate, earlier. I'll ask Clive to have a hunt for it later."

Brian winked at her.

Mentor in Life Feature letter: *Dear Eliza, I go out with a bloke who seemed alright at first. He's got a lovely little daughter who I'm well fond of. He's a bastard, though. He is nice one minute and horrible the next. A right Heckle and Jide. I found out he used to beat up his ex-wife. She is a pain in the arse but she didn't deserve that. Now he's turned on me. I do love him, what should I do? Thanks, My-identity-is-secret.*

Dear I-know-who-you-really-are, He's a vile man who treated his ex-wife abhorrently. She's taken years to get over it and will be forever haunted by the actions of that man. However, she's since found happiness with one of her first loves. He's her Venetian blind in a world full of flimsy voiles (something like that, I think she said). Anyway, my point being, she found love afterwards and this one doesn't beat her up. Plus he has a voice which makes your stomach gurgle (in a good way, not like when you've had too much cheese). Some people do not deserve love; he is one of them. Find someone worthy of such a wonderful emotion. I will give you this piece of wisdom and hope you are able to find the strength to leave him: "No matter how many times a snake sheds its skin. It will always be a snake."

Chapter Thirty-seven

Billington Gazette Headline: ***Billington Nightclub, Vertigo, Reaches Dizzying New Heights With its Own Label Gin Launch*** (Pun Points – five)

Eliza paced the hall waiting for the door to open. Jude had barely stepped over the threshold when she pounced on him.

She hunched over and put her fingers to her lips and whispered loudly.

Eliza: "Ssshh…"

Jude, in a state of confusion: "Er, ok. Are you alright?"

Eliza batted her hand up and down.

Eliza: "Tsssk. Quiet…"

She pointed at the ceiling.

Eliza: "Listen."

Jude: "Eh?"

Jude looked to the ceiling.

Eliza: "Wait…"

They waited for a few moments then a loud groan emanated through the ceiling.

Jude straightened and cocked his head to right.

Followed by another groan after which came a wail.

Jude looked at Eliza and frowned.

Jude: "Is Tom still staying at your parents, Eli?"

Eliza: "Yes."

Jude's shoulders sagged with relief.

Jude: "Good."

Just then another loud squeal came through the ceiling.

Eliza: "It sounds very dubious, doesn't it?"

Jude scratched his head and turned his mouth down with disapproval.

Eliza led him through to the kitchen.

Eliza: "I need to have a word with you about a few things I've witnessed today. I came home and caught George in the act with Ellington."

Jude looked horrified.

Jude: "Good god! As in how I found Lydia the other year? Shackled to the bedposts with the wind in her hair sort of 'caught in the act'?"

Eliza: "No, worse than that, Jude."

Jude went slack-jawed.

Eliza: "He taught him to pick up road kill squirrels."

Jude exhaled and patted his chest with relief.

Eliza, in full flow: "I can't have Ellington bringing them home willy-nilly. It's bad for the vibrations. Your house will become a vortex of deathification. He also has an unnerving amount of..."

An almighty grunt came from upstairs.

Jude put his hand up to stop Eliza.

Jude: "I'm sorry, I'm going to have to put a stop to this. I've just come home from work. Hang on, Eli."

Jude turned tail out of the kitchen and ran upstairs, quickly followed by Eliza.

They stood outside the bedroom door where the noises originated.

From inside the room: "... no, no harder... left a bit... you put it here... that's it... AARGH!"

Eliza and Jude looked at each other and shook their heads. Jude banged on the door.

The talking quickly stopped followed by the sound of a hastily closing laptop. George opened the door and poked his head round.

George: "Yes?"

Jude, awkwardly: "Erm, everything alright?"

George: "Why wouldn't it be?"

Jude: "We heard some, erm, commotion."

George: "Oh, er. Ok. Sorry bro. I'll keep it down a bit in future."

Eliza nudged Jude.

Eliza, whispering: "Ellington."

Jude: "Ok, thanks. Oh, and Eli would like it if you didn't bring roadkill into the house in future. She's gone very spiritual lately and it upsets her, er, is it ethereal pipes... what does it upset, Eli?"

Eliza: "Me. All of me."

Jude: "Oh right. Her. It upsets her."

Eliza nudged Jude again.

Eliza: "And you."

Jude: "And apparently, me."

George: "Fair enough. Her dog is a bit dopey. He's not a very good hunter gatherer. Pampered, that's the problem. Am I allowed to have a bash with the cat?"

Jude and Eliza, in unison: "No!!"

George shrugged.

George: "Anything else?"

Jude: "Erm, I don't think so. Is there anything else, Eli?"

Eliza: "Yes, tell him he shouldn't keep piles of Spam by the front door and out of date condoms are useless... Oh and he needs to mend his side gate... Oh and he can stick his request for a new pillow where the sun doesn'..."

Jude cut across.

Jude: "Yes, that's it."

George: "Good."

He slammed the bedroom door in their faces.

Jude waved Eliza away and directed her to lead the way downstairs.

Once they were downstairs, Eliza proceeded to fill Jude in on her and Brian's findings from the morning at George's house.

Jude looked stupefied.

Eliza: "Anyway, I don't think he's a very positive influence for a seven-year-old. I spoke to mum and she's happy for Tom to stay over for a few extra days as it's the Easter holidays. They've managed to get a last-minute break to a lodge by a lake with a hot tub.

We can get George's house in some semblance of order whilst he's away and then get George back in. Do I have your word, he's not going to kill us in our beds whilst he's here?"

Jude: "I'll talk to Dorothy. She's been more in contact with him than me throughout the years. He hasn't killed anyone; I would have written about it in the paper."

Mentor in Life Feature letter: *Dear Eliza, It's me again, I'm-an-Adonis. Thanks for answering my previous letter. I did what your suggested and went on that dating site. There were a right load of old weirdos on there but one profile did quite catch my eye. Shakespearesister1. Should I send her a picture of my penis? Cheers, I'm-an-Adonis.*

Dear Adonis'-do-not-send-pictures-of-their-penises, That is a dormant account and has now been removed so no pictures of your parts are required, thank you very much. May I take this opportunity to advise against any such carry on, it's in frightfully poor taste. I shall leave you with this quote: "Beauty is not in the face; beauty is light in the heart" – Kahlil Gibran. (Please replace the word face with willy).

Chapter Thirty-eight

Billington Gazette Headline: ***Popular Owner of Billington Game Store Celebrates Birth of Daughter, Annie-May*** (Pun Points – six – however it should be noted this is due to baby name choice and nothing to do with any headline wittism.)

Eliza was sat at her desk, absentmindedly ramming a packet of crisps into her mouth whilst listening to Charlotte talk to a friend on the phone.

Charlotte-long-hair: "...Uh huh... Well, I said life was too short to take a USB out safely but what with him being heavily into IT he didn't take it well...Uh huh... Can you believe he said I was condescending? That means I talk down to people...Uh huh... I don't think it would have worked. I'm part Australian; a natural adventurer but he wanted to stay in a static caravan for the week... Uh huh... That put the cat amongst the apple carts."

Eliza, instinctively mid crisp: "Pigeons."

Charlotte turned to Eliza and huffed.

Australian footed Charlotte-long-hair: "What? Get on with your work. I'm on the telephone."

Eliza: "Cat amongst the pigeons. You upset the apple carts."

Charlotte-long-hair: "Are you listening to my private conversation, Eliza?"

Eliza put a Hula Hoop on each finger and started to bite them off.

The one you're having in a non-private setting, completely within ear shot of the whole office. That one?

Eliza: "Yes."

Just then Jude walked back into the office.

Charlotte-long-hair to her friend on the end of the phone: "Gotta go. Catch you later."

She hastily put the phone down.

Jude's mouth twitched when he saw Eliza and smirked.

Jude: "Busy?"

Eliza: "Erm…"

I'll take his mind off my laziness by being sexy.

Eliza started to suggestively lick around a Hula Hoop on her finger whilst looking at him in what she deemed an alluring manner.

Jude didn't seem to be that impressed and ruffled his brow.

Jude: "They'll go soggy; just shove them in."

Tut, you try and be sultry.

Eliza was swiftly sucking them off her fingers when her phone rang. She wiped her hands on her trousers and picked it up.

Eliza: "Good Afternoon. Billington Gazette, how may I help you? Oh hello, Henry."

Henry: "I found out how much those magazines are worth. The ones I put aside on your friend's bathroom sink should achieve approximately £30 each."

Eliza: "Ooh, lovely. We can get a skip and some new furniture if they all sell. Thank you."

Henry: "I've also found out about that clock."

Eliza: "Oh, how marvellous. Well done you."

Henry: "I've shown it to our senior valuer and it's as I expected. It's Archibald Knox's."

Eliza: "Shall we give it back to him?"

Henry, patiently: "No, Eli. It's by Archibald Knox. One of THE designers of the early 20th Century. Designed for Liberty. It's worth a lot of money."

Eliza: "Oh, that's nice. I'll give it back to George and tell him."

Henry: "Erm, I'm not sure we should be so hasty, Eli."

Eliza: "Why?"

There was an awkward pause.

Henry: "I think it might be stolen."

Eliza, spluttering: "STOLEN?!"

Charlotte pricked her already fervent ears up and got her pen and note pad out.

Uh oh, she senses a story.

It's Jude's brother. I can't tell her he's been nicking antique clocks.

George must have stolen it when he was in the Boots smash and grab soap and condom phase.

Think fast.

Eliza: "Stollen, you say?! I love stollen. German fruit bread is my favourite. Nom nom nom!"

Charlotte frowned slightly but kept hold of her pen and pad.

Henry: "Pardon? I said, I think it might be *stolen*."

Eliza flicked another look at a highly poised Charlotte.

Eliza: "Indeed you did and I fully understood that so let's meet, have stollen and discuss. A newspaper office is such a busy place full of people writing articles about things. Things that happen now and things that have happened in the past. Good things, bad things, things that have moved from their original place and ended up in another. All those things. It's all about the writing of things and telling people. Lots of people."

Henry, with penny dropping: "Oh goodness! He's a friend of yours and he may be a pilferer. You don't want the local paper getting hold of that, do you? Of course, let me know when and where and I'll tell you what I've gleaned."

Eliza: "Perfect. I'll text you if that's ok to arrange?"

Henry: "Yes, ok. Let's meet up next week. I'll try and find out more about it in the meantime."

Eliza: "Thank you, Henry."

Henry: "No worries, Eli. Please can you also find out what you can as I don't feel comfortable having potentially misappropriated artefacts in the auction house. Speak to you later."

Eliza, over brightly: "Bye! See you for stollen!"

Eliza plonked the receiver down, stared at it and tutted.

Charlotte watched Eliza drop the receiver down, stared at her and tutted.

Charlotte-long-hair: "Who was that?"

Feign ignorance.

Easy.

Eliza: "No one."

Charlotte-long-hair: "It was a Henry, I heard you. What did he want?"

Eliza: "Nothing."

Charlotte-long-hair: "Nothing except stollen?"

Eliza: "Exactly."

Charlotte glowered at her.

She's a bloodhound for a story.

Stare her out.

Don't blink.

Oh my eyes, my eyes!

Charlotte shook her head with disdain, looked away and put her note pad and pen down.

Charlotte-long-hair, mumbling: "It's not even Christmas."

Ha-ha, I win the staring.

Victory is mine!

Mentor in Life Feature letter: *Dear Eliza, No matter what I do, I can't seem to find any reason for living. I can't get a job; I can't find a partner and I just can't see the point in it all. Please, help. Yours, I'm-at-my-wits-end*

Dear Please-don't-be-at-your-wits-end, I know life can be desperately hard and unfair at times but people are there to help and listen to you. I'm definitely not qualified to dispense advice on such a serious matter: I only got this job because I'm sleeping with the management (Not all of them, just the one in charge). I have sent you a list of numbers you can contact. Please reach out to them, they can help. However, after years of self-help and my mother, I am enormously qualified in quotes and will leave this one with you: "Just when the caterpillar thought the world was over, it became a butterfly."

Chapter Thirty-nine

Billington Gazette Headline: ***Hold the Door Open and Pull out a Chair - Award Winning Billington Restaurant, Manners, Due to Re-opcn Next Month After Extensive Refurbishment.*** **Use our exclusive promo code for £10 off a main meal: M1NDYOURPSANDQS** (Pun Points – Not Applicable – No one should play about with food.)

Later that evening Eliza and Jude were in bed.

Eliza: "I tried to lick my Hula Hoops for you earlier."

Jude: "Is that a euphemism?"

Eliza: "In the office, when you walked in."

Jude: "Oh, when you were cramming a packet of crisps in your face."

Eliza: "I was being seductive."

Jude looked at her with amusement.

Jude: "You are quite ridiculous. Come here."

He stretched out his arms for a hug and Eliza snuggled into him.

He kissed her on the top of her head.

Jude: "Don't be seductive at the office, just do some work. I like it when you work."

Eliza sat up.

Eliza: "Oh, you like being the boss. I see. Shall I wear a power suit? Would you like that? I can get one with shoulder pads and be all 1980s. I saw one in the charity shop the other day. I can be Alexis Carrington."

Jude: "Will you shut up. Just be normal."

Eliza: "I don't know if I can."

Jude: "Just do your best."

Shall I tell him about my call with Henry today and George having Archibald's clock?

No, hold off until you know all the facts.

And what do I do when I get the facts?

No idea.

I'll ask Lydia what to do.

Ooh Lydia.

Eliza: "That reminds me. Last time I went to the Merrythought Café, Lydia asked me to talk dirty. Dave's not been back since; it really upset his equilibrium. Belinda says he's booked an extended stay in a bed and breakfast in Bude. Do you want to talk dirty?"

Jude looked at Eliza, astonished.

Jude: "Do we have to?"

Eliza: "Lydia does it with Tony and, apparently, he's stopped paying his monthly maintenance to the Smurfs as a result of it. You try it first, let me see if I like it. Apparently, men can do it quite easily."

Jude: "Can they? I feel remarkably uncomfortable. Can't we just do what we normally do? I know where I am with that."

Eliza: "You mean, silence?"

Jude: "Yes. I leave my words at the office."

Eliza: "Ok. Stop talking then."

****

Eliza closed her laptop and looked across at a bacon sandwich eating, George.

Eliza: "Right that's the skip ordered. It's being delivered next Tuesday so we can start filling it then."

George: "Oh."

Eliza: "Oh, What, oh?"

George: "I won't be available next Tuesday."

Eliza: "Why not? You don't work, do you?"

George: "No, working's a mug's game."

Eliza: "Thank you."

George: "I'm going away for a few days."

Not to a lodge by a lake with a hot tub?

Eliza: "Anywhere nice?"

George: "I'm going to a boot camp."

There's definitely no way he'd run into my parents and Tom then. Phew.

Eliza: "As in a fitness one?"

George: "No."

Eliza: "What then? A survival boot camp?"

George: "Exactly one of those."

How very Bear Grylls.

Eliza: "Fair enough. I'll ask Jude if I can take the day off and will make a start."

George, ramming the last of his sandwich in: "Thank you."

George wiped his hands on his trousers and scraped his chair back, handing his plate to Eliza as he left the room.

What did your last slave die of?

Mange, probably.

Mentor in Life Feature letter: *Dear Eliza, Are you the woman who ran off after our first date? I'm the chap who ate liver for breakfast and spat my dinner out over you. I've got to the bottom of my allergies and am now a vegan; I haven't had the squits since. Would you consider giving it another whirl? Yours, meat-is-not-my-friend.*

Dear meat-is-not-my-friend, Yes, I am indeed that woman. Glad to hear your digestive tract has fully recovered. I'll decline the kind offer of another whirl, if that's ok. I hope you find your quinoa to your Quorn.

Chapter Forty

Billington Gazette Headline: ***Billington Appliance Retailer Closed Down After Cooking The Books*** (Pun Points – six)

Eliza sat on the park bench and watched as a swan chased a duck across the pond. She looked up and saw a flustered looking Henry approaching.

Henry: "Hi, sorry I'm late, Eli. The phone rang just as I was about to leave."

Eliza: "No problem, Henry. I'm relieved to be out of the house to be honest. Hello."

Henry sat down next to Eliza,

Henry: "You know I mentioned I'd spoken to our senior valuer, Ernest, about the clock? Well, he recognised it."

Eliza: "Off the Antiques Roadshow with Napoleon's toothbrush holder?"

Henry: "No Eli, not from there."

Henry opened his bag, pulled out a dog-eared auction catalogue from the mid 1980's and flipped through to a page he'd book-marked. He opened it across his lap.

Henry: "Ernest keeps all the auction catalogues. Look at lot number twelve."

Eliza bent closer to Henry's knee and shot back up with her eyes wide.

Eliza: "Is that our Archibald?!"

Henry: "I do believe it is. I used to spend many an hour flicking through old catalogues when I first joined. It must have been where I recollected seeing it."

Eliza: "If you think it's stolen, I'm assuming George didn't buy it?"

Henry: "No. According to our records, the owners of Billington Manor did. Ernest says they were one of our best customers."

Henry sighed heavily and shook his head, sadly.

Henry: "It's such a pity. Ernest said they were lovely people. They were renovating the manor in the mid 1980's and had been to our auctions a number of times. Ernest said they were refurbishing the drawing room around the time they bought that clock. They bought a number of items that day for it."

Henry shrugged and sighed.

Henry: "Billington Manor was architecturally astounding, and now..."

Eliza: "What do you mean...shrug... and now? Why are you shrugging and sighing?"

Henry, cheerlessly: "It no longer exists."

Eliza looked at Henry with confusion.

Eliza: "Eh? What happened to it?"

Henry: "It burnt down."

Eliza: "Oh dear."

Henry: "Very much so."

Eliza: "Where was the house?"

Henry pointed through the park gates towards Billington's new supermarket.

Henry: "Over there."

Eliza: "In the car park?"

Henry: "No Eli, they built the supermarket where it once stood."

Eliza: "Oh."

Henry: "It'd been in the family for five generations. Such a dreadful shame."

Eliza: "Could it be a different clock?"

Henry: "Highly unlikely; they're like hens' teeth. Look, may I make a suggestion?"

Eliza: "Yes, of course."

Henry: "I'll keep the clock in the auction house safe for another week or so if you can look into it a bit more. Something definitely doesn't add up, Eli."

Eliza: "That's a good plan, Thank you."

Henry looked at his watch.

Henry: "Look, I must go, I've left Jessica in charge."

Henry rolled the catalogue up and placed it back into his bag and stood to leave. Eliza went to stand, as well.

Eliza: "Billington Manor, you say?"

Henry: "Yes, that's right."

Eliza: "Five generations, you say?"

Henry: "Yes, that's right."

Eliza: "Who owned it?"

Henry: "Sorry, I thought I'd told you. The Hicks family."

Hicks?!

Eliza: "Oh!"

Shocked, Eliza dropped her bag and the contents spilled out onto the path.

Eliza: "Aargh!!"

Henry doubled back to help her, as she scrabbled about picking up her belongings.

Eliza, on the ground hastily throwing possessions back into her bag: "Are you sure, Hicks?!"

Henry, bending down to help her: "Yes, Eli. Most sure it's Hicks."

Good Lord!

Eliza watched as Henry picked up a biscuit which was wrapped in a tissue and examined it, a look of revulsion crossed his face.

Uh oh, he's inspecting with disgust my half-eaten emergency Hobnob.

Eliza batted him away.

Eliza: "You go, Henry. You don't need to be picking up my paraphernalia; you've a Jessica to sort out. I'll give you a call in a couple of days."

Henry handed the nibbled biscuit to Eliza and wiped his hands on his trousers.

Henry, gratefully: "Ok, great. Speak to you soon."

Henry hurried off down the path before turning back to Eliza.

Henry: "And Eli... Take care, eh?"

Eliza from crouched on the ground.

Eliza: "Of course! I'm a naturally cautious person."

Henry smiled with relief and waved as he sprinted off.

Out of the corner of her eye, Eliza saw a tampon roll across into the path of the now preening swan and, spying a new tasty morsel, it picked it up.

Eliza hastily lunged at the swan and tried pull it out of its beak.

Eliza, shrieking: "You can't eat that! You'll block your bread pipe up and the Queen will be after me!"

The swan reared up and started flapping its feathers in a threatening manner at Eliza, holding fast on to its unexpected snack.

Eliza: "Gerroff!! I'll be put in the tower!"

The swan hissed violently at her.

From behind her came a puffing holler.

Disembodied voice from over Eliza's right shoulder: "What in buggering's name are you doing woman?! Get off it! It'll have your arm off!"

Eliza dropped her grip with surprise and turned round to be faced by a puce park warden.

Eliza: "He's got my tampon!"

I said that out loud to a stranger in the middle of a park with a swan and several ducks as witnesses.

Eliza looked around and saw a woman sat on a nearby bench, watching agog at the side show she'd found herself witnessing; slack-mouthed, holding a half-eaten sandwich midway between her mouth and her lap.

And an employee of the new Billington supermarket on her lunch break. Splendid.

Livid park warden: "Why the buggering bollocks did you give him one of them? Are you out of your mind? We ban bread; it's a given that you don't feed them sanitary products. Am I going to have to update the signage?"

Eliza, indignantly: "I didn't. It took it. I dropped it."

Meanwhile, the swan having realised this wasn't a particularly tasty morsel, spat it out, fluffed up its plumage and waddled off into the pond.

Livid park warden: "Littering, eh? As well as harassing the birdlife."

Eliza: "It went for me. The swan started it."

The park warden's face went from red to blotchy purple.

Livid park warden: "That's it! What's your name? You're barred. I can't be having the likes of you upsetting my angina. I only took this job because those bastard bankers squandered my pension."

I'm nearly forty. I can't be barred from recreational spaces at my age.

The park warden retrieved a dog-eared pad out of his back pocket and a heavily chewed pencil from his shirt pocket.

Livid park warden: "Name."

I'm a respected member of the Billington Gazette. I run an advice column. No-one would write to me again if they knew I'd been banned from Billington Park for wrestling a tampon off a swan.

What advice do I give myself?

Lie. That's my advice.

What's my name?

Eliza: "Felicity."

Oh, very nice. Though I don't think I look like a Felicity.

In my fantasy mind, Felicity's wear jodhpurs. I wouldn't even know where to purchase a pair. If necessary, I'll purchase them online.

The park warden jotted it down.

Livid park warden: "Surname?"

What's my surname, brain?

Eliza: "Flapstop."

Pardon? Is that the best you can do?

The park warden looked up from his pad and eyed her suspiciously. Eliza shrugged.

Blame my imaginary parents.

He looked back down and wrote the surname on his pad.

Livid park warden, a few shades paler on the red tonal chart: "Right then..."

He looked at his pad.

Livid park warden: "...Felicity Flapstop. You are hereby forbidden to indulge in foul play with the fowl and are withheld access from this amenity space until such a time as I no longer work here. Got it?"

Eliza sheepishly nodded, picked up the swan's discarded tampon and went to hand it to the park warden.

Eliza: "Here you are."

The park warden shook his head and pointed to a sign which was affixed to the fence near the park entrance.

Park warden: "Take your rubbish home with you. Number two on the sign, Ms Flapstop."

Eliza shoved it in her pocket and collected the rest of her dropped belongings and made a hasty exit out of the park.

Park warden, yelling after a rapidly departing Eliza: "... And don't even think of breaching the dictum or I'll get you Felicity Flapstop!"

Yes, yes.

What was I doing before I got slung out of the park?

Ah, that's right.

I told Henry that I was very risk averse.

Mentor in Life Feature letter: *Dear Eliza, I met a fabulous bloke who is everything I could ever wish for. He's asked me to marry him and I am over the moon but there's one small problem; he's twenty-five years older than me. When I'm forty he'll be nearing retirement. Do you think this is something I should worry about? Yours, My-fiancé-remembers-life-before-the-internet*

Dear I-remember-life-before-the-internet-too, My best friend lives with a man who is positively ancient but she's never been happier. People search their whole lives for what you've found, who cares if it's last season's design? As the Benjamin Franklin quote goes: "Many people die at twenty-five and aren't buried until they are seventy-five." You could find yourself a young one but he might be really dull. Just do everything now and take lots of photos to remind yourselves how much fun you had before everything dropped off/ceased/started dribbling uncontrollably/ebbed into the long passage of inevitable decline and forgetfulness.

Chapter Forty-one

Billington Gazette Headline: ***Local Clothes Manufacturer Having to Cut to Their Cloth Due to a Downturn in Sales.*** (Pun Points – seven)

When asked for comment, Managing Director, Peter Taylor, undeterminable age but looks late forties, says "We remain hopeful of a turn up in trousers for autumn".

Eliza skidded across the Merrythought Café tiles and threw herself onto a chair.

Eliza, puffing: "I'm so sorry I'm late, Lydia."

Lydia: "Not a problem, darling. Is everything alright?"

Eliza: "Apart from having an altercation with a swan and wandering into an episode of Poirot, I'm fine."

Lydia: "Oh good. I've been doing a crossword. Look!"

Lydia held up a magazine with a half-done crossword.

Eliza: "I've never seen you do a crossword before? What's brought this on?"

Lydia: "Miriam from number fifty-four won a chateau in the Rhone valley doing one."

Eliza: "You want to move to France?"

Lydia: "No, of course not. I prefer a crusty bloomer to a baguette any day of the week. I'd sell it and buy a house with more bathrooms."

Eliza: "Why do you need more bathrooms? Isn't the one enough?"

Lydia: "Absolutely not. Tony's too hirsute; I blame the testosterone."

Eliza: "Eh?"

Lydia pulled a very disapproving face.

Lydia: "Pubes all over the bath, darling. I've told him to rinse it out after he empties the tub, but does he? Hmm? My pamper time is sacred and I don't want to remove my cucumber slices to be faced with wanton pubic hairs floating around my face."

Belinda wandered over.

Lydia to Belinda: "You took your time."

Belinda, wiping hash brown fat across her brow: "I'm rushed off my pissing feet; it's a living hell. I never thought I'd say this but I miss Dave."

Eliza: "Aww."

Belinda, tersely: "It's all your fault. What do you want?"

I'm hazarding a guess that the diploma wasn't in customer service.

Eliza: "Tea and... what's today's cake?"

Belinda: "There isn't one. I missed the ordering day. You can have toast; I bought a loaf from Asda on me way in."

Eliza: "... and toast then."

Belinda nodded.

Belinda: "You can have the china cups. I couldn't give a shit if you talk about cocks."

Eliza: "Most kind hearted of you."

Belinda screwed her nose up and sloped back to the kitchens.

Lydia: "So what's brother George like?"

Eliza: "He's a bit… erm… different."

Lydia: "In what way different? Hanging from chandeliers in pants, sort of different or killing hamsters with bare teeth, sort of different?"

Eliza: "Are they my only two options?"

Lydia: "They are the bench marks, yes."

Eliza: "Somewhere in the middle then.

Lydia: "Oh dear."

Lydia looked back to her crossword.

Lydia to Eliza: "Eight across. Six letters. 'To serve oneself?' Starts with…"

Belinda wandered over and clumsily dropped their order onto their table.

Belinda: "Wanker."

She then turned tail to serve her next customer.

Lydia furrowed her brow.

Lydia: "B…"

Eliza: "Buffet."

Lydia inspected her crossword, scribbled it in and beamed across to Eliza.

Lydia: "Well done, darling, that's another one done! I'm another step closer to France. Shall I be mother?"

****

Later that evening, Eliza was getting ready to go out for dinner with Jude. She looked at her reflection in the cheval mirror.

Eliza to Ellington: "A departure from the norm but rather pretty and floaty, don't you agree Ellington?"

She whisked round and did a turn for him.

Ellington looked up from his bone and did a cursory tail wag at the mention of his name.

Eliza: "Thank you, Gok Wan."

Jude wandered into the bedroom, bent down and stroked Ellington then looked at Eliza with confusion.

Jude: "Is that a nighty? I thought we were going out."

Nighty? When are you from, 1957?

Forty-eight quid in Zara this was. At least the dog likes it.

Eliza, huffing: "I'll just change. Hang on. I've had a very hectic day so I'm running a bit late."

Hide the fact you've spent over an hour getting ready.

Jude: "Oh really, busy day, was it? Lots of letters written? Sat slaving at the lap top all day, were you?"

He's got a funny tone on.

Eliza looked at Jude, carefully.

Eliza: "Yes, absolutely. Type, type, type. Solving one personal problem after another."

Jude, lightly: "Oh, that's most odd then... Most odd indeed..."

He rubbed his forehead and furrowed his brow.

Eliza swiftly pulled off the dress and yanked on her trusty jeans as Jude took out his mobile phone and stared at it, intently.

Jude, levelly: "You've got a doppelganger as well then."

Uh oh, I've been rumbled. He knows I went out.

Eliza, expansively: "Ok, ok. I did see Lydia, alright. We normally see each other on a Thursday, which is my day off but she's having problems with Tony and his pubes so we met up today instead. I promise I'll work on Thursday instead. I would have told you but I'm naturally furtive. I'll seek crystal guidance to make sure I address this attribute of my character. How did you know?"

Jude looked up from his phone.

Jude: "Oh, I didn't know about that bit..."

Jude held up his phone to Eliza.

Jude: "... Felicity."

Oh dear god, no.

Jude hit play.

There in full technicolour was Eliza fighting with the swan and hollering at the park warden earlier that day.

Eliza's eyes widened with horror.

Eliza: "... But how?!"

Jude: "The news desk was emailed this video this afternoon by a..."

He hit pause and scrolled through his emails.

Jude: "Shannon Fisher."

Eliza, incredulous: "She must have been the sandwich eater on the bench! Cheeky cow. I'll never frequent that supermarket again."

Jude's eyes crinkled with amusement.

Jude: "She wondered if we'd like to put it on our newsfeed. She reckons it could go viral. Just imagine the exposure it'd give the paper, Eli."

Gulp.

Where does his allegiance lie? The paper or me...

Eliza: "But you wouldn't, would you? I'd be a laughing stock."

Jude put his phone down and opened his arms to Eliza.

Jude, pulling Eliza into his embrace: "Of course, I wouldn't."

He's chosen me.

I truly love this man.

He kissed her on the top of her head then held her at arms' length.

Jude, smirking: "It is tempting though!"

He dropped his grip and headed out of the room.

Jude: "Come on, we'll be late. The table's booked for half seven."

Mentor in Life Feature letter: *Dear Eliza, I got some Danish pastries which are on the turn and Dorothy's told me to mention, she has some chrysanthemums which are wilting if you fancy popping by after work to pick them up. Ps. Your cottage has got a team of tradespeople all over it – you'll be back in no time. With Best Regards, Mr Hicks*

Dear Mr Hicks, Thank you for the offer but I'm a bit busy this evening trying to make my boyfriend propose. Thank you for the cottage update – if I'm successful, however, I might not need to dirty the newly refurbished threshold. Send my love to Dorothy. Eli x

Chapter Forty-two

Billington Gazette Headline: ***Mute Swan Refuses Treatment After a Member of the Public Tries to Choke it with Feminine Care Products*** (Pun Points – Not Applicable - this is a very serious matter and one shouldn't create a humorous headline under such circumstances. (As per Charlotte's instruction)).

Eliza and George were sat at Jude's breakfast bar and she opened her lap top.

Eliza: "As those magazines sold for a pretty penny, we've got money left after the skip hire so we can purchase some stuff to make your house more habitable. That will be nice, won't it?"

George shrugged as Eliza rubbed her hands together and brought up an online furniture website.

George watched over her shoulder as Eliza popped a toaster, mug tree and bale of towels into the online trolley.

Eliza: "I thought we could get a nice carpet for the lounge."

George: "Absolutely not."

Eliza: "Why not? Those bare boards would be a devil to sand."

George: "I'm not ripping up a perfectly good carpet in an emergency."

What emergency constitutes the ripping up of a room carpet?

You can't reason with insanity. You've spoken to yourself for years and got nowhere.

Eliza scrolled through the online furniture shop and found a large rug with an offer - buy one get a matching smaller one free.

I like that, I could have the small one. That'd look lovely in our newly refurbished cottage.

Or Jude's lounge when we live happily ever after.

When we're married...Snuggled up on the settee together. Ahh.

Where was I? Oh yes.

Eliza: "Ok, no carpet. Perhaps a rug to take the edge off?"

George pondered for a moment.

George: "That could work. They'd never suspect then."

Erm. They? Who is this they?

You want the rug. Just agree.

Eliza: "No, no they wouldn't. So, yes to the rug?"

George nodded.

Eliza: "Great."

Eliza clicked and put it into the online shopping basket.

New rug for Eli... Yay!

Eliza: "Right, I think we're there."

George handed over his credit card and Eliza keyed in the details.

Bring up the clock.

Eliza, in a sing-song voice: "Oh George, that clock. The old dusty silver one that was on your mantelpiece. You don't happen to know where it came from, do you?"

There. Matter brought up in a non-confrontational way.

George: "Who's asking?"

Eliza: "Er. Me."

Be subtle.

Eliza: "Only I thought it might be stolen."

Perfect. Just perfect.

George's eyes narrowed.

Eliza gulped.

Eliza, hurriedly: "Did I say stolen? I didn't mean stolen. I meant something else. Another word which doesn't mean that at all. It's just my sense of humour. Hahaha!"

Eliza laughed somewhat hysterically.

George, levelly: "If you're referring to that Art Nouveau one; it was a present."

Eliza: "Oh. Who from?"

George: "What is this?"

Eliza: "Answer the question."

George tutted.

George: "Dorothy."

Huh?

Eliza: "As in Lydia's bezzie and Blooms and Bloomers, Dorothy?"

George: "As in my sister, Dorothy. I don't know about the Lydia bit but yes, she does now own Blooms and Bloomers."

Eliza, slowly: "Dorothy gave you that clock?"

George: "Is there something wrong with you? Yes."

Eliza: "Are you sure?"

George, sarcastically: "No I made it up."

Eliza: "When?"

George: "Does it matter?"

Eliza: "Yes. When?"

George: "God, you're belligerent. I dunno. Five years ago. Ten? A while ago. It was a birthday present."

George got off his stool.

George: "Are we finished?"

Eliza nodded.

George, muttering to himself as he left the room: "My brother needs a medal putting up with that nutcase..."

Mentor in Life Feature letter: *Dear Eliza, I recently went for a night out with my friend and got absolutely ~~shitfaced~~ inebriated. My friend put a well dodgy clip of me attempting to hula-hoop with a discarded bicycle tyre up on her social media feed. I'm not happy. I'm a laughing stock. What should I do? Yours, I've-given-up-drinking.*

Dear, Glad-to-hear-you've-given-up-drinking, Cameras are everywhere these days, I managed to avert a similar fiasco when I was filmed having a fight with a hostile bird and providing a park attendant with a false name. However, I couldn't blame drink, just misfortune for the incident. I shall give you this quote by Jay Baer: "Content is Fire, Social Media is Gasoline". One must be on one's mettle at all times if one is to evade the ever-seeing eye of Big Brother (or Shannon from the supermarket).

Chapter Forty-three

Billington Gazette Headline: ***Mayor Cuts the Ribbon on New Billington Gift Shop*** (Pun Points – five)

Eliza pulled up outside Blooms and Bloomers and smiled grimly; momentarily despondent, at the familiar shop.

If only we could have made it work.

If only we weren't pushed out of business.

Life is full of, if onlys...

Eliza pushed through the shop door and the bell jangled.

Out from the back popped Dorothy. She beamed broadly as she spotted Eliza.

Dorothy: "Hello Eliza!! How absolutely wonderful to see you! We've missed you dreadfully. We keep up with your excellent advice column, though. Most informative and insightful."

Eliza: "Hello, Dorothy. You look well."

Dorothy: "Thank you, I am. Mr Hicks has me whipping his cream. It's quite a strenuous activity."

I bet. I've seen Bunty's biceps.

Dorothy: "What can I do for you, today? I'm afraid I had to chuck those chrysanthemums but I've some Gypsophila that's dropping all over the place, if you'd like a bunch of that? We've also got an offer on batch loaves and potted marigolds."

Eliza: "I wanted to ask you something, actually."

Dorothy: "Oh, shall I put the kettle on then, dear?"

Eliza: "That would be lovely, thank you."

Dorothy beckoned for Eliza to come through to the kitchens and busied herself with the kettle.

Eliza: "You know we have your brother staying with us at the moment?"

Dorothy: "Ah yes, George. Thank you so much for helping him with the house, Eliza. You truly are a gem. Jude was telling me how tremendous you've been. I don't have the time now we have the shop or I would have offered my assistance."

Eliza: "He's the opposite of you, Dorothy. He doesn't stack cushions. He doesn't even own cushions."

Dorothy grimaced.

Dorothy: "He always did lack the acknowledgement of grime. None of the family have been over to his house for years. I understand it was in a bit of a pickle."

If pickle means utterly squalid then indeed, it was in a bit of a pickle.

Eliza: "You could say that."

Dorothy pointed to a jug.

Dorothy: "Milk?"

Eliza nodded.

Dorothy: "Anyway, dear. What did you want to ask me?"

Eliza: "When we were tidying out George's house, we found a clock on his mantelpiece."

Dorothy: "Did you? That's nice."

Eliza: "Yes. A silver one. Do you recall it?"

Dorothy furrowed her brow and handed over a cup to Eliza.

Dorothy: "A Clock? Hmmm. Silver?"

Eliza: "Yes, Dorothy. An old one. He said you gave it to him."

A look of recognition sprang across Dorothy's face.

Dorothy: "Oh, that clock! Yes, I do recall it. Delightful, isn't it?"

Eliza: "Where did you buy it? I'd love to get one for Lydia. She likes telling the time."

She likes telling the time. Is that really the best you can come up with, brain?

Dorothy: "You might struggle, dear. I found it in a box."

Eliza: "In a box?"

Dorothy: "Yes. In the shed."

Eliza: "In the shed? Whose shed? Your shed?"

Dorothy: "No dear, Kenneth's. He had a big box with all manner of bits in there. I wasn't allowed in his shed, but I saw a baby bird trapped in there one day and I went to let it out."

Dorothy rubbed her chest, her earlier joviality instantly erased with the recollection. She looked down, sadly.

Dorothy: "One has to have small rebellions in a life full of suppression and I wasn't prepared to let a bird die thanks to his mandate. He found out, of course, and was outraged. He put a lock on the door so that was that, but at least I was able to get the clock for George."

Dorothy shrugged and shook herself; physically shaking the memory away.

Dorothy: "It was serendipity; worth the upset. Beautiful items such as that shouldn't be hidden away in a dusty old shed."

Eliza gently patted Dorothy's hand.

Eliza: "No, you're right. I'm so pleased you've found happiness with Mr Hicks, Dorothy."

Dorothy: "Thank you, dear. I am very lucky to have been given another chance. He's the Rock Hudson to my Doris Day."

Perhaps now not the time to tell her about Rock Hudson.

Mentor in Life Feature letter: *Dear Eliza, my boyfriend is lovely but has a weird fetish which unnerves me a bit, not to mention it's proving a bit costly. He has a fixation with Danish pastries. He uses them in all manner of sexual situations; last night he asked me to pretend to be Princess Leia with Danish pastries as my hair buns. Is this normal? Yours, I-used-to-quite-like-a-continental-breakfast.*

Dear, You-could-try-bacon-and-egg, Humans are a funny old bunch and it's best not to dwell too much on their predilections. If he treats you well and this is the only concern how about you go down to Blooms and Bloomers in Pilkington - Mr Hicks is sometimes knocking them out cheap as they lose their flake quite quickly. He also does loads of lovely baked products you might want to experiment with. Might I suggest, however, you steer clear of the macaroons.

Chapter Forty-four

Billington Gazette Headline: **Billington Fish and Chip Shop Tips the Scales with Magnificent Cod Piece – Get Yours Whilst Stocks Last** (Pun Points – seven)

Eliza stretched and resumed her task; flicking through films on the ancient microfiche reader.

Behind her, the door opened and hesitantly a head creeped around the door. It was Valerie.

Voluptuous Valerie, relieved: "Oh, it's you Eliza. I thought we had an interloper. I've called for back-up."

From behind Valerie, Gaz could be heard approaching.

Gaz: "Yo, yo, yo! Freeze or there'll be con-see-quences. I's got a baguette and it's a crusty one."

Back-up had, apparently, arrived.

Gaz burst through the door brandishing a tuna and sweetcorn baguette.

Gaz: "Oh, it's you!"

Gaz put down his bread weapon.

Gaz: "What you snooping about for, laydee? Abandoning your station in broad daylight. Good job you's got the nepotism or we'd have to report you to the boss."

Valerie batted Gaz away.

Voluptuous Valerie: "Go away now, Gaz."

Gaz: "No probs. Glad to be of service to the workforce."

He cheerily waved goodbye with his baguette and wandered out of the back room.

Valerie shut the door behind him.

Voluptuous Valerie: "What are you doing, Eliza? If you're looking for something in particular, perhaps I can help you; I've been at the paper for many years."

I've been sat here for hours and not found anything.

Maybe a bit of assistance wouldn't go amiss.

Just don't go into specifics…

Eliza: "You may be able to help, actually."

Valerie's face lit up. She dragged across an old stool, perched her bottom on it and pulled her button-strained cerise blouse down over her plentiful bosoms. She rubbed her hands together and leant towards the microfiche.

Voluptuous Valerie: "What are we looking for?"

Eliza: "Well, Tom is doing a project for school. He needs to find out the history of the Billington Manor fire and what happened to its internal artefacts, specifically the drawing room antiquities. He needs to concentrate quite heavily on that room."

Voluptuous Valerie: "How old is your child, again?"

Eliza: "Seven."

Voluptuous Valerie, surprised: "That's a very advanced project for a year two pupil."

Eliza: "He's a genius. Can we just try and find the information, please?"

I've been sat here for so long my bum's gone numb.

Voluptuous Valerie: "Well, let me think…"

Valerie looked to the ceiling and tapped her chin.

Voluptuous Valerie: "... Our Lorraine's youngest was just out of nappies...Yes. 1987... Summer... Could be the tail end. I had very swollen ankles due to the heat."

Valerie hopped off the stool and pulled open one of the microfiche draws. She flipped through them, checking the dates on the top labels until she found the one she wanted. She pulled it out and handed it to Eliza.

Voluptuous Valerie: "Try that one."

Eliza pulled out the film reader, took out the film she had in there and slid the microfiche under the glass, clicking it back into place.

She pulled the lever, whizzed over to the top left-hand box and looked at the screen in front of her.

It was the front page of the Billington Gazette Headline - Wednesday, October 21st 1987: **Billington Manor Razed to the Ground in 'Suspicious' Fire. Exclusive!**

Eliza read the accompanying article.

A Devastating Fire has completely gutted the once Majestic Grade II listed House, Billington Manor.

First built in 1762, the Hicks family bought the residence in 1851, during the height of the Industrial Revolution.*

Twenty fire crews across three counties were called to the house at 03:10 BST on Saturday, 17th October with the blaze finally extinguished at 11.03 BST on Monday, 19th October. The family, who were asleep at the time, raised the alarm. Sidney and Constance Hicks and their son, Montague, escaped along with their beloved dog, Drummer. Sadly, at the time of going to press, their cat, Octavia, remains unaccounted for.

Fortunately, much of the building's contents were salvaged as, whilst the fire took hold, the family and nearby locals worked tirelessly throughout the night to retrieve priceless works of art, fine furniture and rare stoneware; carrying them away from danger by storing them in the ground's stable block and outhouses.

* Editor's Note: The Hicks family have long been an important part of Billington's industrial heritage. Opening the textile mill off Tributary Road in the 1840s, Edwin Hicks was much revered in the town as, spurred on by public discord caused by the meddling of Charles Dickens and other such social reformers who thought cholera and children working long hours were unacceptable, he set about improving the working conditions of those at the mill and built much of the cottages along Bobbin Street for the workers; most of which still remain to this day. The clock in the market square was erected in his memory as he was a stickler for time keeping; historic records note locals fondly joked about having to work double shifts for no pay if they were as little as two minutes late. A timely memorial in every sense of the word.

Ah ok, so Archibald must have ended up in one of the outhouses.

Eliza stopped reading the article and looked at an over-the-shoulder reading Valerie.

Eliza to Valerie: "So lots of the bits and bobs, like Archibald clocks and other stuff ended up in the stable block and outhouses?"

Voluptuous Valerie: "Well, yes but they didn't stay there. If your son needs to explain what happened to the 'bits and bobs' it may prove more difficult."

Valerie stood and went back to the microfiche drawers, flicked through and pulled out another slide.

Voluptuous Valerie: "Take a look at that one."

Eliza replaced the slide with the new one and slid over to the top left-hand corner and read the front page.

Billington Gazette Headline - Wednesday, October 28th 1987: **More Anguish for Billington Manor Owners as Salvaged Fire Damaged Family Heirlooms Ransacked**

Just when the owners of Billington Manor thought their luck couldn't get any worse.

As reported in last week's edition, during the fire, the family's prized possessions were put for safe keeping in the ground's stable block and outhouses.

The Billington Gazette has been told, once given the go ahead by the fire crews, the family returned to the burnt-out shell of their once grand home to retrieve their rescued belongings to find a number of the items had been removed and many of the remaining possessions damaged or destroyed.

The police have questioned the fire service which remained at the scene in the preceding days to the family's return to the property. We have been told nothing untoward was observed and the police enquiries remain ongoing.

If you spotted anything unusual between Sunday 18th October and Wednesday 21st October, please call Billington Police with any information.

Oh, that's awful!

So it definitely was stolen. Henry was right.

Along with everything else in those boxes.

The ones in the shed.

Oh. My. God.

Kenneth's shed!!

Eliza screeched back her chair with such speed, Valerie almost toppled over.

Eliza: "Can we print this off, Valerie?"

Voluptuous Valerie: "Yes of course. Press this green button here."

Valerie pressed the button and the page printed out.

Eliza: "Thank you. I've got to go."

Voluptuous Valerie: "What immediately?!"

Eliza: "Yes."

Voluptuous Valerie: "Is your son's project that overdue? You really ought to have allowed more time. It doesn't teach children good time keeping skills, leaving things to the last knockin's."

Eliza: "What?! Oh, oh, yes. No you're quite right. I'll never do it again."

Eliza gave Valerie an impromptu hug.

Eliza: "Thank you, Valerie. I can't put into words how much help you've been. Leave the film things, I'll sort them out later."

Valerie blushed and busied herself putting the films back into the drawer.

Voluptuous Valerie: "It's alright, I'll tidy up after you. You remind me a bit of our Lorraine. She's a messy little bleeder as well."

Valerie stopped tidying and patted Eliza on the arm.

Voluptuous Valerie: "I'm pleased you've joined us. You've been like a breath of fresh air and Jude is so much happier since he's been with you. Mandy and I thought he'd never settle down."

Valerie sighed.

Voluptuous Valerie: "And what a waste that would have been."

Valerie sidled up to Eliza and gave her a conspiratorial wink.

Voluptuous Valerie: "Charlotte's livid, of course. Which makes it even more delightful."

On any other day, I would cheerfully indulge in the misery my existence causes old Charlotte-long-hair but I don't have time for this.

Eliza: "Really, that is an added bonus. I've got to go, Valerie. Thank you."

Social Media Meme: *Very few of us are what we seem – Agatha Christie.*

Chapter Forty-five

Billington Gazette Headline - October 28th 1987: ***Charred Remains of Billington Manor: Page 6 Picture Special***

Create your own version of the manor with our cut out and keep pop up replica of the ravaged house. Fun for all the family.

Jude hollered from the hallway as he opened the front door.

Jude: "Evening, my little mystical pixie! It's pouring out there. I'm taking my clothes off; care to join me?!"

Jude strode into the kitchen mid dis-robe and stopped suddenly upon seeing Lydia sat on a stool dunking a biscuit.

Jude hastily pulled down his untucked shirt.

Jude: "Ohhh, it's you. I didn't know you were here."

Lydia raised an eyebrow.

Lydia: "Evidently. Hello."

Jude: "Er, yes. Hi. Where's Eli?"

Lydia: "The little mystical pixie in the loo."

Lydia pointed her thumb towards Jude's downstairs toilet.

Jude tucked his shirt in his trousers.

Lydia, chuckling: "Oh, don't let me stop you."

Eliza bounced into the kitchen and Jude's shoulders visibly sagged with relief.

Eliza, beaming: "Hello Jude! Ooh, you look wet through. Get out of those clothes, you'll catch a chill."

Jude nodded eagerly.

Jude: "Yes, do excuse me."

Lydia: "Tut. Killjoy."

He hot-footed it out of the kitchen and returned a few minutes later. Eliza handed him a freshly brewed cup of tea and he smiled, appreciatively.

Lydia: "You have a very nice house, Jude. I never got to see it when we had our brief dalliance. I like your breakfast bar."

Jude: "Er, thank you."

Lydia: "I wish Tony had a breakfast bar. Saying that, him hopping up onto a stool might be an event I don't need to witness. Never mind, we'll have one, Eli, when we're old and live together."

Eliza: "Ooh yes, I'll put it on the list."

Jude: "What about me?"

Lydia: "Oh, you'll be dead by then."

Jude: "Oh."

Jude sighed and finished his tea.

Jude: "I'm popping out for a bit; I'll leave you both to it. Text me when you're done, Eli."

Eliza: "Ok, we won't be long."

Jude kissed Eliza on the forehead, nodded at Lydia and left them to it.

When the front door had shut, Lydia leant in to Eliza and rubbed her hands.

Lydia: "Right then. That's him gone; my mere presence has made him vacate his own house. Where were we?"

Eliza: "I was saying about the clock."

Lydia: "Oh, yes. Some chap called Archibald."

Eliza: "That's him. He was on George's mantelpiece."

Lydia: "Run by me who George is again."

Eliza: "Jude's brother."

Lydia: "Ah yes. Same eyes but he's got a non-functioning kitchen with Henry's grandmother's cooker."

Eliza: "Yup. That's him. Well, the clock was a present from Dorothy."

Lydia: "That's nice."

Eliza: "Dorothy found the clock in the shed."

Lydia rubbed her temples in exasperation.

Lydia: "Eli, is this really something I needed to leave a leg half waxed for?"

Eliza: "Let me finish. The clock came from Billington Manor."

Lydia: "Never heard of it."

Eliza: "That's because it doesn't exist."

Lydia: "Have you been sniffing fairy dust or chanting in the wrong direction? The clock came from an imaginary manor?"

Eliza: "It did exist but doesn't now. It burnt down."

Lydia: "Oh. When?"

Eliza: "Three ten am, British Summer Time, Saturday, 17th October 1987."

Lydia: "That's unnecessarily specific but okay. How did the clock end up in Dorothy's shed? What's the connection?"

Eliza: "I think it's stolen. Read that."

Eliza took the copy of the Gazette page she'd printed off the microfiche and put it on the counter top.

Lydia read the clipping and looked at Eliza, incredulously.

Lydia: "Are you kidding me?! Are you seriously suggesting Dorothy, our meek, bird-loving, flower arranging Dorothy, ransacked some stable during a clean-up operation, took a clock and put it in her shed?! Have you gone mad? You've been working at the newspaper too long; you've gone all Kate Adie and journalistic."

Eliza: "Not Dorothy. It wasn't her shed. It was Kenneth's. He wouldn't let her go in there but she rescued a bird. She said it was in a box with a load of other stuff. What if the other stuff is from the manor?"

Lydia: "Why would Kenneth steal from a burning manor house?"

Eliza: "Because it belonged to Mr Hicks's family. They had it for five generations."

Lydia's mouth dropped open.

Lydia: "Our bread-making Mr Hicks lived in a burnt-out manor in Billington for five generations? He doesn't look that old."

Eliza: "Yes. Well, it wasn't always burnt out, was it? Henry said it was really grand."

Lydia: "Oh my goodness, Eli. We could solve forty-year-old mystery! I feel like Jessica Fletcher in Murder She Wrote."

Eliza: "Exactly. Do you think we should go to the police?"

Lydia: "What if the box has gone? Dorothy hasn't lived there for ages. There's nothing to say it's still there. We'd be stirring up a right hornets' nest if we go rattling Kenneth's cage on the strength of an Archibald clock. Anyway, he could have bought that off Mr Hicks when they were friends, or something. It's not enough; I've watched Silent Witness. We need to have indisputable evidence. They've got very limited resources; we need to hand them the case on a plate."

Eliza: "Yes, you're right. We need to get into Kenneth's shed."

Lydia looked to the ceiling and huffed.

Lydia: "But how do we do that?"

Eliza: "Ah well, I think I might be able to help you there."

****

Francesca punctured the film on her fish pie, slid it into the microwave and hit eight minutes on the timer.

She opened the fridge, pulled out a bottle of Sauvignon Blanc and poured herself a glass. She was taking her first sip as her mobile beeped.

She picked it up and saw it was an email. Her brows knitted as she read the contents:

Dear I-don't-want-to-be-just-his-mistress,

I hope you don't mind me writing to you in a personal capacity and not as the Billington MILF. I am in need of your help, please. You may well hold the key to solve a mystery, in a very literal sense. If you feel happy to help me, please can you reply to this email? Many thanks in advance, Eliza.

P.S. In a MILF capacity, I hope you're ok and my advice helped in some way.

The microwave pinged, Francesca opened the door and unceremoniously dolloped the fish pie onto a plate. She pulled open the cutlery draw, took out a fork and whilst she ate, replied to the email.

Mentor in Life Feature letter: *Dear Eliza, I am 16 and went to Maccy D's with a boy from school. He bought me a McFlurry and when he handed it over, he said he'd dipped his willy in it. I think he was joking, so I ate it as I love McFlurrys but what if I'm pregnant. Love, I'm-only-having-fillet-of-fish-in-future.*

Dear I'm-only-having-fillet-of-fish-in-future, Firstly, what school do you go to because I'll be sure not to send my child if the level of sexual education is that poor you believe you can fall with child from a willy dipped ice-cream. Secondly, I think he was being silly – that's what 16-year-old boys are like. Thirdly, even if he had put his willy in it, unless the McFlurry was up your own McFlurry you have nothing to be concerned about. I have attached a YouTube video link for your perusal to help you understand about the act of procreation, but you might have to turn off your child settings to watch it.

Chapter Forty-six

Billington Gazette Headline: **Billington Police Close the Net on Illegal Butterfly Trader** (Pun Points – seven)

Eliza was sitting at Jude's kitchen breakfast bar answering a letter for the paper when George came shuffling down.

Eliza: "How was your survival course? Did you abseil down a mountain and hoof a passing goat?"

George: "Don't be ridiculous. Goats would have to fend for themselves in such circumstances."

George opened a couple of kitchen cupboard doors and inspected their contents. He pulled out a couple of packs of dried noodles and put them in his dressing gown pocket.

George, muttering: "Hmm, might come in handy."

I'm busy trying to clear the mess and he's hell bent on replacing it.

Eliza: "I don't understand how you can live like that, George."

George: "Like what?"

Eliza: "Living amongst mountains of crap. What bothers me most is you don't even appear to use what you're amassing. What's the point?"

George, popping a tin of sardines in his pyjama bottoms: "The point is, Eliza, that when the situation arises that 'mountain of crap' could well save my life and, if you are in the vicinity at the time, yours."

Eliza: "I don't wish to be saved by thirty-five bars of Lux and a pocketful of haslet, thank you."

George shrugged.

George: "Fair enough. I'll cross you off the list."

Perhaps he's got emotional problems. That would explain a lot.

Be gentle and tease it out of him.

Eliza: "Did something happen to you?"

That's it. Let him enter the circle of trust.

George: "Like what?"

Hmm, indeed like what?

Eliza: "As a child, did you feel a sense of inadequacy stemming from the indisputable fact your brother is a demigod and nothing you could ever do would come close to his magnificence thus rendering your life superfluous therefore resulting in an inevitable downward spiral of self-loathing and Spam stacking?"

George: "What?"

George scratched his head.

George: "Magnificence?! He collected Sindy dolls."

Oooh. That's not something I needed to know.

Move on.

Maybe it is something less historical. Be gentle. Lead him to the path of clarity through careful exploration of his own consciousness.

Eliza: "You know in your house? Did a structural beam drop on your head?"

Direct. Not exactly leading down the path.

George: "I don't think so. My bathroom ceiling caved in though. Wet rot."

Quelle surprise.

Eliza: "Anything else? Something physical? A catalyst?"

George pondered for a few moments.

George: "Now you ask. Yes."

Ahh, you see.

Chapter 46, paragraph five, 'Examination of Self – Manifestation of Fixation; Sourcing the Genesis'.

I knew I'd get to the crux of it.

George: "I read a book."

Well done.

George: "It transformed my life."

I'm assuming it wasn't the bible.

I don't think teaching domestic pets to retrieve road kill was in there.

George: "It taught me the importance of resistance, resilience and readiness."

Perhaps it was Star Wars.

George: "My house will be a safe zone."

For The Rebel Alliance?

Eliza: "Who for?!"

Even the rats have moved out.

George: "Well, you've taken yourself off the list, so not you. Julian, Dorothy. I quite like your friend Brian, so him and his husband, if I can get to them in time. What about your son, do you want him rescued? We could all look after him when we form the commune."

Eliza looked at George completely non-plussed.

Eliza: "Tom in a commune?!"

He might enjoy living with the Rebels, though. He'd lose his mind if he got to meet Luke Skywalker.

George: "I'll teach him the pressure points. Life skills. Much better than the old new age piffle you fill his head with."

New age piffle?! How dare you!

It's thanks to the grace those teachings have afforded me that I find myself having this conversation with you.

Eliza: "Pressure points?"

George: "Yes, I was watching a YouTube video about it the other day. You know, the one you and Julian told me to keep the noise down on."

Pressure point porn?!

They definitely didn't cover this revelation in 'Manifestation of Fixation, Sourcing the Genesis' chapter. I'm a bit out of my depth.

Eliza: "The day you were watching porn?!"

George looked taken aback.

George: "PORN?! I'm not some sort of tea-time pervert! What do you take me for?! I could never collude in such ignominy of the human form! No, it was a self-defence video. For example, if I grab you here. "

George jumped up, grabbed Eliza in a head lock and put his fore finger knuckle on her bottom lip.

Jeeezus!

I'm too close to his arm pits! Don't breathe in or you'll faint!

George: "You'd be dead in ten seconds."

And that's just from the pits!

I'm being man-handled! And incorrectly, at that.

She moved George's knuckle to the cleft of her chin and pushed.

Eliza: "There. Not in my mouth; in the dip of my chin. That's a pressure point."

Eliza flapped him off her and straightened up. George sat back down.

George: "Well, you made me turn it off. I missed the end bit. At least you know how to protect yourself, that's good."

Eliza: "I did a self-defence course with Lydia."

George: "I don't feel so bad about leaving you to fend for yourself now. Perhaps you could go ahead of us, remove the adversaries so we could have a clear passage to my safe house."

Eliza: "Who are these adversaries I'm killing with my ninja chin prod move?"

George looked at Eliza in astonishment.

George: "Zombies of course!"

Huh?

Eliza: "Come again."

George: "I'm a prepper. I'm prepared for the zombie apocalypse."

Of course you are.

Not only did a structural beam fall on his head, half the roof caved in with it.

Just when I thought the world couldn't get any weirder, along comes zombie boy.

Eliza: "The survival boot camp wasn't Bear Grylls, was it?"

George: "No, of course it wasn't. I have no wish to drink my own urine and traverse a cliff – I've got bunions. It was truly realistic and thoroughly immersive. I feel completely ready for it now. Bring it on!"

George punched the air in readiness then sat down and looked bashful.

George: "I met a lovely zombie, when I was there."

Well, that's not a sentence you hear every day of the week.

Eliza: "Did you, that's nice."

George, blushing: "She's really quite special."

In a way only a zombie can be.

Eliza: "Does she know all the moves to Thriller?"

George: "Don't be silly. That's not a requirement to be a special zombie. I might ask her out; she gave me her number."

Good lord. Other zombies must have eaten her brain.

Eliza, flabbergasted: "Did she?!"

George: "Do you have any ideas where I could take her? I'm a bit out of practice on dating."

Eliza: "To the butchers?"

George: "She's a vegetarian."

Call herself a zombie.

Eliza: "There's a new gastro pub opened up along the towpath. They do a nice veggie lasagne. Do zombies eat lasagne?"

George looked sideways at her.

George: "You're a bit odd but quite pleasant."

Oh charming.

Eliza: "Thank you."

George: "You're different to the sort my brother used to go for. They were right stunners. But you're kind enough, which is a nice trait to have."

Could I be any more insipid in your opinion?

Just because I'm not a zombie.

Eliza, tightly: "How kind of you to say."

Excuse me whilst I watch my self-esteem gauge plummet.

Jude loves you... Jude loves you...

But I'm not as stunning as his other girlfriends.

Jude loves you...

Eliza: "Right then. I must get on with things. I've got a column to write."

George: "Yeah, your MILF thing. Ha-ha... Saying that, I might."

Eliza: "Can you go away now, please."

George: "Yeah man."

Social Media Meme Film Quote: *"What If I'm not the Hero? What if I'm the Bad Guy?" Edward Cullen, Twilight*

Chapter Forty-seven

Billington Gazette Headline: ***Burst Water Main in Billington Housing Estate Causes Locals to Have a Dip in the Road*** (Pun Points – six)

Eliza and Lydia sat in the car, waiting.

Lydia: "What time did she say?"

Eliza: "Eleven."

Lydia pulled up her sleeve and looked at her watch.

Eliza: "Is that one of those fit watch things?"

Lydia: "Yes, I bought it as part of my Tony induced fitness drive. It's marvellous, it tells me when I've done enough steps to have a slice of cake."

Eliza: "How many is that?"

Lydia: "Three thousand. I don't want to overdo it; I twisted my knee doing a burpee the other day."

Eliza looked in her rear-view mirror.

Eliza: "Ah, she's here."

Eliza and Lydia got out and ran to the car that had just pulled up and jumped in the back.

Eliza and Lydia, leaning over to the front: "Hello, Francesca."

Lydia: "Why are we getting into yours to go down the road?"

Francesca: "Because the neighbours are used to me being there."

She paused.

Francesca: "Well, they were."

Eliza: "Thanks for helping us."

Francesca: "Not a problem. I've still got a key."

Lydia: "Not that we're ungrateful but why are you, though?"

Francesca chuckled a hollow laugh.

Francesca: "Perhaps, I woke up and got a life."

Eliza and Lydia looked at each other and raised their eyebrows.

Francesca: "I'll reverse up to the back gate. You stay in the car until I've gone in and unlocked it. It's pretty shielded from view by the oak tree in the front garden; you should be able to get in without being seen."

Eliza and Lydia nodded.

Francesca duly reversed up the drive, got out and let herself in through the front door.

Lydia: "I'm sensing she doesn't like him very much anymore."

Eliza: "He is very hard to like."

Lydia nodded in agreement as they watched Francesca undo the back gate and beckon them through.

Eliza and Lydia went to leave the car, when Eliza grabbed Lydia's arm.

Eliza: "We must be stealth, ok? He must not suspect anything."

Lydia tapped her nose.

Lydia: "Clandestine is my middle name. Years of stalking Roy afforded me that ability. Come on."

They hopped out of the car and ran through the gate which Francesca promptly shut behind them.

Francesca: "Did Dorothy say where the shed key was?"

Eliza: "No. I didn't ask her."

Francesca huffed with irritation.

Well I do beg your pardon. I didn't think it prudent to announce to her that her husband's mistress was assisting her new best friend and me by breaking into the former marital home.

Eliza: "Has he got a fiddly-diddly drawer?"

Francesca and Lydia, in unison: "A fiddly-diddly drawer?"

Eliza: "Yes. An oddment drawer. Has he got one of them?"

Francesca: "Actually, he has. I came across it when I was looking for the garlic crusher. Wait here."

Francesca dashed back through the back door and came out a few minutes later.

Francesca: "This might be it."

She held aloft a single key fob.

Francesca: "I found it at the bottom underneath an expired library card."

The three of them went to the shed and Francesca tried the lock, gave it a few wiggles and the door sprung open.

Francesca: "Bingo!"

The three of them stood on the threshold and looked at each other. All fully aware that they were in unchartered waters. Lydia nudged Eliza.

Lydia: "You go in Eli; this is your whodunit."

I feel a bit wibbly.

Eliza, nervously: "Should we just wait for karma to get him?"

Lydia: "You are his karma, now get in the shed."

Eliza nodded, gingerly stepped forward and looked around the shed.

Under a potting shelf was a box, covered in an old tapestry wall hanging; corners nibbled by a resident mouse.

Eliza carefully lifted the tapestry and peered inside.

Eliza: "Hello, 'ello... What's this?"

Eliza bent down and pulled out a copper Art Nouveau picture frame. She wiped the front on her t-shirt and it revealed an old, faded picture. She put the picture frame in her handbag and carried on rifling through.

A couple of minutes later, she went out into the light and joined Francesca and Lydia.

Eliza: "There's allsorts in that box. I've taken an old picture frame and a couple of bits of silverware. Any more than that and it'll be obvious things have gone. I'll see if I can find out anything about them. I've put the rug thing back over it as before."

Lydia: "Ok, let's get out of here."

Francesca: "I'll lock up and meet you back in the car."

Francesca swiftly locked the door, let Eliza and Lydia back out of the gate and ran back into the house and put the key back into the drawer.

Eliza and Lydia threw themselves into the back of Francesca's car just as she strode out of the front door and walked, purposefully, to the car and opened the driver's door.

Francesca, a hissing whisper: "Slide down, the postman's coming."

Eliza and Lydia slid down the back seat foot-well as the postman sauntered up the path.

Postman, jovially: "Hi, Fran. I haven't seen you here for a while."

Francesca, equally spritely: "Hi, Jim. I had some business to take care of. I'll see you around."

Postman: "I hope so. Take care."

Francesca waved him back down the path and slithered into the driver's seat.

Francesca exhaled loudly.

Francesca: "Coast is clear. Let's get out of here."

Social Media Meme posted from the back of the car: *The Axe Forgets but the Tree Remembers – African Proverb.*

Chapter Forty-eight

Billington Gazette Headline: ***Billington in Bloom Judges Rose to their Feet to Award Budding Newcomer Top Prize*** (Pun Points – six)

Kenneth pulled into the drive, turned off the engine and looked at the house.

He sighed and chewed his lip as he took an uncustomary moment to ponder on matters.

He didn't enjoy coming home to an empty house; it wasn't something he envisaged a man of his stature having to endure. Perhaps he should sell it; move somewhere smaller. But doing that would be an admittance that his marriage was over which it most certainly was not. Dorothy would come to her senses sooner or later; when she tired of that dead beat Hicks. It was taking longer than anticipated and this was proving to be an ever-expanding festering boil which he could see he would need to lance soon. He huffed as he hauled his briefcase off the passenger seat and bleeped the central locking on the car.

He turned the familiar front door key and strode into the dark house. Switching on the hall lights, he threw his briefcase on the console table then, mid-stride, suddenly stopped. Twitching his head, he sniffed; flicked his head around and scanned the hallway. It smelt different.

Like a dog catching a trace in the air, he tracked it to the kitchen with the scent becoming more pungent. Kenneth inhaled deeply and felt his groin twitch; it was a familiar scent. Oriental; vanilla with a hint of cinnamon hung in the air. He growled, malevolently. Francesca.

He darted back out to the hall and yanked open the console table drawer. He leafed through a folder of documents and pulled out an envelope. He checked through and breathed deeply when he realised all the money and credit cards were intact.

He raced upstairs and checked the bedrooms. All present and correct.

Why was she here? Nothing's damaged or has been removed.

Maybe he was imagining it. He berated himself for being paranoid and went back downstairs.

He needed a coffee; he'd had a long day. He went to fill the kettle. Then he saw it. The undeniable truth; open a matter of centimetres was a drawer. Kenneth never left any drawers open. Everything was perfectly aligned and closed properly. He saw to that.

His spine stiffened and his breathing became ragged; urgent. He snatched the drawer out and unceremoniously dumped its contents on the floor; desperately searching through until he found what he was looking for.

Crouched on his haunches he audibly exhaled as his hand located the key.

He hastily unlatched the back door, scurried down the path, unlocked the shed door and slammed the door open.

In the half-light he scrutinised the box. The rug was still thrown over it; but was it like that when he last saw it? Was the tapestry the other way up? Was the box further under the potting shelf? He ran his fingers through his hair and fell to his knees.

Shaking, he ripped off the tapestry and started rifling through the box's contents. Was anything missing? He can't remember what was in there; it'd been years since he'd checked. The last time was when Dorothy unearthed it saving that blasted bird. He continued scouting through the box then looked to the ceiling.

Think man; what was in there? Then Kenneth caught himself. What was he doing; Kenneth Cuthbert knelt amongst the grime and mouse droppings sifting through a box full of junk?! He shook his head and berated himself as he stood, threw the tapestry back over the box and kicked it back under the potting shelf.

He wiped his hands on his trousers, locked the shed door and went back into the kitchen. He rebuked himself as he stared at the contents of the drawer strewn across the floor. Maybe he had left it slightly open when he left that morning; he was under a lot of stress at work and it had been nothing but work, recently. Yes, that had to be it. He must have imagined Francesca's perfume because he needed female attention.

Perhaps he'd been a bit hasty ditching her so fast; she did provide a welcome diversion to his timetable. He'd call her; she'd be so grateful she'd run back with open arms. He smirked a libidinous grin as he thought of her and adjusted his trousers.

He continued making his coffee and as he sat down to drink it, he made a mental note to himself. That box needed to be disposed of. The satisfaction of the win had lost its potency; its presence was no longer testament to his supremacy. It was affecting his sanity. He'd take it to the tip this weekend. End of. It was a chapter that needed closing.

Social Media Meme: *Of all the animals, man is the only one that is cruel. He is the only one that inflicts pain for the pleasure of doing it – Mark Twain*

Chapter Forty-nine

Billington Gazette Headline: ***Grammarian Local Author Turns Over a New Leaf and Writes Book in Text*** (Pun Points – Seven)

Francesca stiffened as she watched the familiar shape walk up her garden path.

Kenneth banged on the knocker and stood back from the door step.

A few moments later the door clanked opened, chain on the latch.

Francesca, curtly: "What do you want?"

Kenneth was the picture of unctuousness.

Kenneth: "Francesca. May I come in?"

Francesca, firmly: "No. I'm busy."

Kenneth's eyed narrowed.

Kenneth: "Now, now. You're never too busy for me. Open the door, there's a good girl."

Francesca: "I said I'm busy. I've got a friend over."

Kenneth's composure faltered and his smile dropped momentarily, before he slapped it back on again.

Kenneth: "Ah, how delightful. May I meet your little friend?"

Francesca: "No. Please go away."

Kenneth: "I can come back later, no problem."

Francesca: "I don't want you to come back later. You've made your feelings perfectly clear."

Kenneth: "Ah yes, well that is why I'm here. I've thought about it and I'm happy to give us another go."

Francesca, perplexed: "You're happy to give us another go?!"

Kenneth: "Yes. I would be willing to take you out for dinner. It wasn't my wish to offer whilst stood on your doorstep, however."

Francesca started to laugh. A low incredulous laugh.

Francesca, shaking her head: "Unbelievable. Go away, Kenneth."

Kenneth, utterly flummoxed: "I beg your pardon?"

A voice called out over Francesca's shoulder.

Disembodied voice: "Who is it, Fran?"

Francesca turned back into the house.

Francesca: "Oh nobody. A cold caller."

Kenneth spluttered.

Kenneth, slack-jawed: "A nobody?!... A cold caller?!"

Francesca turned back to him.

Francesca: "Yes, a short-lived fascination. Good-bye, Kenneth."

And she shut the door in his face.

Francesca leant on the closed door whilst she composed herself then went back into the kitchen.

Francesca's Guest: "Fancy getting a cold caller this time in the evening?! Don't they have anyone to be with on a Friday night?!"

Francesca, starkly: "That one doesn't."

Francesca fetched two glasses from the cupboard, opened the fridge and took out a bottle of wine.

Francesca: "Shall we celebrate?"

Francesca's Guest: "Most definitely!"

Francesca poured the wine, handed her guest a glass and they clinked them together.

Francesca: "Cheers. To us, Henry!"

Henry: "To us!"

Francesca: "And our new pumping station!"

They both took a swig and beamed at each other.

****

Kenneth pursed his lips with indignation. How dare she rebuff him? He was the one who called the shots, not her.

Kenneth got into his car and pulled off down the road and parked up two cars away.

He put on the World Service and waited…

Mentor in Life Feature letter: *Dear Eliza, You've been round the block a bit. Answer a debate me and my mates have – do women prefer muscles or beer bellies? Cheers, Make-mine-a-large-one.*

Dear Make-mine-a-large-one, For your reference I have not 'been around the block'. I am very pure, actually, I just look a bit haggard, but that's having a child for you. However, I can assist you with your debate. Both. Not at the same time – what I mean is, as the saying goes, it's 'horses for courses.' There's someone for everyone.

Chapter Fifty

Billington Gazette Headline: ***Hearts Sink as Billington Swimming Baths Announce Closure*** (Pun Points – Eight)

Eliza pushed open the door to Blooms and Bloomers and the familiar little bell tinkled as she entered.

Dorothy skipped out from the kitchens and a wide beam spread across her face.

Dorothy: "Eliza! How marvellous to see you again! What brings you to our little shop this bountiful Saturday morn?"

Eliza: "Hi, Dorothy. I was wondering if Mr Hicks was in."

Dorothy: "He is, let me just go and fetch him. He's busy licking some iced fingers."

Dorothy went back out to the kitchens and came back with Mr Hicks who was preoccupied wiping icing off his chin.

Mr Hicks: "Hello, Eli. You're looking well. Dorothy's brother looks like he's putting some colour on your cheeks. They are a family which brings happiness to the soul."

Eliza: "We're living together at the moment; maybe permanently, I don't know. I need to convince him he can't live without me. Brother George doesn't bring quite so much happiness to the table, though, Mr Hicks. Pocketed cured meat, yes. Happiness, not quite so much. He's living with us, presently. He's a bit of a trial but will come in very handy if there's a zombie apocalypse and if I ever run out of soap. He has also procured an unnerving collection of cleavers but they do come in handy with the ivy."

Dorothy and Mr Hicks exchanged glances.

Dorothy, brightly: "Cup of tea, dear?"

Eliza: "Yes, please."

Dorothy slipped off out the back.

Mr Hicks: "What can I do for you, Eli?"

Eliza: "Well, erm. I'm not sure where to start..."

Mr Hicks pulled up a chair for Eliza.

Mr Hicks, patting the seat: "Sit down. Start at the beginning."

Eliza searched around her mind for a few moments.

Eliza: "Are you Montague?"

Mr Hicks blinked.

Mr Hicks: "That is my name, yes. Why?"

Eliza: "I read about you in the Billington Gazette. About your manor house... And the fire."

Mr Hicks looked visibly winded. He gave a grim smile.

Mr Hicks, quietly: "Yes, Eli. It was I who raised the alarm that night."

Eliza: "I'm so sorry, Mr Hicks. It must have been awful."

Mr Hicks emitted a low murmur.

Mr Hicks: "My father died a broken man and my mother never physically recovered; she suffered dreadful smoke inhalation."

Mr Hicks shook his head, sadly.

Mr Hicks: "To add insult to injury we lost most of our possessions after the fire. People can be so unkind; taking advantage of misfortune."

Eliza: "You never told me about this, when we spent all that time together with the shop."

Mr Hicks shrugged.

Mr Hicks: "Life moves on, Eli. There's nothing that can change it now."

Eliza: "Well, that might not necessarily be true."

Eliza ferreted about in her handbag and pulled out the Art Nouveau frame and handed it to Mr Hicks.

Eliza: "I found this."

Mr Hicks took the frame and gazed at the picture, he looked aghast at Eliza then back at the frame and crumpled to his knees.

He gently traced a face on the photograph within the frame with his forefinger; lost in a memory.

Mr Hicks, his voice barely audible: "Papa."

Dorothy came out with a tray of tea and clattered them hastily on the counter when she saw Mr Hicks on his knees.

Dorothy: "Oh my darling, what's wrong?!"

Mr Hicks held up the picture frame to Dorothy and she studied it for a few moments.

Dorothy turned to Eliza with great concern.

Dorothy to Eliza: "Did you give him that?"

Eliza nodded.

Dorothy helped Mr Hicks to his feet, his gazed transfixed on the photograph within the frame.

A tear rolled down his cheek and dripped onto the counter.

Eliza delved into her bag and pulled out the silverware she'd also taken from the box.

Eliza: "These are yours too, aren't they?"

Mr Hicks's mouth dropped open and he nodded, mutely.

Dorothy, urgently: "Where did you get them?"

Eliza: "It was where the Archibald clock was."

Dorothy clasped her chest.

Dorothy, breathlessly: "George's?!"

Eliza: "No, where it was before that."

A look for horror flashed across Dorothy's face as the penny dropped.

Eliza pulled out the news clippings regarding the Billington Manor fire. Dorothy skim read the article.

Eliza: "It was him, Dorothy. The clock too."

Dorothy tugged at her cardigan with anguish.

Dorothy: "You've been in there?!"

Eliza nodded.

Dorothy held her head in her hands.

Dorothy, desperately: "He'll know... He'll know."

Fear shrouded the whole of Dorothy's being and she started to shake.

Eliza: "He won't know. We didn't disrupt anything?"

Dorothy's eyes widened.

Dorothy: "We?!"

Eliza: "Lydia and Francesca came with me."

Dorothy's face darkened.

Perhaps a bit too much information.

Just then 'The Girl for Ipanema' started blaring out of Eliza's handbag.

Saved by the bell.

Eliza pulled out her mobile and looked at the caller display.

Eliza: "Hi Henry."

There was no reply.

Eliza: "… Henry?! Hello!"

Eliza rolled her eyes at Dorothy who was still clasping her chest.

Eliza: "He's man-bag called me."

Eliza: "HENRY! Put the pho… oh hang on…"

Eliza cocked an ear to her mobile and concentrated.

Dorothy started to speak but Eliza put her hand up to silence her.

Eliza: "Tsk. Hang on, Dorothy. Something's occurring…"

Eliza continued to listen and a look of panic crossed her face.

Eliza: "HENRY!!... Oh my god, I can hear Kenneth's voice."

Eliza turned to Dorothy and Mr Hicks.

Eliza, gabbling: "It's Saturday morning - he's at the auction house. That's where Henry has the Archibald clock. Kenneth's there. He must know we found out. "

Mr Hicks, tearing his gaze from the photo: "Who? Found out what?"

Dorothy gently stroked Mr Hicks's arm.

Dorothy: "Kenneth. Eliza believes it was he who took your family's heirlooms. I had no idea. I lived with them right under my nose for fifteen years without any clue. I even gave one away to George...Oh, it's too awful... The depth of contempt I have for that man."

Dorothy wrung her hands in despair.

Mr Hicks put down the frame and took Dorothy in his arms, gently soothing her whilst digesting the information he'd just received.

Eliza: "They were in Kenneth's shed, Mr Hicks. That's where I found your photograph in the frame. We need to get help for Henry. Shall I call the police?"

Mr Hicks let go of Dorothy and shook himself into action. A rage suffused years ago started to rise to the surface as every muscle in his body visibly clenched and determination flooded through every fibre of his being.

Mr Hicks, with authority: "Dorothy you are to call the police, explain the situation and send them to investigate, please. You are to stay here. I insist upon it; I'm not having you anywhere near that man. "

Mr Hicks turned to Eliza.

Mr Hicks: "You and I will go straight over to the auction house. This needs finishing once and for all."

Crikey, you're very masterful in a crisis.

I can feel a bellow of Big Bear coming out there.

Dorothy, sobbing: "Be careful, please."

Mr Hicks held Dorothy's face in his hands and gently kissed her on the lips.

Mr Hicks: "I love you. Look after the shop... and don't lick my fingers."

Mr Hicks released his hold and motioned to Eliza to follow him as he sprinted out of the shop. Eliza hastily picked up the Art Nouveau frame and followed him out.

Dorothy watched them leave and waited until they'd driven from sight. Satisfied they'd gone, she ran upstairs, picked up her coat and handbag, shut up shop and jumped into Mr Hicks's car.

****

Eliza pulled up outside Billington's Auction House and spotted Kenneth's car haphazardly parked across two parking bays.

Eliza: "He's still here."

Mr Hicks jumped out of the car and hurried inside leaving Eliza to trail on behind.

Upon entering the Auction House, they caught sight of Henry stood in the doorway of his office facing Kenneth who had his hands on his hips, his back to the main door.

Henry spotted Eliza and Mr Hicks enter and he ostentatiously beamed and waved them over.

Henry: "Hello!! What an unexpectedly welcome surprise! This chap was just leaving."

Kenneth spun around and as his eyes locked with Mr Hicks's, the air in the room disappeared; a tide of hatred billowing through the void.

Kenneth with swagger: "Ah, Montague. Looking sorrowful as ever."

Montague Hicks, curtly: "Why are you here?"

Kenneth: "This chap, Henry, and I were just having a nice little chat."

Mr Hicks: "You don't do nice little chats."

Kenneth thumbed towards Henry.

Kenneth: "Like you, this chap has something of mine."

Oh that's rich.

Eliza: "You're a fine one to talk, you flip-flopping filcher."

Kenneth: "Who are you? Oh, of course. You're the silly little girl who ran that abysmal failure of a furniture shop."

How dare you!

My pip is well and truly squeaked.

Eliza, about two octaves higher than usual: "It was not an abysmal failure until you decided to open in direct competition. Why did you do it?"

Kenneth shrugged and chuckled.

Kenneth: "Because I can. The problem with society these days is individuals fail to know their place. You needed to be kept in your lane."

Oh, you really are vile.

Mr Hicks started shaking with anger.

Mr Hicks: "Is that what you did with Dorothy for all those years? Made sure she knew her place? You contemptuous piece of scum."

Kenneth: "What rubbish you spew. My wife had a cosseted life of luxury with me. I tried to teach her and I did what I could to bring her up a level but dead weights always sink to the bottom eventually."

Kenneth flourished a hand at Mr Hicks.

Kenneth: "She is, of course, growing tired of you. When she telephoned me last week, she was practically begging me to take her back."

Mr Hicks's composure faltered for a moment before he raised his chin again.

Mr Hicks: "You're lying."

A supercilious smirk stretched across Kenneth's face.

Kenneth: "The truth can be unpalatable at times, Montague; much like your cooking. Ha-ha."

Kenneth laughed heartily at his own weak joke then leant in to Mr Hicks and hissed in his face.

Kenneth: "She's mine and I expect her back."

Mr Hicks squared up to Kenneth and stood his ground.

Mr Hicks: "Dorothy is not a possession."

Kenneth jabbed his finger towards Henry and Eliza.

Kenneth: "Nobody takes anything or anyone from me. Not you, not him and not her."

Mr Hicks took half a step back to distance himself from Kenneth's spittle.

Mr Hicks: "You live your whole life doing just that. If anyone should have stayed in their lane, it was you. You've stolen from everyone you ever come into contact with. Well today, Kenneth, you luck has finally run out."

Uh oh. There's a ceiling fan up there and a lot of poop is just about to hit it.

Kenneth: "What are you talking about?"

Mr Hicks: "Your nefarious actions have been exposed."

Just then there was a clatter at the main doors and Jude bustled in.

Thank the lord for perfectly timed perfect boyfriends.

Jude: "I came as soon as I could. Eli, Mr Hicks, are you ok? Hello, Henry."

He literally is a knight in shining armour. I have to make him marry me.

Eliza: "Yes, just about. Kenneth is being very loathsome, as you'd expect, but no-one's hit each other... yet."

Kenneth: "Julian?! What on earth are you doing here?"

Jude: "Dorothy called me. She was worried."

Jude turned to Eliza.

Jude, seriously: "I thought you were dropping Tom off at his dad's?"

Uh oh, I'm in trouble.

Eliza: "Ah, well yes. I did but then I went to Blooms and Bloomers about something."

Jude: "About the picture frame."

Eliza: "Ah. Hmmm. You know about that... Then Henry man-bag phoned me so we..."

Henry looked around with confusion and pulled his mobile out of his back pocket.

Henry: "Did I? I'm most frightfully sorry. I've got new trousers on. They're a bit tight round the old sea..."

Kenneth cut in.

Kenneth: "Picture frame? What are you all talking about? I haven't got time for this; I've got a tip run to attend to. I only came by here to warn this fellow about Francesca... If you'd excuse me."

Kenneth started to push his way past Mr Hicks and Jude.

They both stopped him.

Mr Hicks: "Oh, I don't think so Kenneth... Show him Eli."

Oh must I? He looks rather angry.

They're all watching me. I have no choice.

Eliza reached into her hand bag and pulled out the Art Nouveau frame as Kenneth shrank back with panic.

Jude's mobile rang and he picked it up.

Jude: "Hello... Gone?!... Are you sure?"

Jude turned to Mr Hicks.

Jude: "Dorothy is in the shed. The box has gone."

Kenneth, raging: "That's breaking and entering! She will pay for this."

Mr Hicks: "What's sauce for the goose, Kenneth. Perhaps some of your teachings did rub off on her after all."

Kenneth sneered at him.

Eliza beckoned to Henry.

Eliza: "Come on Henry, I think we should check his car."

Kenneth urgently pushed against Mr Hicks and Jude also restrained him.

Kenneth, puce with rage: "Let me go, this instant! Stop man-handling me! This is utterly unacceptable!"

Mr Hicks, sadly: "You are utterly unacceptable. To think we were best friends once, Kenneth. Marianne was so disappointed in you."

Kenneth, spitting at him: "Leave my mother out of this. We couldn't all be a rich paragon of virtue like you, could we?"

Meanwhile, Henry and Eliza hot-footed it to Kenneth's car.

They peered through the windows and sure enough, slung in the back seat was the box of heirlooms he'd stolen from Billington Manor on the night of the fire.

Henry, high-fiving Eliza: "Well done, Miss Marple. You've got him."

Social Media Meme: *Good Books Don't Give up Their Secrets All at Once – Stephen King*

Chapter Fifty-one

Billington Gazette Front Page Headline: ***Billington's Maestro Breaks Down after Wheels Fall off his Business Empire*** (Pun Points - nine)

Kenneth Cuthbert, 53, owner of several businesses within Billington and the surrounding area has been released on bail after being charged with the historical theft of heirlooms from Billington Manor. The theft took place during the aftermath of the fire which rocked Billington in 1987; the sadness of the event was shared by many local residents; such was their fondness of the grand manor house and the Hicks family.

As a result of this development, a police spokesperson informed the Billington Gazette that they are also re-examining the circumstances of the fire; a case which remains open. Any persons with relevant information are asked to contact the police on 101 quoting crime reference number 54236.

Eliza was sat at Jude's breakfast bar, answering an email and George sauntered in.

George: "I'm moving back in today."

Eliza: "Oh, thank god."

George: "I, er, wanted to say thank you for doing my house. I've bought you a present."

Eliza: "Oh, you needn't have done that. How thoughtful."

George presented a hastily wrapped gift.

It's something with a handle.

Boxes of chocolates don't have a rubber grip.

Eliza tore off the wrapping paper and stared at George.

Eliza: "It's a duster."

George: "It is."

Eliza: "Why did you feel that was an appropriate present?"

George: "I had a load of cobwebs left so presumed you hadn't got one."

I haven't got the energy to hit him.

Eliza: "You have it, do the cobwebs for me."

George: "Oh, ok. But then you won't have a thank you present."

I'll cope.

Eliza: "You going is present enough."

George: "Oh."

Eliza: "How does the new rug look?"

George: "Splendid. I've put it over the door."

Eliza: "Rugs, go on floors. There's much you need to learn about interior design, George."

George gave her a look.

George: "The trap door in the lounge. It's where I've put a majority of my inventory. Now I'm with Helena, I feel I should have more floor space for entertaining."

Eliza: "Helena?"

George: "The lady I told you about; I met her at the survival course."

Eliza: "The vegetarian zombie."

George nodded.

Eliza: "Don't use the condoms. They're over a decade old."

George pulled a disapproving face.

George: "They aren't for that sort of activity. What sort of man keeps out of date condoms in his lounge for sexual activity?!"

Quite.

George, continuing: "They're perfectly serviceable for holding water. Non-spermicidal, obviously. I've popped them in the cellar with the batteries. Anyway, I just wanted to say thanks and wondered if we could pair up and go on a foursome together sometime – me and Hel's and you and my bro."

Absolutely not.

Eliza: "Absolutely."

Just then the doorbell rang.

George: "I'll get it. I've got to finish packing."

George wandered down the hallway and opened the door.

Stood on Jude's doorstep was Lydia, holding two outfits up in front of her face.

Lydia, from behind the outfits: "Which one says sex goddess?"

George: "At a push, the one on the right says sex worker."

Lydia flung down her garment holding arms.

Lydia: "You're not Eliza. Move out of my way, please."

George stepped aside and Lydia pushed her way into the house.

George: "She's in the kitchen."

Lydia: "Yes, thank you. And for your information sex workers are very highly skilled so less of your tawdry insinuations and stereotyping please, Brother George."

George: "Whatever."

Lydia wandered into the kitchen.

Lydia: "Hello, darling. Why's he still here?"

Eliza: "Hello, he goes today. Cup of tea?"

Lydia: "Yes please. I want your opinion. Which outfit for tonight's do?"

Lydia held her choices aloft again.

Eliza: "Left one."

Lydia nodded and slid onto one of the stools.

Lydia: "Where's the Mighty Sword?"

Eliza: "He's dealing with the nationals with the Kenneth drama. Any closer to winning your chateau?"

Lydia shook her head and tutted.

Lydia: "I've given up the crosswords. I went to see Miriam to get some tips as all I'd won was vouchers for oven chips. Turns out it was a bottle of Château Neuf-du-Pape from the Rhone valley she won."

Lydia sighed and rolled her eyes.

Lydia: "When she told me about it originally, she was chewing a Twix so I'll cut her a bit of slack but, honestly, she needs to be more eloquent with her story telling. For someone who spends her life doing crosswords she isn't very concise!"

Eliza: "I thought you needed the French residence to rid yourself of bath pubes?"

Lydia: "I've developed a coping mechanism. I shut my eyes and aim the shower head down the bath for five minutes prior to running it. I then pretend it didn't happen and I run my bath in self-imposed ignorance."

Eliza: "Well, as Rita Mae Brown once said, 'one of the keys to happiness is a bad memory'."

Eliza handed Lydia her cup of tea.

Lydia: "Did I tell you? Charmaine has left Roy. I think with the stress of it, she's taken up the sauce. When she brought Freya back the other day, she asked me the most peculiar question. She asked where she could find a Venetian blind as she's sick of voiles. Freya wants to keep in touch with her. I'm not keen if she's bonkers."

Eliza: "Oh, erm. I'm sure it's just a phase of moving on with her life. We've all had them."

Lydia: "You're right, we're only human, aren't we? Even me."

Eliza: "As the expressions goes, 'Strength lies in differences, not similarities'."

Lydia: "You've become a walking MILF."

Eliza: "As Buddha said, 'What we think, we become'."

Lydia: "Stop it now."

Eliza: "As the great wordsmith Gaz once said, 'there's no off switch on awesome'."

Lydia glugged her tea and slid off the stool.

Lydia: "I can't take any more, I'm off to start applying my make-up."

She picked up her outfits, whisked off down the hall and opened the front door.

Eliza, calling after her: "As the saying goes, 'as one door closes, another one opens'."

Lydia, hollering back: "Yes, my car door. Now stop thinking in quotes and go back to the hippy incarnation. See you later, darling!"

Social Media Meme: *I never look back darling, it distracts me from the now. Edina Mode, The Incredibles.*

Chapter Fifty-two

Billington Gazette Headline: ***Net Finally Closes in on Billington Big Fish as Dorothy Delivers Damning Dossier of Documents Detailing Dodgy Dealings.*** (Pun Points – ten out of ten. Plus bonus for double bubble – Boom!!)

Kenneth Cuthbert's estranged wife, Dorothy, (age withheld), now co-owner of Pilkington-on-the-Moor's Blooms and Bloomers, presented the police with a damning dossier detailing a number of illegal transactions pertaining to his business activities including a number of bogus insurance claims as well as highlighting several accounts irregularities.

Furthermore, investigations regarding misappropriation of funds pertaining to the Hardy Family Trust are ongoing and Trustees of the Trust have been assisting the authorities with their enquiries.

Asked for comment, Mr Cuthbert told us to shove our tawdry rag where the sun doesn't shine. We presume he means Glasgow.

We will keep you up to date with this unravelling story.

Shared with all the tabloids and mainstream media, HMRC and the Charities Commission.

Brian ran up to Eliza and welcomed her with an extravagant air kiss.

Brian: "Mwah, Mwah. How marvellous to see you. Carlos is so stressed; he's popped a vein in his temple!"

He turned his attention to the next incomers through Manners' restaurant door.

Brian: "Jude! Wonderful to see you again!"

Brian and Jude shook hands, warmly, as Jude looked around.

Jude: "Hello, Brian. The place looks fantastic! May we write a piece on it for the paper?"

Brian: "You most certainly may! It's cost an arm and a leg. All positive coverage is most welcome."

Brian looked down at gawping Tom who had just trailed in.

Brian: "And you, Master Tom. Good Evening."

Tom: "Hello, Brian. Gaff looks nice. You had a change round?"

Brian: "We have!"

Tom: "I approve."

Eliza: "I do too! It looks fantastic!"

Brian: "Thank you! Be sure to tell Clive – the whole process has tested the delicate fibres of our marital bond so he'll be pleased to receive positive feedback."

Eliza: "Where would you like us to sit?"

Behind them more people queued up to get into the restaurant and Brian looked around, urgently.

Brian: "Hang on... CLIVE!"

Clive stopped talking to a couple by the bar and came bustling over.

Clive: "So sorry! I was drowning in a conversation about real ale. Hello, Tatty Head! Jude, Tom. Follow me, let me take your coats and get you seated."

Clive took their coats and led them away as Brian continued to greet the guests as they came through the door.

Clive, bustling back to Eliza: "Carlos grabbed me on the way from the cloakroom. I must attend to him. You're over there to the left of the stuffed rhino."

Clive pointed to a large round table over his right shoulder and rushed off.

Eliza took in Manners' newly refurbished decoration and marvelled. The walls were chestnut brown panelling. Adorning the panelling were elaborate light sconces, interspersed with gold flock animal busts, around their necks were garlands of intricately arranged peonies, hydrangea and eucalyptus leaves which matched centrepieces on the tables. Nestled within the centrepieces were pillar candles and delicate entwined pale pink ribbon.

She felt a gentle tap on her shoulder as Mr Hicks caught up with them.

Mr Hicks: "Hello you three. What a splendid little family you make."

Jude, Tom and Eliza turned round and smiled

Eliza, looking behind Mr Hicks: "Hello Mr Hicks, no Dorothy with you?"

Mr Hicks: "It might have been a step too far, but she was more than happy to do the arrangements and sends her best wishes."

The group wandered over to their table and were greeted by a joyous Lydia who jumped up and enveloped her in a perfumed hug whilst the others said their hellos.

Lydia: "Hello darling! Isn't it simply bewitching?!"

Lydia wafted her hand around, expansively.

Eliza: "It is. You look lovely!"

Lydia: "Good. Sometimes the only ammunition I have is my face."

Lydia went to hug Tom but he put his hand up to stop her.

Tom: "No need, Auntie Wydia. Not before I've eaten me dinner."

Lydia: "Oh, hello then."

Tom: "Hello. Hello Freya, Mr Old Man. Scoot up, I'll sit over 'ere. Those chairs hurt me bum."

Ah, the infamous chairs from the man on Dragon's Den.

Clive re-joined them as Tom shuffled behind the table and gently shouldered Freya and Tony along a sumptuous, navy blue velvet buttoned banquet seat.

Clive: "It's ok, Tom. Brian was recommended some designer wadding by an exotic chef he encountered. Apparently, they'd used it in their al fresco eatery. Bums have never been so cossetted!"

Brian wandered over, caught the end of the conversation and winked at Eliza.

Lydia: "We were all commenting how wonderful the restaurant looks."

Clive: "It's been a nightmare but Eli came to the rescue with the wall colour choice."

Freya gazed round and looked at Eliza with distaste.

Freya: "You're responsible for poo brown?"

Lydia: "Freya! Don't be so rude!"

Eliza, somewhat piqued: "I think you'll find it's Caramel Soil. And a very tasty one at that."

Plus, I hadn't seen the colour chart but it had to be better than Burnt Broccoli.

Lydia, hissing to Eliza: "She's inherited that from Roy. He doesn't have an interior bone in his body."

Brian: "We must leave you to it. Clive, we've got to chat to the happy couple."

Clive: "Of course. Catch up with you all later."

Eliza and Jude sat themselves down and Eliza stared at an enormous ornate baroque picture frame which contained a masterfully painted life work.

'Allo 'allo.

Jude gently touched her elbow and started to speak. Eliza put her hand up to stop him.

Eliza: "Tsk... I'm looking."

Jude followed her gaze.

Jude: "At the painting of a nude man with a strategically placed Lobster Thermador?"

Eliza: "Yes. He looks familiar. I'm sure I recognise those biceps."

Jude's eyebrows shot up.

Think brain... who is this beautiful person?

Good Lord...I think I've got it.

Eliza waved at Lydia across the table and pointed to the painting.

Eliza: "That naked man behind your head, Lydia, is that who I think it is?"

Lydia followed her gaze and beamed.

Lydia: "Yes, darling. It's Daniel. He's mine."

Well, this is all a bit blatant! Maybe, the tromp l'oeil wasn't gender specific.

Perhaps, they've roped Daniel in.

Eliza pointed to Tony.

Eliza: "What about him? He's sat there eating olives."

Tony looked up from his bowl of olives and raised an inquisitive single, stomach gurgle inducing, eyebrow.

He didn't even need words.

Lydia, patiently: "No, Eli. The painting. I did it. There's two more around the place. Look, there's one over there under the ostrich head."

Eliza followed her gaze to another renaissance inspired painting of a naked Daniel, reclining upon a dining table, table cloth draped over his shin whilst holding a platter over his lap.

Eliza: "Is that a plate of Beef Wellington over his willy?"

Lydia: "Vegan actually, without nuts. One needs to cater for all inclinations these days".

Eliza: "They're brilliant, Lydia! When did you do them?"

Lydia: "We stayed in contact after our meet up at Pilkington Park and met up every Wednesday. We bartered – he posed and I got a personal trainer. You should see my abs, darling!"

Eliza: "Ohhh, Wednesday. Now I understand."

Lydia: "I told Tony I was seeing you. I wanted to surprise him with my artistic efforts."

Tony stopped eating and gazed longingly at Lydia and she flushed under its intensity.

Tony, growling: "I'm so proud of you, my darling petite mort."

Oh blimey, my pants have actually combusted.

He tore his eyes away from Lydia and spoke to Jude.

Tony: "You must be proud of dear Eliza, too. Solving that awful business with that philandering pilferer."

Jude: "I am. I can safely say, hand on heart, the day I met Eli my life changed forever."

The whole table: "Awww!"

The group smiled and went back to their previous conversations; Tony, Lydia and Mr Hicks chatting about baked products and their genitalia covering prowess. Tom and Freya competing for the best face made with green olives.

Eliza quietly to Jude.

Eliza: "For the better?"

Jude smiled at Eliza and nodded.

Jude, quietly back: "Yes, Eli. For the better."

Eliza: "For ever together, under the same roof, better?"

Jude beamed at Eliza.

Jude: "If you'd like to."

Eliza beamed back.

Eliza: "I'd like to."

Just then there was a chink of metal on glass as Brian grabbed everyone's attention and the restaurant chatter subsided.

Brian: "Thank you, everyone! Hello!! Firstly, Clive and I would like to say a massive thank you all for coming along this evening. It means a lot to welcome so many friends and their families here tonight. It's the first time we've opened since our extensive refurbishment and for our first night open to be such a special occasion is absolutely wonderful. Whilst I have your attention, we have a few mentions, don't we, Clive?"

Clive: "We do indeed. Thank you to Blooms and Bloomers for the exquisite floral displays and the tremendous cake which we'll all delight in later. To our dear talented friend, Lydia, for the remarkable art work and we're over the moon to discover she been commissioned to undertake further similar works for Billington Bowls Club."

Eliza looked over at a pleased as punch Lydia who nodded ecstatically. Tony gave her a big squeeze and planted a delighted kiss on her cheek.

Clive whispered something in Brian's ear and he dashed off to the kitchen. He came back a few moments later with a very food splattered, red faced Carlos.

Clive, continuing: "We'd also like to thank Carlos, our long-suffering chef. Without him there'd be no ox tongue on a bed of goat's cheese and citrus beetroot."

Carlos looked bashful and waved Clive's compliment away. Suddenly, there was an almighty bang in the kitchen and the whole restaurant leapt in the air.

Carlos, shrieking: "Sheeet! I forgot to put the weight on the pressure cooker! My liver has exploded! I must go!"

Carlos ran off and left a stupefied restaurant. Brian nudged Clive.

Clive: "Yes, well, anyway. Less about us. To the happy couple!"

Brian ran out the back, ushered them in and thrust a glass of champagne in their hands.

Brian: "To Francesca and Henry!!"

Everyone Else: "To Francesca and Henry!"

Mentor in Life Feature letter: *Dear Eliza, you seem to have the answers to everything. You must have it all going on. Please tell me your secret. Regards, I-want-to-be-the-oracle.*

Dear, I-would-love-to-be-the-oracle. The greatest lesson I have learned in life is I still have a lot to learn in life.

Epilogue:

The elderly lady looked out of the window and sighed deeply as she gently ran her right-hand fingers over her liver-spotted left hand; lost in contemplation.

She turned when she felt a gentle nudge on her shoulder and smiled at the aproned lady, with a name tag, Karen, on her bosom pocket.

Karen, kindly: "You called for me? Would you like to go out into the garden?"

Elderly Lady: "Not at present, Karen. Would you be so kind as to fetch me the telephone?"

Karen: "Of course. I'll just see to Arthur; he is having a confused moment."

Karen went over and soothed an agitated pyjama-wearing Arthur and the elderly lady watched as Karen delicately cupped his elbow and calmly guided him back to his room.

Karen returned a few minutes later with a mobile phone.

Karen: "Would you like me to dial it for you?"

Elderly Lady: "No, no. I'm fine now. I'll call you when I've finished."

Karen smiled and left her to it whilst she went off to attend to another lady who was calling her.

The elderly lady inhaled slowly and dialled the number.

Elderly Lady: "Yes, hello. I have some information regarding..."

Picking up the paper to her side, she quickly scanned the page.

Elderly Lady: "... Case number 54236... My name? Oh of course, Marianne... Marianne Cuthbert."

****

They say everyone's got one book in them; it turns out I had three.

I hope you enjoyed them x

Printed in Great Britain
by Amazon